Miss Charlotte Ralston has always appeared to harbour an affection for Julien Revel, ninth Earl of Clandon. So, when a broken heart makes her agree to a wealthy, but loveless, connection with the dissolute Lord Braybridge, it becomes the Earl's task to dissuade Charlotte.

Smarting from his own rejection by Charlotte's pretty sister Penelope, Julien proposes himself as a more amenable husband – yet Charlotte fears to accept this most eligible suitor. How can she entrust her future to his hands when her heart has already been secretly broken by the Earl's longstanding indifference to her?

By the same author in Masquerade

JOANNA

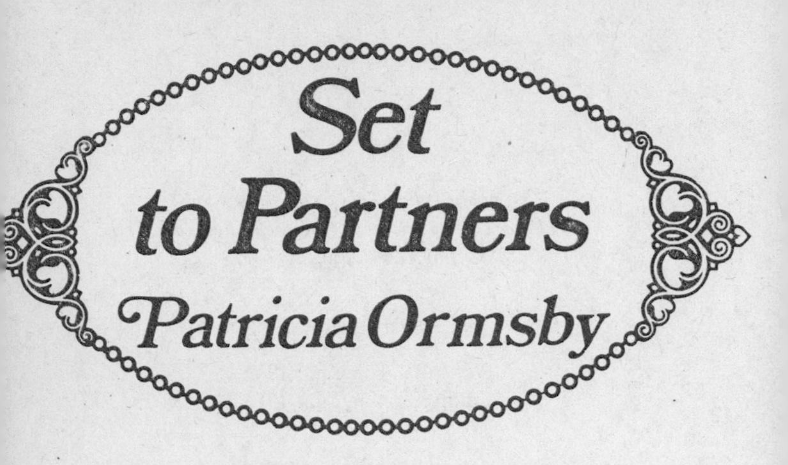

MILLS & BOON LIMITED
London · Sydney · Toronto

First published in Great Britain 1978 by
Peter Davies Limited, 13 Queen Street,
Mayfair, London W1X 8BE

This edition published 1979 by
Mills & Boon Limited, 17–19 Foley Street,
London W1A 1DR

ISBN 0 263 72874 9

Set in Monotype Ehrhardt

Made and Printed in Great Britain by
C. Nicholls & Company Ltd
The Philips Park Press, Manchester

TO RENEE M.
for whom this book was written

CHAPTER ONE

It was generally conceded by persons of consequence, and indeed by those of less account also, that Julien Robert Valentine Revel, ninth Earl of Clandon, was a singularly fortunate young man. None but the most benign of fairy godmothers had attended at his christening, and if later unhappy events had left him almost totally bereft of family at an early age, it was held that the earldom with its attendant wealth and possessions offered very fair compensation for this regrettable occurrence.

His mother, a French lady, who had decreed that his name be spelled 'Julien' rather than 'Julian' as was customary in England, had died when he was a child; his father, the eighth Earl's only brother, had quixotically risked his life by visiting France at the height of the Revolution in an attempt to rescue a relative of his wife's. The attempt failed and both gentlemen lost their lives, leaving young Julien heir to his bachelor uncle who promptly removed him to Chalice, the family seat situated on the Hampshire borders, and an upbringing befitting the future Earl. The eighth Earl's indignation was, therefore, understandable when, upon attaining the age of twenty-one, his nephew announced that he had purchased a commission in the army and at once left the shores of England for the Peninsula. Nor did he return to his native land until five years later when the death of his uncle forced him to sell out and come home to take over the responsibility of his great inheritance.

Some two and a half years after this event, the Earl, now approaching his twenty-ninth birthday, sat in the library at Chalice, partaking of a belated breakfast and reading a letter which appeared to afford him considerable amusement. As Sefton, his elderly butler, entered with a fresh pot of coffee, he tossed the letter from him with a low chortle of laughter and addressed himself with enthusiasm to a dish of coddled eggs and home-cured bacon. Sefton, with the assurance of a privileged old servant who has known his master since boyhood, ventured to enquire as to the source of his lordship's mirth.

'My godfather, Lord Biddlecombe,' explained the Earl in his clear pleasant voice, 'seems to be suffering concern on my behalf. In a word, Sefton, he gives it as his opinion that it is high time the nurseries at Chalice were put to their proper use.'

'Meaning that you ought to be thinking of marriage, my lord?' Sefton set the refilled coffee-cup by the Earl's elbow and stood looking down on the engagingly disarrayed black locks with more affection in his gaze than most employers have any right to expect. 'There is the succession to be thought on, my lord.'

'Yes.' Julien, suddenly serious, pushed away his plate and got up to look out of the window to where, in the bright spring sunshine, a line of scythemen were starting the first cut of the east lawn. He was in riding dress for he had been out and about his estates since before eight o'clock that morning, but he had flung off his coat and the careless grace of his beautifully proportioned figure gave much credence to his normally phlegmatic valet's considered opinion that any sculptor would give his heart to use his lordship for a model, which statement had never been taken in dispute by those less favourably positioned to judge the matter, for its veracity was all too apparent. While in Spain he had earned the soubriquet of Sultan among his fellow-officers because, they declared, his hosts of female admirers were so vast as to form a harem, ranging from those who were contented with a glance from the celebrated deep-blue Revel eyes to less inhibited ladies who declared that if those finely-moulded lips were not shortly pressed to theirs they would fall into a decline. The Earl, ever-thoughtful of others, invariably did his best to avert such catastrophes.

Once home in England, where stricter codes of conduct

obtained, Clandon's position and consequence were so immense, and his looks so striking that, while susceptible maidens fell readily under the spell of his charms, their mothers as readily fell victims to the lure of his fortune. How he had contrived to escape the matrimonial traps set for him it was difficult to say. There were those who would have it that he put too high a price upon himself, that he knew his own worth to the last inch. His few intimates thought this conception to be untrue and wondered if, beneath his easy well-bred manner, the Earl might not hold the intricate social structure into which he had been born in considerable contempt. Though he spent little time at his town house, much preferring to be at Chalice, he was well esteemed in fashionable circles. While always dressed to a nicety, he was no dandy, and an inborn skill in handling his horses and guns, added to more than competent swordsmanship, made it not entirely absurd to suppose that, had he cared to exert himself, there was small doubt he must have been acclaimed a nonpareil, the highest honour the world of fashion could bestow upon the gifted amateur.

A quick sigh broke from him as he picked up Lord Biddlecombe's letter again: 'A wife', he mused, half-aloud, 'might bring about problems.' Hopefully, Sefton awaited further confidences but Julien, recalling that however old and trusted a friend his butler might be, he was hardly the person with whom the Earl of Clandon could discuss his future marriage, thrust the letter into his pocket and resumed his seat. 'Bid Chivers lay out my morning dress and Brereton have the bays put to the curricle in say –' He paused to consult the fine water-clock on a nearby stand. 'God! Nigh on half-past ten already! If I am to pay a call on Lady Ralston I must be gone within the hour.'

'Very well, my lord.' Sefton withdrew and hastened to the kitchen quarters where he informed all and sundry that they had best look to their affairs for his lordship was seeking a wife and maybe one not far distant either. Admittedly the Earl had known Lady Ralston's three daughters all their lives, for their mother and his had been close friends, but that might be regarded as an asset in the present circumstances since the Earl's heart did not necessarily have to be engaged.

The staff at Chalice bore the news with philosophical calm. That the Earl must take himself a wife one day was, they considered, an inevitable calamity, but should he choose one of the Misses Ralston to be his countess then fortune could not be called too unkind, for the Ralston girls had run in and out of Chalice and its stables for so long they were as well-known to its inmates as their young master.

Mrs Tremlett, the housekeeper, was of the opinion that the Earl must choose Miss Penelope, the youngest of the three.

'Miss Charlotte, of course, would be much more in his style,' she declared, 'but I am informed that she is in hourly expectation of an offer from Lord Braybridge, and Miss Melissa is the least well-favoured. No, I am content that his choice must fall on Miss Penelope and he had best make haste for, as you know, her aunt is bringing her out this month and such a taking young lady will soon be in great favour amongst the gentlemen.' This statement was treated with the respect it deserved, Mrs Tremlett's sister being housekeeper to Lady Ralston, though James, the first footman, did venture to suggest that the young lady would be a queer noodle to turn down an offer from the Earl. With this sentiment Mrs Tremlett heartily agreed. 'Indeed, James, it is not perhaps a great match for his lordship but one he could be comfortable in, and I am sure we would all be pleased to see Miss Penelope here as his lady.'

A general murmur of assent went round the servants' hall. Better the devil you know than the devil you don't was the universally expressed opinion, and Miss Penelope was so taken up with her horses it was not likely she would wish to interfere much with the management of Chalice.

Quite unaware that his household had settled his future for him the Earl, left to himself in the library, found he had lost something of his appetite. The prospect of matrimony was not entirely a new one but, until that morning, he had easily been able to persuade himself that it could safely be left to resolve itself in the future. His heir presumptive, a distant cousin, was an agreeable enough young man, but had not so far displayed any of the qualities which might be looked for in an Earl of Clandon, and the thought of Chalice being left to his care caused Julien some unease when he could bring himself to consider it.

Turning in his chair, the Earl looked up at the end wall of the library where, secure in its alcove, rested the golden chalice that had given the mansion its name. It had been discovered during the re-building of the house, once a monastery, and was generally believed to have been concealed by the monks at the time of the Dissolution and forgotten in their hasty departure. Whatever the reason for its being overlooked, the chalice was one of the proudest possessions of the Revel family, being of extreme antiquity and exquisite design.

'And now you are bidding me find a mistress for your house, are you, my pretty?' Julien mused whimsically, pulling the ears of the spaniel lying close to his chair. 'Well, I'd best be off and fire my opening salvo in this new engagement!' The spaniel thumped her tail vigorously and gave vent to a short bark of approval. 'You consider I am right, Fidela? Then we will put it to the test.'

Thus it was that on the stroke of midday the Earl, resplendent in sleek-fitting pantaloons and finely tailored coat of blue Bath cloth, presented himself at Heatherstone Hall. His elegance was further enhanced by a mildly fanciful waistcoat, gleaming be-tasselled Hessians, and a fall of snowy muslin arranged with deceptive simplicity at his throat. Apart from a single fob and his signet ring, he wore no other adornment, for to be hung about with jewellery except on the most formal occasions was, he considered, to be not quite the thing.

Lady Ralston was at home and overjoyed to see him. 'Julien, dear boy – oh, this could not have fallen out better! I was on the point of sending to ask if you would call. You are quite a stranger and the blame for that must be set at my door for I have been laid low with a tiresome bronchitis this month past.'

'Dear Aunt Emmelina, no one to look at you could dream that you had suffered a day's indisposition.' Julien gallantly raised her hand to his lips, flashing her a sparkling glance from under his heavy lashes.

'You tiresome boy,' she teased him. 'I believe you would flirt with a bed-post! And is hand-kissing still the thing for aged honorary aunts? I had thought it to be quite out of fashion. Come, let us go into the small saloon and Perkins shall bring the sherry, for you must know I am quite solitary, all my chicks have fled the coop.'

'What! All of them?' Julien asked, rather startled, as he followed her into the charming, flower-filled room.

'Yes, indeed.' Lady Ralston established herself in a deep armed chair with cushions of Spanish leather on one side of the fireplace and motioned him to be seated opposite to her. 'Firstly, I must tell you that Charlotte is betrothed to Viscount Braybridge and he has taken her off to Meudon Hall to meet his mother. I should have accompanied them but I was too occupied in preparing Penelope for her London début. She left yesterday, escorted by her cousin, Geoffrey Warner – you know, the Sarum Warners, you have met them here – he is entering on his second year on the town so may be of help in telling her how she should conduct herself. As I have no need to remind you, Penelope is a mite careless of social niceties! Ah, thank you, Perkins. Set the tray here close at hand and his lordship and I will assist ourselves.'

'Indeed, ma'am,' said the Earl at his most formal, 'I must felicitate you on this good news. I had not known of this attachment of Charlotte's for when I last saw Braybridge, a few weeks since at Woburn, nothing was said of it.'

Lady Ralston remained silent until the door had closed behind her butler. 'I would speak to you privately on this matter, Julien. I have met Lord Braybridge only once when he came to ask for Charlotte's hand. He seems a pleasant enough, well-set-up man and his consequence is such as must gratify all but the most ambitious mother's hopes. But – will he make a good husband for my sweet girl? Oh, I know what you will be thinking – that you cannot cry cavey on him. That is not what I am asking. What he has done before he met Charlotte matters little, provided he mends his ways when he weds her.'

There was an understanding twinkle in the Earl's eye as he handed Lady Ralston her glass of sherry.

'It would seem, dear aunt-by-courtesy, that you know more about him than you would give me to believe,' he murmured, sitting down again opposite her, the bright sunshine full upon his handsome person, his dark head sharply outlined against a background of daffodils arranged with natural simplicity in a fine bowl of Chelsea ware. Lady Ralston reflected, not for the first time, with what pride could she accept him for a son-in-law, and not merely because he was one of the greatest matrimonial catches in the country. 'I cannot admit to being closely acquainted with Braybridge,' Julien spoke slowly as if choosing his words, which indeed he was, 'we meet on occasion at our clubs when I am in London.' He paused, his eyes thoughtful, staring into the fire. 'He leads what might be termed an idle life, I suppose, that of the Corinthian, the man-about-town, and yet he is not precisely of that set. As to his fortune, I believe him to be comfortably situated, though he digs pretty deep and is not a gracious loser at the tables. Have I answered your question, ma'am?'

'Yes, I thank you,' she said quietly. 'You have told me you do not hold him in any great esteem.' He made a slight disclamatory gesture of the hand.

'That is only my opinion. I have no doubt there are others who could paint a different picture. But what in Heaven's name does Charby want to marry him for? She surely cannot fancy herself in love with him, he must be near twice her age!'

She was touched by his use of her daughter's childhood name and smiled. 'I think him close on forty, though I will say he carries his years well.' She hestitated and then went on slowly. 'As you know, I married quite late and never made my début at Court, my husband not caring for that style of life.' Julien nodded, recalling with no great excess of sentiment Sir Greville Ralston, a baronet full of starch and self-importance who, mercifully for his lively family, had relinquished his hold on life in the hunting-field some years previously in a characteristically stubborn attempt to surmount an unjumpable obstacle. 'This was why,' continued Lady Ralston, 'I prevailed upon my sister, Lady Oakley, to bring out Charlotte and Penelope, Melissa having no taste for that sort of life. She has no daughters of her own and dotes upon the fashionable world, though I fear a natural indolence is apt to affect adversely her good intentions. I am very conscious that you did more than she in pushing Charlotte off so handsomely in her first season by standing up with her at all the balls and squiring her to places of entertainment.'

He laughed at that. 'Yes, until Lady Oakley hinted that my determined flirtation with Charlotte was discouraging other suitors! Besides, Charby did not need me nor her aunt to tell her how to go on. She may not be a raging beauty but she has more sense and wit in her little finger than any half-dozen of the so-called Toasts that I have met with. By-the-by, what became of that young officer who was hanging on her sleeve last summer? Harry Taverner, wasn't it?'

Lady Ralston sipped deeply of her sherry before replying. 'He was killed by a stray shot at the surrender of Pampeluna a short week after he had rejoined his regiment,' she said at last. 'Julien, it concerns me lest that is why Charlotte has accepted Braybridge's offer. Now that she knows that there is no hope of Harry Taverner – oh, there was no betrothal, but I am persuaded they had an understanding – I feel it may matter little to her whom she marries. There is also the knowledge that she has turned twenty-one and has two younger sisters. With Penny coming out this year – well, I am not precisely put to the pinch, but money must always be a consideration if my girls are to be established comfortably, and of this circumstance Charlotte is, perhaps, too well aware.'

The distress in her face moved Julien to go to her and, sitting on the deep footstool by her chair, take her hand in both of his. 'Aunt Emmelina, why did I not know of this?'

'Why should you have? She told no one save only Melissa, hoping no doubt to save me anxiety for, charming boy though Harry was, he was a younger son with scant prospects. To have another such disappointment befall her –' Tears began to trickle unchecked down her cheeks and the Earl very sensibly removed her sherry glass and produced his handkerchief.

'Dearest aunt, do not distress yourself,' he begged. 'If I can be of use – but what do you mean by *another* such disappointment? Have there been many unhappy attachments?'

'You remember – you know her so well, her warm heart, her sudden excesses of emotion –' Lady Ralston evinced signs of rare confusion as if she had said rather more than she had intended. Julien did not press her for further explanation. He was recalling with affectionate amusement the devotion with which a twelve-year-old schoolgirl had attached herself to him until his departure for the Peninsula.

'I well remember! Let us hope that this allegiance to poor Taverner may prove to be one of her "takings".'

'Maybe,' said Lady Ralston more briskly, 'but she will never admit that for it would bring her constancy into question. But to marry a man she cannot love out of a sense of duty, oh, it will not do! You must understand that to her now it is the only sort of marriage she can consider. The world will comprehend that her affections are forever fixed, so a marriage of convenience may be accepted.'

'I trust Braybridge will comprehend that also.' Julien's tone was dry but she went on as if he had not spoken.

'What troubles me the most is that it is scarce six months since young Taverner was killed, she must allow herself time to recover from that shock before taking any decision that will affect all of her life. If only I could go to her, but I cannot do so now because of Melissa.'

'What has Melissa to say to anything?' His look of complete bewilderment brought a fleeting smile to her lips.

'She is visiting friends at Chichester and I have had a letter from Mrs Pritchard, the mother, telling me that she fears Melissa is forming an undesirable connection with a naval officer, who has been invalided out of the service on the smallest of pensions. This, I apprehend, I must attend to myself for, as I have no need to inform you, once oppose Melissa's wishes and there is no moving her.'

'Stubborn as a mule!' agreed his lordship readily. 'I well recollect her flat refusal to undertake a season in town. Damme! What a tangle!'

'And as for Penelope,' began Lady Ralston.

'Oh, not Penny, too!' he protested.

'I assure you that it was almost beyond my powers to set her on her journey yesterday, she was in such a pet over Sultan.'

'Sultan?' The Earl sounded as if he could not believe his ears.

'Yes, you must know that the horse you so generously gave to her on her birthday has been named Sultan – for you, of course! – and he had the misfortune to become agitated in his stable the other night, a rat or some such no doubt, and injured a hock. Oh, nothing serious, but you know how she is about her horses and, in particular, any one you have given her.'

'May I be informed how the knowledge of that name came to Penny's ears?' he enquired with dangerous calm.

'Why, I imagine everyone knows of it, *and* the reason for its bestowal!' She shook her head, smiling at his obvious annoyance. 'My poor Julien, I declare that you are not yet aware of the engrossing interest your doings and sayings provoke in others. In particular, the haut ton who like their young bloods well-spiced!'

'Well, here's something else to capture their interest.' He drew his godfather's letter from his pocket and handed it to her. 'Now, dear aunt, tell me what I should do about that!'

Lady Ralston, puzzled by his expression, read quickly through Lord Biddlecombe's wordy communication then looked up again to meet his watchful regard. 'What do you want to do?' she asked. He flushed and turned away to look into the fire.

'I came over this morning, Aunt Emmelina, to request if I might –' To his surprise he found that, despite the ease with which he had hitherto conducted his affairs with the gentler sex, offering for a lady's hand in marriage was a very different kettle of fish. Also the case did not seem to be quite as he had thought it to be when he had set out for Heatherstone Hall. His embarrassment afforded Lady Ralston considerable amusement though she took great care to conceal it.

'You came to ask if you might pay your addresses to one of my daughters?' He nodded, thankful for her quick understanding of the matter. 'No, Julien. I am very sensible of the honour you do us, but – no.'

The Earl's chin came up at that and a militant sparkle appeared in his eye. 'May I be permitted to know why my offer is declined, Ma'am?'

'Now, don't come the haughty with me!' she admonished him, using an expression her daughters had coined years before whenever they suspected their noble neighbour of laying undue stress upon his rank. 'Pray, for which one of my daughters are you offering, my lord?'

'What? Oh, Penny, I suppose, since the others are out of it.'

Dear Heaven, she thought, would Penelope ever forgive me if she learned I had turned him away? Maybe I am being a fool but I must be sure of one thing else tragedy could lie ahead for all of us. Leaning forward in her chair, she took his face between her hands.

'Julien, my dear,' she said gently, 'I love my girls and hold them in the greatest esteem, but you have your position to consider. You can and should choose from the highest in the land when it comes to taking a wife.' He made to speak but she silenced him with a finger on his lips. 'No, hear me out. I was your mother's friend and I am yours now. You are too much alone at Chalice. After the hurly-burly and companionship of the army I wonder you can bear it. You need a wife to be both friend and lover to you. You see, I know one thing of your Revel family history, the men love but once and that for all time. Your uncle loved a lady who died before he could wed her and so remained single all his life. Your father was half the man I first knew after your mother was taken from him, and you are cast in the same mould with the same gift for lasting affection. Wait, I beg of you, until you can bestow that affection in wedlock. A sad business it would be if you married for convenience and later met the lady you could love.'

A strained silence fell and Julien, deeply moved after a fashion he could not precisely define, rose and went to stand by the fire, his elbow resting on the mantelshelf, his face averted from her. When he spoke, his voice was so low, she could scarcely hear him.

'How could you guess at the loneliness? There were times when, but for the girls, I was like to have run mad.'

Her heart ached for him, but she affected a cheerfulness she was far from feeling. 'You should spend more time in London. When did you last set foot in Clandon House?' He shrugged and she continued remorselessly. 'Which encourages me to make my outrageous demand of you. You are the only one to whom I can appeal that Charlotte may listen to. Will you go to town and speak with her? She leaves Meudon Hall this coming week and joins Penelope at my sister's establishment in South Audley Street. Julien, please talk to her and make her understand that she does not have to marry Braybridge, nor indeed, to marry anyone if she don't wish for it.'

The Earl, much surprised by her request, made impatient reply. 'My dear aunt, what do you imagine Braybridge is going to think of my interference? I am very likely to find myself at daggers-drawing with him if not at pistol point in the cold light of dawn!'

'I am sorry for him if it comes to that, but I cannot conceive that it should,' she retorted. 'I do not have to remind you that he is no youthful, first-time lover. Charlotte has taken his fancy and he needs an heir. His first wife gave him only girls – four whey-faced misses they are, too! Charlotte is not likely to confide in him anything you may have to say to her.'

'Aunt Emmelina, are you quite certain that she does not hold him in affection?'

'Quite certain.' Lady Ralston spoke with a finality that brooked no further argument. 'And it occurs to me that you should prepare yourself for a prolonged stay in London. When the word is put about that you are on the look-out for a wife then everything feminine that can crawl out of its cradle will be paraded for your inspection. You might, if you would be so kind, also favour Penelope a little and help push her off.'

'With the greatest of pleasure, ma'am. If I am not allowed to marry one of your daughters at least I can put them in the way of receiving the most eligible proposals.' The slightly acid note in his voice was not lost on her.

'Julien, if ever you come to me, hand on heart, and say you love – a girl of mine and wish to marry her on that count alone, then will I welcome you gladly as a son-in-law.'

'In spite of my wretched rank and consequence?'

'Stop quizzing me, my lord! You know my concern for your happiness is as great as for that of my own children. I only pray that, if you do not find someone worthy of your affections, you will not allow yourself to be entangled by some pretty face with no more ideas behind it than that of being a Countess.'

'Depend upon it, I am conversant with most of the lures thrown out by hopeful young ladies and their mamas.'

The scorn in his voice startled Lady Ralston. So that is what has turned him against town life, she thought. Well, it was hardly to be wondered at, he should not have been blessed both with extreme address and extreme eligibility and, in addition, a fastidiousness of mind and person which made him uncommon hard to please. She patted the stool beside her.

'Come then and let us discuss our campaign. I am of the opinion that it might be best if you were to present yourself to my sister as having come to assist at Penelope's launching at my behest. I will write to her to this effect. Then you can be meeting with Charlotte without seeming to seek her out. Do you not agree?'

The Earl drove home that afternoon in a somewhat disturbed frame of mind. While, in all truth, he had to confess that his offer for Penelope had sprung more from the impulse of the moment than from any deep-seated conviction that she was the right wife for him, yet he was fond enough of her to view the prospect of marrying her in reasonable confidence of their being able to deal comfortably together. She was young, of course, and a thought wayward, but a season in town should teach her what was what and he would not be too hard to please. No, what was causing him such an unaccountable sense of hurt was not so much Lady Ralston's refusal of his offer as the lack of reason behind it. Why had she accepted a middle-aged widower for one daughter and spurned his offer for the other? Her argument that she wished her daughters to marry for love was quite overborne by her conduct. The fact that Charlotte was twenty-one and had most likely made her own decision, presenting her mother with a *fait accompli*, was very possible, but Lady Ralston seemed not even to have raised a protest. And then, in a belated fit of conscience, she had prevailed upon him to put the affair to rights! His first impulse had been to tell her to go to the devil and get someone else to do her nursemaiding for her, then his warm feeling for all the family and his natural good breeding overcame his resentment. In additon, there was Charlotte to consider, and as he had always dealt with her as he might with his own sister, it was to be hoped that his intervention might be acceptable to her, though such an outcome could not be taken as assured, Charlotte being endowed with a fair measure of the Ralston obstinacy!

As for Braybridge, he had never liked the fellow – a cool, supercilious creature, very sure of himself and indifferent to the feelings of others. Was there not something else about him, some story – by God, yes! Momentarily, his hands dropped and the bays snatched at the opportunity to break into a gallop. It was coming back to him now but it had all happened four or five years since, while he was in the Peninsula. Steadying his team, he thought on it. Something about Braybridge's wife dying in odd circumstances and it being whispered that her husband had wearied of her and her four puny daughters. But nothing had ever been proven and the rumour had died for lack of confirmation. Nonetheless, there was an unsavoury flavour to the business and he could wish that Charlotte had chosen some other to support her marriage of convenience. If the foolish child thought to use Braybridge as she might some callow youth and dictate on what terms her marriage should be conducted, she was likely to suffer a sad disillusionment.

The Earl's mouth hardened suddenly and his eyes half-closed as at some displeasing thought, then, touching his leaders lightly with the whip, he swung them up the sharp rise to where the great gates of Chalice stood open, awaiting his return. In any event, he concluded, he had undertaken to make his best endeavours on the girls' behalf and there was no drawing out of it now.

CHAPTER TWO

It was May Day when the Earl arrived at his town house in Manchester Square to find that the news of his coming to town had preceded him.

His hall-table was laden with invitations to balls, routs and evening parties of every description. Napoleon had abdicated, the fighting men were coming home from the wars, London was en fête to a degree uncommon in living memory and the heady perfume of victory was sweet on the warm summer air.

Julien, a little put out by a hot and dusty journey, its tribulations added to by having one of his wheelers go lame, no sooner had peeled off his gloves and had his driving coat removed than he demanded an immediate bath and change of attire. His staff, having learned to respect that slight edge to their master's voice, hastened to carry out his wishes. Sefton, who with certain other indispensable members of the household at Chalice, had journeyed to London the previous day, himself ventured into the Earl's dressing-room to set down a tray bearing what he hoped would be acceptable refreshment.

'I presumed to bring the Madeira, my lord.' Julien, fresh from his bath, looked at him in the mirror, eyebrows raised in question.

'Was my ill-temper so apparent? I must mend my ways and try for a little more social grace.' Sefton bowed but deemed it wise to refrain from comment.

'I have also to inform your lordship that Colonel FitzJames has called and awaits you in the small drawing-room.'

'What? Then, I pray you, pour me a glass of the Madeira and

convey the rest to Colonel FitzJames with my compliments. I'll not keep him waiting above a few minutes.'

The meeting of the two friends who had served in the same regiment in the Peninsula, but had not seen each other for over a year, was unrestrainedly cordial.

'Ned, you misbegotten offspring of a Spanish muleteer! Where the devil did you spring from?'

The Colonel, a big, handsome, fair man, whose merry blue eyes and whimsical manner gave an impression of frivolity which was far from being the true case, for his understanding was keen and his sensibilities unusually refined for so seasoned a soldier, ignored the reflection on his parentage and grasped the Earl's out-thrust hand.

'It has all gone quiet over there now that Boney's *rompéd*,' he explained cheerfully. 'I got home last week and, by God, home is where I mean to stay!'

'You're not selling out?' The Colonel nodded.

'Aged aunt – not set eyes on her this century! – slipped her coil and left me her blunt. About £5,000 a year and a little property in Hampshire. It would please me if you could spare the time to come and look it over. It's all to pieces, I daresay, but you would know best what's to be done with it. M'brother says there's no estate better cared for than Chalice because you see to every detail yourself. That's confounded good Madeira you offer your guests, Sultan!'

'I chanced to be drinking it myself which is why you are so honoured! How did you learn I was here, I have but just arrived?'

'My dear Sultan! The gossip of the past few days has been of little else. Clandon on the look-out for a bride! I vow the proposed visit of the Emperor of all the Russias will not equal the excitement!' The look of dismay on Julien's face set the Colonel chuckling. 'And what is this about your helping to push off one of the prettiest little misses of the season?'

'Penny? You've met her then. Well, I did it for her sister – oh, I suppose I've got her aunt to thank for the other rumour. An amiable lady but a sad gossip.'

Much amused, the Colonel allowed himself to be pressed to another glass of Madeira. 'But why, Sultan, with such a prime beauty at your fingertips, must you be putting yourself to the trouble of looking further for your wife?'

'Her mother won't have me,' explained the Earl briefly. The Colonel's jaw dropped.

'Not have you? Is she astray in the attic?'

'No, got some old-fashioned ideas about her girls making love-matches.'

The Colonel uttered a short military term indicative of his disbelief. 'What of her sister? I recall Miss Charlotte's come-out, I was home on leave at the time. A grand girl, I developed quite a tendre for her until –' He checked and then continued in an off-hand way, 'I realized I could not stand up against the competition.'

Julien frowned. 'That is another reason for my being here. She has got herself engaged to Braybridge and her mother don't like it. Ned, did you know Harry Taverner?'

'Who did not! But what has that to do with the case?'

'He and Charlotte appear to have had an understanding before he got himself killed.'

'You don't tell me she is wearing the willow for Harry Taverner?' asked the Colonel in amazement. 'Why he – well, to be blunt, if he remembered the colour of Miss Charlotte's eyes after three months' separation from her, I would be much astonished! Believe me, I liked him and was grieved to hear of his going for he was a good soldier and a cheerful fellow, but constancy was not a first consideration with him and he was the greatest flirt on the Peninsula, not excepting yourself. Not that you were a flirt precisely,' he added with considered fairness, 'women just swarmed in your direction. And I warn you, the hives are buzzing again! In any event,' he went on hastily, seeing the Earl's obvious distaste for that subject, 'why is Miss Charlotte marrying Braybridge if she still yearns for Taverner?'

'Sense of duty, so her mother is persuaded. No one can accuse her of fickleness in affection because she is not in love with Braybridge. Feminine logic, but what can I do to convince her she is being a ninny?'

Colonel FitzJames thought of several things the Earl might do but uttered none of them. Instead he asked curiously, 'So Lady Ralston has commissioned you to sort out Miss Charlotte's affairs and watch over her sister, yet she will not have you for a son-in-law? Odd, ain't she?'

'On the contrary, I have always considered Aunt Emmelina to be blessed with great good sense,' Julien returned calmly, hoping that his irritation on that subject did not show. The Colonel, watching him closely, guessed much of what was passing through his mind. If he knew anything of old Sultan there was going to be the devil to pay in one way or another, but he wondered what deep game Lady Ralston was playing, for it was beyond his comprehension why she should turn Julien down.

The conversation then changed to talk of mutual friends and the last fierce exchanges of the war, while the level of the Madeira sank lower in the bottle. Reluctantly FitzJames rose to take his leave for he had other calls to make.

'If nothing better offers, join me at White's for dinner and a few rubbers of whist,' he suggested.

'I'd like that, but first I must make my bow to Lady Oakley and greet my charges. Can we leave the time open?'

'When you wish – I look to be there by seven o'clock. I pray we do not find poor Brummell gambling away what little he has left with no thought of retrenchment.'

'Prinny still withholds his favour then?'

'Prinny is as spiteful as a woman scorned. Take the matter of the snuffbox he was having fashioned to replace the one he removed from the Beau's collection. Not only does he countermand the order for it, but he has failed to return the original box. By-the-by,' the Colonel added as they strolled to the street door together, 'apart from all the pretty young 'uns, there is at least one lovely widow on view. Sally Warne is back in town and more fetching than ever, I do believe.'

That checked the Earl in his stride. The Marchioness of Warne – Lady Sarah Manners as she was then – had been the toast of his first season in town and he, like most of the young bloods, had worshipped at her shrine. But the Marquess of Warne was too great a catch to be passed over in favour of a very youthful and, at that time, merely prospective earl. Julien's nineteen-year-old heart suffered no lasting hurt, but his visual memory retained a clear picture of Sally Warne's charms, her dainty little person, her exquisite cream-and-roses complexion, her soft brown eyes and swift entrancing smile.

'Hmm!' he said thoughtfully. 'At Warne House, is she?'

'No, in fact staying for a time with near neighbours of yours, the Hertfords, while her place is being put in order. Will you be visiting there to-morrow morning?'

'Very likely,' returned the Earl coolly. 'I always make a point of calling on the Hertfords as soon as I get to town. Do we trip over Prinny there, do you think? Is he still devoted to Lady H.?'

'Very likely!' The Colonel so perfectly mimicked the Earl's tone that they burst out laughing. 'Au revoir, Sultan, behave yourself! Their mother may, but I would not entrust you with the care of any woman under seventy!'

After FitzJames had left him, Julien walked to South Audley Street, bidding his coachman bring his carriage in half-an-hour, by which means he hoped to set a limit on his visit and so arrive at White's at a reasonable hour for dinner. He was startled, as he handed his stick and gloves to Wiggins, Lady Oakley's butler, to hear his name shrieked out from the top of the stairs. Swiftly moving forward, he was just in time to catch a laughing avalanche of femininity which had precipitated itself downwards at such speed that it must surely have terminated its descent on the floor had not his arms been there to steady it.

'Oh, Julien!' gasped this impetuous young lady. 'You are a *darling* to come! I know you will do more for my come-out than *anything*!' Whereupon she threw her arms around his neck and kissed him soundly. The Earl with admirable, if reluctant, self-control, endeavoured with small success to detach himself from her embrace, and read her a lecture on the impropriety of young females making advances to gentlemen in public however well acquainted they might be.

'You must know, Penny, it isn't at all the thing,' he finished, ending his homily on as severe a note as he could contrive in view of the armful of vivacious beauty he held in his grasp. For Penelope was a beauty, on that score there could be no two opinions. Naturally curling locks, the colour of ripe corn, framed an enchanting little face and a pair of direct and sparkling blue eyes gave much character to a countenance that might otherwise have been accounted merely pretty. Even the Earl, who had known this vision for all of its eighteen years, was much taken aback to observe what skilful hair arrangement and an elegant gown could do for his hoydenish little friend whom he was more accustomed to see in bedraggled riding habit, with her hair half down her neck, begging to be allowed exercise one of his horses.

'Oh, Julien, don't be stuffy!' she implored him. 'Of course I don't do that to every gentleman who calls! But I *like* kissing you, you smell so clean – I declare you are as finicking as Charlotte on that score. Not like that terrible old man I danced with last night who stank of the stables and had poured at least a bottle of perfume over himself to conceal it instead of taking a bath!'

The Earl was recovering from this verbal and physical onslaught when a low laugh from the stairway drew his attention.

'Why, Charlotte!' he cried, disentangling himself from Penelope's Medusa-like clutches and adding mendaciously, 'I had not thought to find you here.'

Charlotte descended the stairs to greet him and his heart sank as he noted her pallor and listless air. She was a tall girl with a graceful slim figure that showed to great advantage when dancing or riding, both of which accomplishments she performed with enviable ease. Her near copper hair curled softly around a heart-shaped face which had little more to commend it than a pair of brilliant dark-lashed grey eyes. Her nose was unfashionably retroussé, her mouth unexpectedly firm, giving no hint of the sudden sweetness of her smile. She was still wearing her day dress of white muslin sprigged with dark blue and a matching blue silk spencer gave emphasis to her neat bosom and tiny waist, white kid slippers peeped from under the frilled hem of her skirt and a plain collar edged with lace completed the ensemble. Her only jewel was an enormous diamond ring which gave the impression of being too heavy for her slender hand to uphold. She greeted Julien with evident pleasure, if less enthusiastically than her younger sister, but there seemed to him to be a constraint in her manner and her smile lacked its customary warmth.

'Charlotte, I believe I have to wish you happy.' His good sense held him back from kissing her cheek as he was wont to do, but he carried her hand to his lips and so did not observe the look of unbearable misery she directed at his bent head.

'I thank you, my lord.' She was very formal. 'I understand from mama that you are here on two counts. I hope to be able to return your obliging sentiments before too long.' Not to be outdone in civility, he complimented her on her appearance, while Penelope skimmed away across the hall to inform her aunt of his arrival. 'It is excessively kind of you, my lord, so to put yourself out on Penny's behalf. I had spoken to Braybridge upon the matter, but he gave it as his opinion that you would be his superior in such an undertaking. He does not care to dance greatly nor to attend such entertainment as might divert so young a girl. In addition, your consequence is such as must draw attention to whatever lady you honour with your company.'

'Even in my shirt-sleeves, currying the horses?' That brought the laughter back into her eyes.

'Julien, be serious!'

'Thank God! I thought you must have forgotten my name.'

'That is not likely,' she replied quietly, 'but there is a world of difference between the Earl of Clandon currying his horses at Chalice, and that same Earl in residence at his town house. Well you know that, were it not for the fact of our being close neighbours and our mothers friends, the daughters of a mere baronet and the Earl of Clandon would be no more than bowing acquaintances.'

'Nonsense!' he replied. 'I will wager what you like that no such consideration will restrain the highest in the land from paying court to Penny when she makes her come-out.'

'Paying court maybe, but marrying is a horse of another colour,' replied Penelope's sister coolly. He could not resist the thrust.

'Is Richard Braybridge of so little consequence then that you can accept his addresses without fear of presumption?'

Colour flooded her pale cheeks but she was saved the trouble of replying by the arrival of her aunt, who took her to task for keeping the Earl standing in the hall.

'Though I hope I have no need to assure you that you are very welcome to call in as informally as you please, my lord.'

Lady Oakley had taken note of certain carefully expressed hints contained in her sister's letter which had aroused her quick curiosity, the chief of which had been to suggest that she should encourage Julien to visit South Audley Street as often as he might choose for whatever purpose. Lady Oakley, if not over-endowed with good sense, yet possessed a kindly and affectionate disposition, and was most ready to do all in her power for Penelope though she entertained small hope of her young niece attaching such a man as Clandon. Then Penelope darted back and led him into the drawing-room and her aunt, observing Julien's appreciative regard of the attractive picture she presented, allowed herself to feel more hopeful. One never could be sure with gentlemen, she reflected, and even if the Earl had known the child all her life and thought of her as the merest schoolgirl, very much stranger things had been known to happen and she was never one to despair.

'Come riding with me to-morrow morning, you two, or are you fashionably lazy lie-abeds?' Julien asked. Penelope's happy face fell at his words.

'Of all things, I would adore it!' she cried. 'But, as you know, I cannot abide hacks and Sultan remains at home so we have not been riding. I take it you have brought Rodrigo with you?' she added wistfully.

'Yes, and I will not allow you to ride him!' he retorted, for there was a continuous battle between her desire to master the fiery Arab he had brought back from Spain and his resolve that she should not risk her neck in doing so. 'However, Rodrigo has not journeyed alone. I took the liberty of bringing Jenny,' he smiled at Charlotte whose eyes lit up with pleasure, 'and also that beast of singularly ill nomenclature, Sultan himself!'

'Sultan!' she cried out. 'He is recovered then?'

'Well, I should advise against riding him into the ground just yet –' He got no further for she flung herself upon him.

'Dearest Julien, I must kiss you again for that!' she declared, suiting her action to her words.

'Penelope!' cried Lady Oakley in awful tones. 'I beg of you – a little decorum! My lord!'

For Julien, rather than bend his head to allow his small admirer to achieve her object, had clipped his hands around her waist and lifted her up to the necessary level. At the climax of this interesting scene Lady Oakley's butler flung wide the doors and announced Lord Braybridge.

His lordship checked on the threshold and raised his quizzing-glass the better to take in what lay before him. Charlotte, the laughter gone from her face as by magic, stepped forward to greet her betrothed.

'My dear girl, what have we here?' His lordship enquired in his habitually drawling voice. 'Good God, Clandon, have I to congratulate you?'

'No, no, of course not!' Charlotte burst into hurried speech. 'Penny was only thanking Julien for bringing her horse with him to town. We – they are very old friends, you know.'

'Indeed, so it would appear!' His lordship was smiling but his hard grey eyes were untouched by any real feeling and Julien, setting Penelope down, formed the instant opinion that he did not care for Braybridge any more than he had ever done. However, he greeted him with his customary politeness and offered his congratulations in so easy a manner that the tension that had descended upon the party at Braybridge's joining them soon was dissipated until his lordship turned to enquire of Penelope what pleasures had been occupying her attention during the day.

'For it is what you young ladies come to town for, is it not, to be pleasurably occupied?'

'No more than you do, I daresay, my lord.'

The rapier-like riposte took him by surprise but, before he could collect himself sufficiently to give her the set-down she had invited, Julien intervened smoothly.

'Now that is a palpable absurdity, Penny. Lord Braybridge comes to town to rid his mind of cares and worries such as you have not yet had laid on you. When you –'

'When I am older I will comprehend better? Thank you, Julien, I have had that sermon preached to me before but – but never by you!' With a stifled sob, she fled past him out of the room, leaving considerable confusion behind her.

'I declare I cannot think what has come over her!' Lady Oakley was almost wringing her hands. 'No, Charlotte, I will go to her. Such impertinence passes all bounds, I shall insist that she returns to make her apology.'

'Not on my behalf, I thank you.' Julien was at his most urbane. He was astonished by Penelope's outburst but he had sensed her dislike of Braybridge from the moment of his entering the room. That being so, to be forced to apologize to him for what had, after all, been a mere display of childish petulance would be unutterably galling to her youthful pride. If he disclaimed all need for apology, Braybridge could hardly do less. 'No doubt she has been in and out of everything this last week, ma'am, and is a little overtired.'

'Well, she did admit to having the headache this afternoon,' Lady Oakley agreed doubtfully, 'but your arrival put all thought of it from her.'

'And now it has returned twofold. Lay all the blame upon me, ma'am, my shoulders are a deal broader!' He smiled so sweetly at

Lady Oakley that there is no knowing what she might not have undertaken to do for him had not her butler chosen that moment to announce that the Earl's carriage had arrived and was awaiting his pleasure. He kissed Lady Oakley's hand, accepting with every evidence of pleasure her invitation to dine as soon as could be arranged. In offering the same courtesy to Charlotte, his fingers tightened slightly on hers and he felt her answering grateful response. He enquired at what hour she would care to ride in the morning and if Penny might be expected to be in a more reasonable temper. 'By Heaven, if she's not, just send me word of it and I will leave Sultan in his stall and bring for her the most miserable hack to be found.' She laughed and promised to stand surety for her sister's good behaviour.

'She will be so overset at having flared out at you, her penitence will be pitiful to behold,' she promised him.

'Hmm! For a day or two, perhaps, so I had best make the most of it! Your servant, Braybridge.'

When Julien had left the room, his lordship helped himself to snuff in the most elegant fashion. 'I daresay,' he said languidly, 'that Miss Penelope knows what she is about.'

'What can you mean?' Charlotte eyed him in some misgiving.

'To most men such a display of pertness and forwardness in affection might seem offensive. But Clandon appears to accept it in good part. In another it might arouse an inclination to beat her rather than to marry her.'

'Why do you suppose he wishes to marry her?'

He smiled, dusting the snuff off his fingers.

'If that is not the case then he should be a little more discreet in his dealings with her. I accept your explanation that long acquaintance supplies the reason for his easy manners with – both of you, but prospective husbands are apt to take a less tolerant view of such behaviour.'

The icy note in his voice left her in no doubt that he included himself in the latter category and she was much relieved when Lady Oakley tactfully turned the conversation to more general topics.

In the hall, the Earl had just received his hat and gloves from the butler when a door opened fractionally and a sibilant whisper arrested his attention.

'Psst! Julien!' A small hand beckoned to him imperiously.

'Wiggins,' said Julien, sighing resignedly, 'pray bid my man walk the horses until I am free to join him.'

'Certainly, my lord.' Not by so much as a flicker of an eyebrow did Wiggins betray his inner amusement. Twist the Earl round her little finger could Miss Penelope!

'Penny, what the devil are you about?' The expression on his face as he closed the door of the breakfast parlour and advanced upon her did not guarantee the Earl's willingness to be twisted around anyone's finger.

'Julien, I must talk to you. You cannot allow it, you simply cannot!'

'Cannot allow what?' he demanded, not unreasonably mystified.

'Charlotte to marry that *hateful* man! She does not even *like* him!'

'Well,' admitted the Earl, whose thoughts had been running on similar lines, 'their association does give all the appearance of being unsuitable but it is to be presumed that Charlotte does not find him precisely *hateful*.'

'But she does, I promise you!' Penelope insisted. 'And that business of breaking her heart over poor Captain Taverner was all a fudge, I assure you.'

'Penny,' said the Earl sorrowfully, 'I cannot for the life of me conceive where you acquire such expressions.'

'Oh, fiddlesticks!' She flung away from him to the door and stood, leaning against it for a moment, as if listening for any sound outside, until the full meaning of what she had said came home to him.

'How do you know she is not grieving for Taverner? She told Melissa she was.'

'She told Melissa because she knew Melissa would tell mama and *that* way mama might believe it.'

'What? Penny, can you be sure of this? Your mother was so convinced that it was otherwise.'

'Sit down, Julien, please, and listen.' Taking his arm, she guided him firmly to a chair then promptly seated herself upon his knee, with no more thought for the propriety of her actions than if he had been a piece of furniture.

'Penny!' The Earl, more conscious of the delicacy of the situation than she, endeavoured to remove her, only to discover that no vine can be more clinging than a fragile female when she bends her mind to it. 'What, pray, would Braybridge or your aunt think if they walked in on us now?'

'They cannot. I have just locked the door!' she declared calmly.

'You have *what*? Give me the key at once!'

'Not until you have heard me out. Please, Julien, listen! I enacted that little scene in the drawing-room in order to get out and waylay you as you left, but we have only a few minutes so please do not continue to interrupt what I have to tell you.'

'We may not even have that space of time,' he pointed out. 'My horses are being walked up and down the street and when Braybridge leaves it will require no effort of understanding on his part to comprehend that I have not taken my departure. In any case, Wiggins knows I am here.'

She waved aside his objections. 'Wiggins will say nothing unless he is asked, and my lord always stays for precisely one half-hour. Julien, I discovered quite by chance that mama is not so comfortably situated as she would have us believe. Last Christmas I overheard a conversation between her and my uncle, Mr Edward Warner. He was attempting to persuade her to sell Heatherstone Hall and retire quietly to Bath or some such place, but she refused, declaring that until we girls were settled she could not conceive of doing such a thing. All this I foolishly disclosed to Charlotte and, very soon after that, the present unhappy situation began to unfold itself. Oh, he,' tossing her head in the direction of the drawing-room, 'had already been dangling after her, but she would have none of him. Then, in a trice, the case is altered, he becomes the most acceptable of men and Captain Taverner – who, I declare, was no more to her than any other of her flirts – becomes the first excuse for such acceptance, and indeed the safest choice, poor man, for being unable to refute any claim she might make upon him.'

'Penny, why in Heaven's name, did you not come to me?'

'Charlotte and I did discuss it but she was of the opinion that it would be most wrong to approach you. Indeed, I gave her my word not to trouble you, but things have come to such a pass that I do not feel any great guilt in breaking it now.'

'If what you tell me is true, the devil's in the whole thing!' he growled.

'I see now we were much mistaken in not applying to you,' she allowed. 'The more I think on it the more I am assured you are the only one who can help us. The first thing to be done is to part Charlotte from that man.' Julien shook his head in perplexity.

'Why, of all men, had she to choose Braybridge?'

'Because he offered,' Penelope said simply. 'There he was, completely her servant, well-bred, wealthy, too good to be passed over. But since he is assured of her I am of the opinion he is not so completely her servant but rather addresses her as if she was one of his own daughters.'

Julien kept his counsel on that subject for, while he had observed with indignation Braybridge's possessive manner towards Charlotte, there was no doubt that the acquisition of so youthful and charming a bride was the source of much satisfaction to his lordship, which satisfaction he did not scruple to display.

'Penny,' he said thoughtfully, 'I much fear that if Charlotte is resolved to sacrifice herself on the family altar she will not be parted from Braybridge unless some other solution can be found to your difficulties.'

'There is you!' she pointed out.

'Sweet, if your mama could not feel herself able to turn to me for aid last Christmas, why should she do so now?'

'Then she will have to be provided with a sound reason for turning to you,' Penelope stated roundly. 'Why – Julien! How stupid we are! The solution is so simple!' The Earl eyed her in some apprehension and requested to be further enlightened. 'You must marry Charlotte yourself, of course! Only think how agreeable it will be! So little disruption to either household, and I could still be at Chalice, riding your horses which, depend upon it, might not be entirely acceptable to a strange lady if you should choose to marry one.' The Earl, being useful with his fives, had done an amount of boxing, but he could not recall ever previously having been dealt such a blow as to render him quite so stunned as he was at that moment. Penelope ignored his consternation and swept on to her triumphant conclusion. 'And, of course, when you are mama's son-in-law that will put a very different complexion upon the matter. She cannot then refuse your aid. Oh, Julien, promise me you will do this! It is common gossip you are looking out for a wife, and who could suit you better than dear Charlotte?'

'You have no notion of what you are talking about.' He set her on her feet with a roughness that startled her and rose from the chair. She studied his face anxiously.

'Have I offended you, Julien? If so, please forgive me, I never meant to do so. Perhaps there is already some lady to whom you have given your heart? I pray she is the nicest person in the world for I am sure you deserve no less. But I must go now and so must you if we are not to be discovered. Do please make Charlotte see the folly of what she is doing. Even if you cannot bring yourself to marry her perhaps you know of some gentleman of substance who is less odious than Braybridge!' With that she ran to the door and unlocked it, then hesitated and turned back to look at him. 'And – and, Julien, pray forgive me if I have said anything amiss about any lady you may choose to marry. I am sure I wish you happy with all my heart, only – only she won't be one of *us*, will she?'

Her voice ending on an unmistakable sob, she whisked the

door open and was gone. The Earl appeared to be lost in thought for a few moments then he, too, took his departure, letting himself quietly out of the front door and walking briskly down the street in pursuit of his carriage.

CHAPTER THREE

WHEN the Earl presented himself at Hertford House the following morning it was to find that a number of persons had had the same notion of calling to enquire after the widowed Lady Warne. Lady Hertford, whose air of haughty respectability belied the truth of her being the object of the Prince Regent's gallantries, greeted him cordially.

'Though I am well aware,' she told him, 'that it is not my *beaux yeux* that have attracted this superior company! Nonetheless, I am always well pleased to see you here, Clandon. In my opinion there are too many upstarts in society to-day, and too many who consider that to be in the height of fashion is near to being ennobled.' Her glance flashed significantly towards George Brummell who stood, deep in conversation with Charles Ellis. Julien, accustomed to her sharp tongue, smiled.

'Some men, ma'am, are born to be great,' he reminded her, 'while others achieve greatness.'

'You are too easy, too tolerant in your manners,' she chided him, but affectionately. 'Now go and pay your respects to Sally. She has been longing to see you.'

The Earl did as he was bid, but in his own time. There were old friends to greet and some chaffing to endure while, all the time, he was covertly observing her in the sure knowledge that such observance was being returned. At last, when he had manoeuvered himself to within a few feet of where she was standing, receiving the fulsome compliments of a gentleman whose dress proclaimed him to be the complete dandy, she turned her head to look straight at him. With a murmured excuse to his companion Julien moved to her side, effortlessly ousting the dandy who looked as if he was about to protest then, on seeing who it was, thought better of it.

'Upon my soul, the hermit of Chalice!' she quizzed him. 'And what can have induced you to leave your sylvan lair, my lord?'

'Whatever reason I may have had for *coming* to town,' replied Julien, holding her hand a shade longer than politeness demanded, 'the necessity for my *remaining* has now become crystal clear.'

'You still turn a pretty compliment,' she allowed. 'How do you practise your wiles? On your horses?'

He accepted the challenge. 'They, at least, cannot answer back, my lady!'

'Maybe, but you cannot wed 'em!' The company, as if by general consent, had drawn slightly away, but there were few pairs of eyes in the room that were not observing them. 'It is whispered that Clandon seeks a bride. Not an impossible ambition – or is Sultan more exacting in his requirements than ever Julien was?'

He shrugged, resigned to this constantly recurring topic of conversation. 'Sultan, my lady, died in the Peninsula. I did not know you had ever met him.' The touch of hauteur in his voice warned her to beware of how she spoke on that subject. She smiled bewitchingly up at him.

'Nor did I. Maybe I was just a little jealous of those that did.'

'You, my lady, can have no need to be jealous of anyone. Was I not ever your obedient slave?'

'You, Julien? Why I scarce dare call you Julien now! You are become so grand, so elegant, so – so –'

'So above your touch, you were about to say?' They were laughing at each other openly now, but their moment of privacy was past and, others joining them, the Earl presently relinquished his place beside her and went to greet Colonel FitzJames who had just been announced. 'Gad, Ned, but I'm fatigued! To bed at three and riding with the girls at nine! I'll have need to call in at Jackson's each day to keep myself in trim.'

The Colonel agreed that fulfilling all one's social engagements could prove strenuous. 'And how did you find my Lady Warne?'

he asked idly, but there was nothing of idleness in his regard as he waited for his friend's response.

'As quick of tongue and fair of face as ever.' The Earl's ready reply betrayed nothing of his feelings and they parted, Julien to speak to Mr Brummell and the Colonel to make his bow to Lady Warne.

She received him in the most friendly manner, but her responses to his gallantries were distrait, and he could not help but observe how her eyes followed Julien's graceful figure as he moved across the room to speak to his hostess. The sadness of her expression gave him cause for wonder, but he could not know of the eight years of married misery she had endured and of how it was being brought home to her that, had she flouted her parents' wishes and run off with Julien Revel, her life would have been a very different story. Not that he had ever proposed such an impropriety, but he was young and malleable then, she had no doubt she could have turned him round her thumb. Instead she had submitted to the Marquess who had some very odd notions of how to conduct himself in so intimate a connection as marriage. She had lost no time in providing him with an heir, hoping thereafter to be spared his attentions but, capricious though his tastes might be, the Marquess was fascinated by his beautiful wife and provided her with two further tokens of his esteem. When he died of a broken neck, brought about by attempting to skip down the great staircase at Warne after a very heavy evening's drinking, she had cried for three days from sheer relief. Men in general she held in contempt, while acknowledging there must be good in some of them, and the very thought of marrying again nearly overset her reason. Then to meet Julien and to recall their happy, light-hearted youth together, stirred a forgotten emotion within her. Heedless of her surroundings, her soft brown eyes filled with tears and she bit hard on her lower lip to stay its quivering. Colonel FitzJames was quick to act.

'I am informed that the view from this window,' he said, taking her arm and leading her to that furthest from the company, 'is quite the best in London.' As the window afforded no more than the sight of a few plane trees and Lord Hertford's stables, she could not but laugh and pressed his arm in appreciation of his kindness. The Colonel looked across to where Julien stood talking. 'He is rather a superb creature, isn't he?'

'I had forgotten how superb,' she replied very low.

'Do not allow him to enslave you, too, Niobe,' he implored her. 'For all that he is my friend there are times when I could kill him for his careless conquests.'

'Are they careless?' she wondered.

'Perhaps not now,' he agreed. 'Events have taught him to be more wary.'

'It is astonishing to me that he has never married.'

'Perhaps he is waiting for someone like yourself!' he teased her, and was shocked by her look of revulsion.

'Never will I marry again!' she cried. The anguish of her expression was such as to make him wonder just what the late Marquess had done to arouse such bitter feelings.

'Never,' he reminded her, 'is a mighty long time! Will you be attending the Rutlands' ball to-night?'

'What? Oh, yes, yes, I believe so.'

'Then may I beg the honour of the first waltz?' She had control of herself again.

'Thank you, with pleasure.'

'It would seem I have stolen at least this march on my lord of Clandon!' The Colonel's eyes twinkled down at her.

'Oh, he has not asked me for a dance. He will be too occupied in escorting the Misses Ralston.'

'What? Both of them? Surely Braybridge – ?'

'Does not dance. But, depend upon it, he will be there, keeping guard over his property!'

'You do not care for the gentleman?' Lady Warne expressed herself in terms that would have warmed Penelope's heart had she been privileged to hear them.

'I cannot conceive of Miss Ralston attaining any degree of happiness in such an attachment,' she declared.

'Ah, but Clandon tells me that, happiness being quite out of the question at the present time, she looks for little from Braybridge save consequence and a comfortable establishment.'

'What do you mean by "happiness being quite out of the question"?' she wanted to know. 'Has she lost her heart to another, then?'

'Yes, one who died in the late wars. Or so Clandon is persuaded.'

'It is argued there is no rival so potent as a dead one. But to marry Braybridge solely for his standing and money – is this necessary for so delightful a girl? She cannot be more than one-and-twenty, is it not likely that she will lose her heart again? Cannot Julien do something? Lady Hertford tells me that he stands in the position of elder brother to the Ralston girls.'

'Have you met the youngest Miss Ralston?' enquired the Colonel. Lady Warne laughed.

'Miss Penelope? Oh, an adorable minx! She has all the young bloods by the ears already!'

'Perhaps more than the young bloods find her bewitching,' he hinted.

'What can you mean by that?'

'That Braybridge honoured me with his confidence last night as I was leaving White's. The general trend of his discourse was that, as he considered himself to be the prospective male head of the family, he felt equal to the task of requesting Clandon either to cease his attentions to Miss Penelope or to make them good. I am assured he felt I ought to pass on this solemn warning to Sultan – which I have not done, nor do I intend to!'

'The fool!' said her ladyship succinctly. 'Julien will not brook such interference.'

'But from a prospective brother-in-law?' he suggested.

'Depend upon it, Ned,' she began with authority then, realizing she had let slip his name quite by mistake, she blushed delightfully, thereby giving him no small satisfaction.

'What must I depend upon, Sally?' he enquired, the gentle mischief in his voice transforming her confusion into amusement.

'Penelope may be a sweet child,' she declared, 'but she is no suitable wife for Julien. She is too young, too untried, to suit his tastes.'

'Yet he has offered for her and has been turned down by her mother, so he tells me,' observed the Colonel, quite shamelessly betraying his friend's confidence.

'Doubtless her mother is of the same opinion. But, nonetheless, to turn him down is wellnigh unbelievable!' Her eyes sought his in astonished question but he had observed Lord Alvanley bearing down upon them and motioned her to silence.

'To be continued to-night?' he whispered. Her eyes danced.

'During the first waltz?'

'Supper,' he said plaintively, 'would be so much more agreeable for discussion!'

She began to laugh but, before turning to talk to Alvanley, she gave a quick nod of consent and the Colonel, well satisfied with his morning's work, strolled away to take his leave of Lady Hertford.

* * *

An opportunity to talk privately with the eldest Miss Ralston did not present itself to the Earl for some time. On social occasions Braybridge was ever at her elbow, and though Penny would willingly have tried for an opportunity to leave them alone on their morning rides, their numbers had been added to by the arrival of a niece of Lord Oakley's, a Miss Branscombe, to join the household at South Audley Street. This lady, as she herself explained, had not come to town for the season. That had been done on a previous occasion and, as she had not taken at the age of twenty, it was unlikely she would do so five years later.

The Earl privately considered that she underrated her attractions, for she had a pleasing countenance, an enquiring mind and an impeccable taste in dress. Charlotte explained to him that Miss Branscombe had been forced to cut short her first season in order to return home and tend an ailing mother. When the inevitable occurred and she was freed from this duty, she felt no inclination to return to London. Her present visit was prompted, she avowed, by her wish to join in the general rejoicing in the capital, to renew the acquaintance of her dear aunt and cousins by marriage, and to meet Lord Byron whom, she was assured, could not be half as handsome as he was painted.

Charlotte had taken to her immediately and, very soon, a warm affection existed between the two young women. Penelope she treated with amused tolerance, while the Earl was accorded a measure of respect as befitted his consequence, but he had the feeling that he was ever under the scrutiny of her keen eyes that missed little of what went on around her.

One afternoon, when calling in at South Audley Street upon the chance that Penelope might care to go driving with him, the Earl discovered that young lady gone to her dressmaker's with Lady Oakley, Miss Branscombe visiting a sick friend, and Charlotte seated alone in the book-room, reading a novel. She rose to greet him with a ready smile.

'Julien, why do you not keep Miss Austen's books at Chalice? I do declare she works so upon my imagination that I am quite out of patience with her Mr Darcy though, to be sure, it is plain that all will come right in the end.'

'The course of true love in such works must always run fair,' he reminded her.

'How unfortunate it is,' she sighed, setting down the book, 'that we cannot bend our own lives to such happy endings.' That gave him the opportunity he had long been seeking.

'Are you so unhappy, Charby?' She looked away but made no answer. 'In God's Name, have done with this nonsensical affair and send Braybridge about his business! Look at me.' He put a finger under her chin and raised it so that she was forced to meet his regard. 'The fact of your having lost your heart to a gallant soldier is no reason for you to yield your body to an ageing roué!' That shocked her, as he had intended it should, and she answered him with a touch of her old spirit.

'My b-body is my own to b-bestow as I please, I thank you!'

He did not fail to notice the slight stammer which always afflicted her in moments of stress, and his voice was very kind as he made reply.

'My poor innocent, you cannot be aware of what you are saying. Have you any notion of what it may be like to give yourself to a man whom you cannot love – nay, whom I suspect you truly dislike? You, Charby, of all people, so warm in heart, so generous in your affections!'

'My name is Charlotte!' she reminded him in a small, stifled voice.

'Miss Ralston, if it pleases you, ma'am!' The Earl was not to be deflected from his purpose. 'My dear, is your heart so sore for Taverner?'

She stared at him in momentary lack of comprehension. 'H-Harry?' she got out at last. 'Yes, of course, but how could you know?'

'From your mother, who had it from Melissa.'

'Oh, yes,' she said, rather too quickly. 'I held poor Harry in – in great affection. M-my life was quite at an end when he went.'

'Maybe,' he said dryly, 'but you could scarce recall his name when I mentioned it just now. It won't do, my girl, you never were a good liar! Come, confess, what is the true story?' She stood silent, head bowed, her fingers pulling at Braybridge's great diamond in her agitation. 'And take that confounded ring off!' He caught her hand and suited his action to his words, flicking the jewel away from him until it came to rest in the middle of the hearthrug. Then, resting himself comfortably against the edge of the library table, he pulled her into the crook of his arm. 'Once you were used to bring all your troubles to me. Are we not still friends? May I not help you now?'

His lips were brushing her ear, the indefinable perfume of her was in his nostrils and, to his amazement – for, after all, this was Charlotte whom he had known all her life! – his heart beats quickened in the most affecting way and only the knowledge that such conduct would not advance his present case restrained him from giving her further proof of his friendship.

Gently, she detached herself from his clasp and moved away while Julien, feeling his judgment to be sadly at odds, could not, for the life of him, understand why he had never before noticed what a wholly desirable woman she had become. Grief or anxiety had lent maturity to her youth, the shadows under her eyes were not unbecoming and, as now, when there appeared a soft flush of colour to warm her cheeks, she bore all the appearance of beauty.

'Julien, you must know there is much I cannot disclose to you. B-but I am obliged to contract as good a marriage as may be, and there are few likely to offer so much as Braybridge.'

'And, I collect, no sooner will the wedding knot be tied than you expect him to throw open his coffers for your family's use?' Her astonishment at his knowledge was plain to see. 'Oh, I have had it all from Penny. But, depend upon it, Braybridge has less generosity in his whole person then you have in one hair of your head.'

'This I did suspect,' she admitted, 'but perhaps he could be per-persuaded – if I pleased him well – ' A natural shyness prevented her from saying more and he was quick to seize upon it.

'The doting husband and the bewitching young wife – is that the picture? You are not cast in such a mould, Charlotte, and I doubt that Braybridge is either. No sooner does he discover you are after his money-bags than you will pay for your cupidity and go on paying for the rest of your life with him. All men like to believe they are loved for themselves, even as astute a one as Braybridge, but that deception will not survive the rigours of marriage.' She winced at that, closing her eyes involuntarily at the prospect his words conjured up for her. 'Why did not your mother call on me? She must know I would help her in any way I could. If only she had accepted – ' He stopped abruptly but she completed his sentence for him.

'Your offer for Penny? Oh, yes, she told me, Julien.' The Earl mentally apostrophized his Aunt Emmelina for her lack of discretion. 'She was troubled by it for she was confident your offer was prompted less by affection than convenience. Is that still the case, my lord?'

'What can you mean?' His surprise was so evident that she had to smile.

'You are paying Penny very great attention. So much so that, Braybridge informs me, the betting runs high in the clubs that you will offer for her before long. Though, I am given to understand, another contestant has now been entered in the lists against her – my Lady Warne!'

Julien flushed with annoyance. There was no doubt he had been seeing a lot of Sally Warne, but he had been careful to ensure that it had always been in the company of others. Their flirtation consisted of a light-hearted teasing on his part, on hers a responsive pleasure in his company, but no more nor less than she appeared to derive from that of others.

'You can tell my lord Braybridge to keep his money in his purse!' he rapped out, walking over to the window to stare, unseeing, at the carriages passing along South Audley Street.

'Then you don't love Penny?' The question so amazed him that he spun round to face her.

'Of course I hold her in affection, and if I married her I would do everything in my power to make her happy, that I swear. But,' he made a curiously despairing gesture, 'perhaps your mother has the right of it. Penny is too young, she knows me too well.'

'As a brother, a mentor, a dear friend,' she agreed, 'but never as a lover. That, I do believe, Julien, would distress her. It would be like Jupiter condescending to notice the least of his nymphs!'

'Don't gammon me! She pays me as little respect as any other.'

'Which puts me in mind of something I would discuss with you,' she said briskly. 'There is a pleasant young man, a Mr Robert Beaumont, who has not been scared away by your constant attentions to her and who, I suspect, meets with her approval.' He frowned, taken aback at this unexpected turn.

'Beaumont? Yes, of course, grandson to the Duchess of Arlesford. Rumour has it she dotes upon him and has made him heir to her personal fortune. No title likely there since it was his mother who was Her Grace's only daughter. But he is a mighty high connected young man and carries himself well.'

'I am glad you approve,' she said demurely. 'He is calling to take Penny driving at five o'clock.' But if her plan had been to distract the Earl's mind from the purpose of his visit she had failed in her object.

'Then I had best say what I have to and be gone. Charlotte, you cannot go through with this marriage. I do not know what maggot has got into your head but there must be some reason other than that you have told me to drive you to such an extreme.'

'There is,' she confessed, 'but none that I may confide in another.'

The devil! thought Julien. Does that mean an unrequited love or an attachment for some unsuitable person? Aloud, he said lightly: 'Well, then, if you are resolved on forming a wealthy connection, I beg you throw off Braybridge and marry me!'

The noise of movement in the street outside sounded unnaturally loud in the stillness that followed and he had to strain to hear her reply.

'Is your case so desperate, my lord, that your ch-choice must fall on one of us?'

'It appears to me that your case is so desperate one of you must direct her choice to fall on me. My fortune will ever be at your convenience, while your mother may not refuse the help of a son-in-law as she might a mere neighbour. And,' he went on, warming to his theme, 'I see no need for her to be informed of this arrangement. Sufficient to tell her that you find Braybridge will not suit then, a little later, that you have accepted me in his place. She cannot cavil at it for the situation will be unchanged – a marriage of convenience, you still being all to pieces because of young Taverner.'

'That fiction is to stay, then?'

'I think it must,' said the Earl thoughtfully, 'else she will be on her high-horse again about love-matches and you will not wish her to know the real reason for your marrying me.'

'No, no, of course not!' she said hastily. 'But, Julien, what advantage can you gain from our – our alliance?'

The Earl considered this aspect of the case and was amazed to discover how much he might profit thereby.

'We deal together very comfortably, you understand my ways, and I believe you would cherish Chalice as I do. That, as you know, must be a first consideration with me when choosing a wife.'

'Is there not another reason which prompted you to contemplate marriage in the first instance?'

'Well, yes, there is that, of course.' Julien looked anywhere but at her and, of the two, Charlotte appeared to accept frank discussion of such an intimate nature with more composure than he. 'If we – if I might prevail upon you to grant me an heir, then you have my word I'll not presume further upon your kindness.'

She bowed her head as if to accept the inevitable. 'Upon consideration,' she said in an odd little voice, 'I find that a small price to pay in return for the consequence and security you will bestow on me. After all, I had r-reconciled myself to giving B-Braybridge an heir and cannot feel that I am in any worse case by offering to do a like service for you.'

Julien's knuckles showed white as he gripped the edge of the table behind him.

'Thank you!' he said with exaggerated courtesy. 'That may not rank as the greatest compliment paid to me in my life, but if you are satisfied that your situation has not been worsened by my intervention, then I am well content.'

'Forgive me if my words sounded less than gracious!' She was all contrition at hearing the anger in his voice. 'There is so much that commends itself to me in your proposal and I do th-thank you for it and assure you that I am deeply sensible of the honour you do me. I shall use every endeavour to be an amiable and dutiful wife – ' Her voice quavered and broke in the midst of her dignified speech. Julien took her by the shoulders and swung her round to face him.

'What is it, Charby? What have you not told me? Or does the thought of marrying me disgust you?' Her head dropped forward on his shoulder, he sensed that she was very near to tears and contented himself with holding her lightly until she should recover her composure.

'Thank you, Julien,' she whispered presently. 'You are more kind to me than I deserve. I – I will endeavour not to t-try your patience too far.' She then withdrew from him and began to walk about the room, while he leaned his elbows on the back of a chair and watched her closely. 'I can do little, I fear, immediately, to turn things about,' she explained, 'because Braybridge has, this very day, left town for two or three weeks. He has estate business to attend to and, did I wish it, I could not imagine how to reach him because I do not know his precise direction from day to day. No doubt his man of business here in London could inform me, but I am of the opinion that a letter will not do in this case. I owe him the courtesy of plain speech and so must wait until he returns to town.'

The Earl silently applauded her courage while deploring the necessity for it. 'And then?' he asked.

'Then we must wait for a time. Th-there must be nothing done to give the impression that you are in any way associated with the breaking of my engagement.' While being in full agreement with the need for quelling any possible scandal, Julien experienced a sharp sense of disappointment, as unreasonable as it was unexpected. 'In the meantime,' Charlotte continued firmly, 'this will be our secret, to be told to no one. I think, also, that it would be best if you left now before the others return and speculation becomes general as to the nature of our tête-à-tête.' The sound of a carriage drawing up to the street door gave emphasis to her words.

'I will await your further directions, ma'am,' said the Earl, with a demureness that did not match up to the sparkle in his eye.

As he stepped into the hall the street bell pealed imperiously. Wiggins came hastening to the door and opened it to admit Miss Branscombe, looking very fine in a rich silk pelisse with white feather muff and elegant matching turban. The Earl made her a bow and was gone before she could take in the significance of his presence in the house. Then, slowly stripping off her gloves, she enquired of Wiggins where Miss Charlotte was to be found.

That damsel was, to all appearances, once more immersed in the affairs of Miss Elizabeth Bennet and Mr Darcy and presented a calm appearance to her friend when she entered the bookroom, though Miss Branscombe did wonder just how difficult it was to be reading a book held upside down.

'Anthea, my dear, I trust you found poor Mrs Fortescue in better spirits?'

'I imagine her to be in better health,' Miss Branscombe declared, 'but her spirits continue obstinately low. So much so that I have yielded to her entreaties and, with Aunt Oakley's permission, will remove myself and my chattels to South Street in the course of the week. It is most unfortunate that Mr Fortescue has to be in Brussels at this time, but his work in the Diplomatic Service must, of course, come first.' Charlotte expressed her concern but regretted losing the company of Miss Branscombe. 'As to that, I shall be no distance away. I daresay we shall see as much of each other as if I continued to live here. Clandon appeared to be in some haste,' she added, dropping her gloves and reticule on the table and sinking gratefully into a chair.

'I told him that Mr Beaumont was calling to take Penny driving,' said Charlotte composedly. Miss Branscombe raised a questioning eyebrow.

'And he took it in good part?'

'With every appearance of stoicism,' Charlotte assured her. 'Indeed, he agreed with me that Mr Beaumont's pretensions could well be encouraged.'

Miss Branscombe placed the tips of her fingers together and assumed a judicial air. 'I almost begin to pity Clandon. No sooner does he pay court to a lady than it sets the fashion for someone else to do so.'

'What do you mean?' The question came out more sharply than Charlotte had intended but her friend appeared not to notice anything amiss.

'Only that I was passed by my Lady Warne driving out with

Colonel FitzJames – no, they did not see me. So absorbed were they in each other's conversation that I could well have been a cobble in the street!' This time Miss Branscombe did steal a glance at Charlotte's face and was afforded considerable satisfaction at seeing her expression of relief. 'It is not to be supposed, of course, that if Clandon really applied himself to the task, he could fail to win the lady from FitzJames. But then,' she added kindly, 'he is only trifling. I doubt he will marry anyone he cannot feel deeply for.'

'That is what mama says,' Charlotte began, and then realized that the trend of the conversation might involve her more than she cared to contemplate. Miss Branscombe rose and went to study her reflection in the overmantel mirror.

'Do tell me, is this turban a trifle overpowering, would you say?'

'Not on you,' Charlotte hastened to assure her. 'I think it suits wonderfully with your pelisse – and what pretty slippers you are wearing!' A moment later she was to regret uttering this last remark for Miss Branscombe, glancing down at her feet, saw something glittering near them on the rug. She bent down to pick up the ring and looked at Charlotte in surprised enquiry. 'Oh! It must have s-slipped off! It – it is a shade large, you know!'

Her flushed confusion hardly bore out such a simple explanation, but Miss Branscombe merely handed her the diamond, saying in her matter-of-fact manner: 'Then perhaps you had better slip it on again, my dear!'

She could not, however, fail to observe the shudder that passed through Charlotte's slight body as she replaced the ring on her hand. Happily, further discussion on that subject was rendered impossible by the return of Penelope and her aunt, and the Earl's visit was not again mentioned.

CHAPTER FOUR

If anyone had thought to put the question to him which, needless to say, they did not, Julien would have assured them that he preferred Braybridge's space to his company. In spite of this, the few weeks that succeeded his talk with Miss Ralston were the most interminable he had ever endured. He might not attend Penelope because of frightening away Mr Beaumont who, to do him justice, gave no indication of being easily frightened, and Charlotte was not yet his to escort. He greeted with relief a politely worded request from his agent at Chalice, to the effect that, if his lordship would be so condescending, the moment was opportune for a meeting with Mr Macadam with whom the Earl wished to discuss the reconstruction of part of the drive which suffered from flooding in inclement weather.

On his return to London he called at South Audley Street, and recounted to Charlotte the details of his talk with Mr Macadam. 'He proposes to raise and drain the level of the drive for a full mile in such a manner as to deflect any flood water away from the Home Farm. The new surface of the drive will consist of layers of hard stone, of which there is an ample supply in the nearby quarry, broken into very small pieces, not one to weigh more than six ounces. Constant usage will wear this surface comparatively smooth in a short time. The pity of it is Macadam will not be there himself to oversee the doing of it, for he is in as great demand as Mr Telford for the construction of roads, but he has given me his word that he will engage the services of an engineer who resides in Newbury and who, he assures me, has done much satisfactory work for him.'

Miss Branscombe, who was sitting with them working on her

embroidery frame, thought the subject a bore, but was ready to allow that her interests did not lie in drainage and road construction. The Earl and Miss Ralston, however, sitting together on a sofa, gave all the appearance of a comfortably married couple, amicably discussing improvements to their home.

'This work will doubtless also greatly ease that sharp bend in the drive that so many of your whipster friends appear to think they can take at the gallop!' remarked Charlotte sagely. He laughed.

'And finish up in the furze bushes! Yes, the firmer road surface should hold vehicles more securely, though I'll not answer for Ned FitzJames and that new curricle of his!'

'Which puts me in mind to tell you that he left a message if you should call here before he had the opportunity to speak to you. He has arranged to take a party to visit Vauxhall to-morrow evening and hopes you can be one of us. It will be almost a family gathering, my aunt and uncle, Penny and Mr Beaumont, Anthea here, Lady Warne, you, the Colonel, myself and Braybridge.'

'He's back, then?' The change in the Earl's demeanour was not lost on the attentive Miss Branscombe.

'He returned to town to-day.' Much though she strove to give an outward appearance of calm, Charlotte's heightened colour betrayed her inward agitation. 'He is in good spirits for he has been able to procure a fine example of porcelain from the Girl-in-the-Swing factory which, he tells me, may be of great value in the future, being something of an oddity.'

'I envy him that.' Julien rose to take his leave. 'My collection is mostly in the orthodox Chelsea style, with a few good foreign pieces. I have been idle, I suppose, in not adding to it in recent years.'

'You idle?' She shook a playful finger at him. 'Now you are really on the catch for a compliment but I'll not oblige your vanity!'

'If I am not appreciated in this house then I will take myself off to some other place where my worth is held in better esteem!' He was quizzing her, but she replied in all sincerity.

'There is, I swear, no place in England where you are more truly held in esteem than in this house.'

'If I may never receive a more gracious tribute than that, then am I well content.'

Watching them, Miss Branscombe thought she might be forgiven for assuming that she did not exist at all, but the delicate moment was shattered as the door was flung open and Penelope floated in, a radiant picture in silver gauze over leaf-green satin, adorned with tiny rosettes of pearls and silver ribbons down the length of the bodice and on her satin pumps.

'Well, now!' Miss Branscombe set down her tambour and turned in her chair the better to survey this vision. 'Let us see what we have done.'

'Oh, Anthea, I think it delightful! I vow I shall turn all heads at Almack's this evening! Julien, do you not agree?'

'Beyond any doubt!' He raised his quizzing glass the better to inspect her and she stamped her foot at him.

'Do not do that, I beg you! You know how it teases me! Anthea – Miss Branscombe – advised me on this gown for I have never before worn this particular shade of green.'

'I congratulate you, Miss Branscombe, on your choice. It is most becoming,' said the Earl gravely. 'Who is escorting you to Almack's to-night, Penny?'

'Mr Beaumont and his aunt, Lady Winslow, are to be there and they have kindly offered – ah, here they are, I should suppose.'

Her expression of delighted anticipation caused Charlotte and Julien to exchange amused glances. Under cover of Penelope's conferring with Miss Branscombe on some detail of her dress, she whispered to him: 'Can you stay a moment to meet him? I think she would like it.' He nodded, surprised to find himself so little resenting another man's intrusion into Penelope's affections. Confound her mother's perspicacity, she would laugh him out of countenance for this!

Mr Robert Beaumont was a slim young man of four-and-twenty, with a countenance sufficiently pleasing to justify being called handsome, while his hazel eyes were alight with humour and intelligence. Another emotion was also apparent in them as they took in the charms of Miss Penelope, so much so for the Earl to feel a certain sympathy with this promising suitor and to greet him with cordial civility.

To be thus received by one who, though not five years his senior was, in consequence and worldly experience, far his superior and, in addition, one whom he had feared to be his rival in Penelope's affections, not surprisingly supported the young gentleman's confidence, and he found himself talking to the company with an easy affability that did much to raise his standing in Penelope's regard.

When the couple had gone to join Mr Beaumont's aunt in their waiting carriage, Charlotte looked a mute question at the Earl. 'Yes,' he said, 'he will do very well, I daresay.'

'Thank you, grandpapa!' she whispered. Lady Oakley, who had entered the room on Mr Beaumont's arrival, caught the low-voiced exchange and at once made herself part of it.

'You like him, Clandon? I must say he is becoming very particular in his attentions and, for myself, I have nothing to say against him.'

'I think him a well-behaved gentlemanly man, perfectly at ease with himself. They should suit well together for his would seem to be a stable character, capable of handling Penny's more volatile disposition,' declared the Earl in a downright pontifical manner.

'Oh, Julien, you don't believe he would beat her, do you?' The mischief in Charlotte's face taunted him to reply.

'No more than I would you!'

It was fortunate that Lady Oakley was obsessed by consideration of Penelope's prospects and so did not pay heed to the silence that fell after his words, but Miss Branscombe's sharp glance missed nothing of Charlotte's confusion nor of the Earl's discomfort at having uttered words which need not, after all, have meant anything significant. He quickly covered up his lapse by asking for details of the proposed visit to Vauxhall and, upon learning that no definite arrangement had been made for dinner, suggested that the party dine at Clandon House prior to their departure for the Gardens.

'I will, like as not, run Ned to earth at White's or Watier's this evening and will sort the matter out with him.'

Miss Branscombe was much struck by the questioning look he directed at Charlotte as he bade her good-night and her slight shake of the head in response. Rarely had she known her friend so gay and light-hearted, even Braybridge's return having failed to cast her into the dismals. She promised herself to keep a close watch on events but to make no premature suppositions as to how the cat might jump.

Clandon House bore an unwonted appearance of gaiety the following evening. The fine dining-room of truly Palladian proportions was lit by three magnificent chandeliers that cast a rich light on the long table, bright with glass and silver and bearing a graceful tribute of early roses by each lady's cover. While his guests murmured their appreciation of the delightful setting, Julien bowed Lady Oakley to the head of the table, opposite to him. Lady Warne he placed on his right hand and Charlotte on his left. As Lady Warne's other partner was Mr Beaumont, who had Penelope beside him, and Charlotte had Lord Oakley on her further side – a taciturn gentleman who had long since been overwhelmed by his wife's eloquence – the Earl found himself fully occupied in keeping both ladies entertained.

The conversation throughout the meal was lively and varied. Penelope described in great detail the appearance of the Emperor of all the Russias at Almack's the previous evening. 'Such condescension, such charm! And he dances the waltz so elegantly!'

'I hear he has declined Prinny's hospitality and is staying at Pulteney's Hotel with his sister,' remarked Colonel FitzJames, wishing he was not so placed as to be unable to observe Lady Warne and Julien without craning round Penny and Mr Beaumont.

Lady Oakley was enjoying herself. 'Clandon, this salmon is quite excellent,' she declared. 'Could you prevail upon your chef to let me have the recipe for his sauce?'

The Earl, knowing full well that the perfectionist in his kitchen would no more divulge one of his culinary secrets than send anything to table that was not superb, was saved the trouble of inventing some excuse for not obliging the lady by a sudden bark of laughter from Braybridge.

'The Prince Regent has a mounting score to mark up against the Emperor!' he drawled. 'His verdict on a certain lady who lives not a mile from here is reported to be "She is mighty old"!'

'And I am informed he is not too punctilious in attending his sittings with Mr Thomas Lawrence,' added Lady Warne.

'I understand Prinny has commissioned Lawrence to paint them all.' Julien motioned to his butler to refill Braybridge's glass. Contrary to his usual custom, that gentleman gave all the appearance of enjoyment and was presently absorbed in an animated discussion with Miss Branscombe on the subject of his porcelain collection.

'Marshal Blücher, no doubt, is the favourite of the people.' Lady Oakley was happily watching a second large helping of salmon being piled on to her plate. 'They say it was all Lord Burghersh could do to get him safe into the house t'other day as he was nearly crushed to death by the mob.'

'Poor old fellow! Said he had never been so frightened in his life!' Colonel FitzJames tasted appreciatively of his wine. 'Sultan, if ever you feel the need for disposing of any of this hock I am entirely at your service.'

'Talking of being frightened,' Charlotte put in, 'I am told the cows in Green Park are yielding little milk for they are scared to convulsions by the constant huzzas and the press of people.'

Julien glanced at her quickly. She had been noticeably silent throughout the meal and he was sure that the coming ordeal of confronting Braybridge was weighing upon her spirits. That she had not had an opportunity to broach the matter already was apparent from his lordship's cheerful temper. Julien bitterly regretted his promise to stay out of the affair for he feared that the Viscount was going to be exceedingly angry at his dismissal, but his own commonsense supported her decision. It would be leaving her open to attack by every bitter tongue and pen in London if it became known that she was planning to become the Countess of Clandon while still betrothed to Braybridge, and though some women would have thought little of such notoriety, Charlotte's sensitive nature must recoil from anything of the kind. His lordship, also, might reasonably feel that his honour had been touched and Julien, cool hand though he was, had no fancy for a duel that would reflect on Charlotte's good name.

'A penny for them, mine host!' Sally Warne broke in on his reverie, but he declined to satisfy her curiosity.

'Will you be attending the Gala Performance at the Theatre Royal on Monday?' he asked.

'Indeed yes. Colonel MacKinnon has a box and has invited me to join his party.' He pursed his lips in a silent whistle.

'The gay Dan? Have a care, my lady!'

'Care,' she replied recklessly, 'has never been my first object.'

He wondered if it was his excellent wine or some undisclosed emotion that had brought the colour to her cheeks, but whatever the cause, she was looking very lovely. Then the table was set into a roar by Miss Branscombe's announcing that she had quite gone off Lord Byron.

' "Mad, bad and dangerous to know"! What a nonsense!' she declared. 'Oh, I grant you his writing, that justifies his fame, but as for the rest he is just a great show-off, no more dangerous than any gentleman at this table!'

'Miss Branscombe, that remark would seem to hint at some special knowledge of those present to-night!' Colonel FitzJames teased her.

'Or of Lord Byron!' Penelope's quick tongue brought the censure of the party upon her, and Miss Branscombe was glad of the opportunity to get on with her dinner and leave Lord Byron to fend for himself.

When the time came for them to leave for Vauxhall, Lady

Oakley expressed her amazement at how quickly the evening had passed. 'Depend upon it, Clandon, good food and good company never fail to give pleasure and we have had an abundance of both here to-night.'

The Earl disclaimed any undue merit in his arrangements but, privately, he was much gratified at the success of the party. Being a bachelor, he entertained but little and that informally, and the sight of even such a small company enlivening Clandon House made him contemplate the prospect of entertaining in a grander style, with a wife by his side, with perfect equanimity. Even Braybridge came out of the evening with credit. Julien almost found himself pitying his lordship, so blissfully unaware of any Sword of Damocles suspended over his head.

Colonel FitzJames had had the capital notion of conveying his guests across the river by boat to the water gate of the Gardens. Penelope had never before visited this famous place of entertainment and she was determined not to miss any one of its pleasures, so they started off at the Rotunda to gaze at the marvels of the Grand Cascade, then listened to a short concert, after which they walked out to view the fireworks. This display quite enthralled her and Mr Beaumont's were not the only eyes to derive satisfaction from watching her amazed delight.

Charlotte, who was secluded in a corner with Julien standing beside her, had quite forgotten her worries and was enjoying herself as much as her sister, if less volubly. Once she flung out a hand to draw his attention to a particularly effective display and her knuckle scraped sharply on the edge of the low wall beside her. Her exclamation of pain made him grasp her hand and examine it for possible injury.

'It is nothing, just a graze,' she protested, but the Earl was not taking her word for it until he had satisfied himself that blood had not been drawn, then he lifted her hand to his lips and held it there for a moment.

'May I kiss and make it well, Charby?'

Her pleasure at his use of one of her youthful expressions was tempered by the fear that someone might have overheard him but the others appeared all to be absorbed in watching the fireworks. Braybridge she could not see because he was standing behind Julien. Her anxiety would have been greatly increased had she known that he had taken note of every gesture of the incident, for my lord had not joined the party solely to be amused by the public entertainment. He had another source of interest to engage his attention.

When they had had their fill of watching the display, Colonel FitzJames confessed to having reserved a table for a light supper. The ladies protested they could not touch a morsel after the excellent dinner they had enjoyed, but the Colonel was adamant that no visit to Vauxhall would be complete without tasting the fine-cooked ham for which the suppers were famous and, perhaps, a confection of peaches in brandy roasted with sugar, and almonds to follow? As the party moved off in search of their supper table, Julien noticed that Lady Warne hung back as if reluctant to leave off watching the fireworks.

'Not hungry, Sally?'

'Julien, could you summon a carriage for me? I – I feel rather unwell.'

'My poor girl, I'll take you home at once.'

'No, no, do not disturb the others, please,' she begged. 'It would be most unfair to N – Colonel FitzJames.'

'I cannot allow you to go by yourself at this hour of night,' he told her. 'You won't care for the water if you are feeling queasy, so we will leave by the other gate.' Just then Mr Beaumont returned in search of Penelope's scarf which she had left lying on a chair. 'Beaumont, be so good as to inform FitzJames that I am escorting Lady Warne home as she is not feeling up to snuff.'

Mr Beaumont expressed concern and sympathy for Sally's pale face. 'It is only that fireworks give me the most dreadful headache,' she explained. 'Each time I assure myself that it will not happen, but it does! I just could not support having to eat supper at the moment.' Mr Beaumont promised to convey her apologies to the Colonel and, retrieving Penelope's scarf, took himself off.

Many people were already leaving the Gardens and Julien was fortunate in securing a hackney carriage immediately. On arrival at Warne House he paid off the driver and turned to escort Sally up the steps but she caught his arm and murmured to him to wait. He had already observed that the house was in complete darkness and wondered if he was going to be forced to wake the neighbourhood by resorting to the use of the enormous brass knocker or the antiquated bell-pull by the side of the door.

'I use the gate into the garden,' she said, 'come this way.' Just past the house was a narrow alley, much overhung by trees, and the small wooden door was almost totally concealed by ivy. She felt amongst the twisted roots for a moment then triumphantly produced a key which Julien fitted into the lock. The formal paved garden at the back of Warne House was bright with moonlight, throwing into sharp relief the iron balcony that ran the length of the first floor. A dim light showed in one of the rooms opening on to this balcony and the Earl looked in question at the lady. 'Those are my apartments. I told my maid not to wait up for me but to leave candles burning.'

'But there is no stair – how do you get there?' he asked.

'I have a key to that door set just below – do you see?'

Deep under the shadow of the balcony there was indeed a door to which the Earl escorted her and waited while she fumbled in her purse. 'Julien, I have not got it! Oh, great Heaven, what to do? Wait, perhaps someone has noticed and left it out for me.' But a hurried search brought no key to light and the door was firmly locked. 'There's nothing for it but to climb up to the balcony.'

'Could we not rouse someone?' he suggested.

'There is only my aunt who sleeps on this side and she is stone-deaf. The servants are all at the top of the house and would never hear. The gardener must have a ladder, could you please look over there by the wall?'

The Earl, feeling that the adventure was getting a little out of hand and that the simplest solution would be to awaken the household, nevertheless was loth to disoblige a lady, and soon had the ladder placed against the balcony, remarking as he did so that it was not very wise to have it left so convenient for any thief to use.

'So unromantic, Romeo?' My lady was clearly much recovered in health and instructed him to go up to the balcony and be prepared to receive her and assist her over the rail.

'What if all the windows are locked?'

'Then we break the glass!' she said firmly.

'Best look about for a brick, then!' he advised her. 'May I suggest it would be a better plan for me to get in and come down and open the door for you?'

'What? Have you stumbling about a strange house in the dark, frightening everyone to fits, when I can be up there in a trice? In any case, the painters are still at work and there are pots and ladders lying about in the most unexpected places which you could fall over.'

If it occurred to him that she appeared to be presenting difficulties where few were likely to exist, he kept his thoughts to himself and, with a resigned shrug, started on his upward journey. A few minutes later he received her in his arms and lifted her on to the balcony. Cautiously she tried the dimly-lit window which, to Julien's relief, yielded to her touch. As she entered, the candles, set on a spider-table just inside, flickered and almost went out.

'Quickly, light these!' He lit the fresh branch of candles she thrust at him from the guttering remnants of the old and, as the flames steadied and soared he was more than a little astonished to find himself in my lady's bedroom, for when she had mentioned her apartments, he had taken this room to be her private sitting-room. He turned to ask if she would like more candles lit and found she had thrown off her cloak and was standing close to him with a look of appeal on her pretty face. 'Julien, it is quite ridiculous – but could you release me from this wretched gown?'

'Now what,' said he, trying to conceal his amusement, 'would you have done had I not been here?'

'Gone to bed in it!' she retorted promptly. 'I would not dare rouse Nellie at such an hour! But as you *are* here – '

'I warn you that my services as a lady's maid command a high price! Turn your back to the light, ma'am!'

His task was almost completed when, with a swift movement, she turned to him, her hands clutching his coat, her face raised to his in supplication. Not unnaturally misreading her gesture, he drew her into his arms and kissed her, at first lightly and then more searchingly as, to his surprise, he felt her body stiffen and draw away as if to repulse him.

'Sally, my dear, what is it? What do you want of me?'

'Just to talk with you, Julien,' she whispered, hiding her face on his shoulder. 'Oh, I pray you – I could ask no other and I must know!'

'What must you know?' He was holding her to him as he would a frightened child, until her trembling should cease.

'It is so difficult to be alone with you,' she went on in a distracted sort of way, 'and in the hackney I felt so wretchedly ill – it did smell so, did it not? – so I conceived this little ruse to draw you up here!'

'I see.' He was smiling over her head. 'I was trapped, was I? An assault upon my virtue?'

'You might be forgiven for supposing that but – ' She hesitated, then took a deep breath and continued in a firmer voice, 'I do assure you it is not so.'

'Then if I might presume to offer advice, my lady, the next time you wish to hold private conversation *only* with a gentleman, do not invite him to your bedroom and ask him to unloose your frock!'

His tone was light and teasing but there was no denying that holding her warm loveliness close to him was, to say the least, disturbing and she, as if suddenly aware of the utter impropriety of her conduct and its possible outcome, shrank from him. Releasing her, he picked up her taffeta cloak which had fallen to the ground and wrapped it around her bare shoulders.

'Now,' he said cheerfully, 'since there is no improving this outrageous situation, let us sit down and you shall tell me what it is that troubles you.'

'I cannot,' she almost sobbed. 'Oh, what have I done? I am so – so ashamed! It is so – '

'What is it so?' he asked gently. 'What do you need to know?'

She caught at him again, clinging as a drowning man to a spar, and he had to strain to catch her almost inaudible reply. 'If I can ever again give myself to any man!'

For an instant his hand, stroking the soft curls at the nape of her neck, was stayed and then resumed its soothing motion. If he found her remark a curious one, taking into consideration her eight years of marriage and three children, no hint of his perplexity sounded in his voice when he replied.

'Why should you not? Are we poor men so repugnant to you?' She could not answer him and he went on, still in the same half-teasing way. 'Is that the reason for my being lured up here to-night? To put me to the test? Oh, Sally, Sally!'

'It is because you are the dearest, most perfect gentleman I know, and – and – '

'Flattery, let me tell you, ma'am, will avail you nothing!' He tilted her head back to look into her eyes. 'Nor am I, I suspect, the *dearest* gentleman you know, however perfect!'

The kindness of his regard quite overcame her resolution to reveal as few as possible of the unhappy circumstances that had led her to seek his advice. It all came out then, the whole sad story of her marriage, with its indignities and degradations, its terrors and misery. He listened in total silence, the pity mounting up inside him at what she had suffered. When, at last, the tired little voice ceased, he picked her up and laid her on the bed, drawing the covers up around her.

'Sally,' he began diffidently, 'there is only one man can answer what you want to know and he is the man you can love.' The devil, he thought, am I taking a leaf out of Aunt Emmelina's book?

'But don't you understand?' she wailed. 'I cannot enter into marriage with any man until I know I can be a true wife to him.'

'Then tell him what you have told me and let him put you to the test.'

'But if I cannot – '

'Then it is best that you do not marry him.'

'But he would be so humiliated – I could not bear it!'

'It is Ned, isn't it?'

'Yes,' she admitted, very low.

'Has he made you an offer?'

'Not yet, because I – I will not permit it. Oh, twice the words have been on his lips and I have turned him aside. If I do it once again he will think I wish to spare him the pain of refusal. He – he is a proud man, Julien, and a shy one.'

Ned FitzJames shy? The Earl could not quite envisage such a thing but supposed it might be so in certain circumstances. 'Then you must let him declare himself,' he said firmly, 'and after, tell him the whole story.'

'But if it should give him a disgust of me?' she sobbed.

'Sally, you goose!' he admonished her. 'You know little of love if you think he would be so easily discouraged.'

'I know nothing of it,' she allowed. 'You might have taught me once had not things fallen out differently.'

'I well might,' he agreed. 'But not now, my dear! That is for Ned to do.'

'Julien,' she confessed, twisting the lace of the coverlet between nervous fingers. 'I did – at the first – have in mind to – to seduce you!'

'I know,' he said comfortably. 'And you might have succeeded had not your courage failed you!' She looked at him wonderingly.

'You guessed at my intention?'

He had to laugh at that. 'Ladies are not usually so inviting unless – and in any case,' he motioned towards the dressing-table where her silk purse lay open, several things spilling out of it, including a heavy door-key, 'when I saw *that* I suspected a snare!'

'I – I wasn't very good at it, was I?' she murmured, a shy smile arousing the dimples in her cheeks.

'The first rule to be observed when luring a gentleman into your embrace,' he explained gravely, 'is to convince him that such an outcome is what you truly desire.'

'Oh!' she said in a small voice. 'And I did not so convince you?'

'On the contrary,' he assured her. 'I was persuaded you held me in the strongest aversion!'

'Well, I don't!' she asserted with spirit. 'It is only that – that – '

'That you love Ned!' He got up from where he had been sitting on the edge of the bed and went to the mirror to study his appearance. She watched him as he smoothed his hair and shook out the folds of his neckcloth. 'There!' he said, turning to face her. 'Will I pass?' An involuntary gurgle of laughter broke from her.

'If by that you mean do you look as if you had almost been ravished – no, dear Julien, you do not, and I take it as a great reflection upon my physical attractions, let me tell you!'

'Another such remark and I will have the sheets off you!' he threatened her.

'I know you will not, and I do beg your pardon for having thought to – to use you as I did to-night.' He kissed the hand she slipped out from under the covers. 'Be happy, Julien.'

'As I am sure you will be, Sally. Sleep well and pray God I do not break my neck going down that ladder!'

She heard him go out on the balcony, descend the ladder and put it away, then his quiet footsteps crossed the paving and, with the soft click of the gate latch, he was gone. She lay for a long time thinking of him, of his charm, his gentleness, his almost feminine sensibility. 'Oh, Charlotte, you great ninny!' she cried out aloud. 'If you do not know what you are throwing away you must be brought to understand it!'

Meantime, the Earl walked briskly along the leafy alley into the street. Though taking reasonable care to avoid being observed, his mind was much preoccupied. Not being one to delude himself about his own failings, he was aware that if Sally's naive attempt to seduce him had been mounted a month earlier the outcome could have been very different, for he was by no means insensible to her charms and he held her in considerable affection. Then he thought of Charlotte and knew, with piercing clarity, why he had not been tempted to accept the conquest that had been his for the taking.

Several carriages passed him, bearing revellers home from their various pleasures, but he took scant notice of them. This lack of vigilance was particularly unfortunate as he stood, in full moonlight, at a street corner, while an elegant chaise went by on the other side of the road. A lady seated in it leaned forward to stare at him intently, then sank back against the squabs with an almost inaudible gasp. Her companion, sitting opposite, looked out quickly to see what had caught her attention. The other two occupants of the carriage were absorbed in each other.

'Hmm!' said Lord Braybridge, very low. 'Clandon, was it not?' Charlotte made no reply, but the moonlight shining upon her hands showed them to be clenched tightly in her lap. 'I would have said it was – some time since he left us. I imagine that is Warne House we have just passed?'

Still she did not answer and his expression as he watched her stricken face was frighening in its intensity, though a chance observer would have been hard put to it to decide whether anger or triumph had gained the upper hand. By the time they had arrived at South Audley Street and she and Penelope were handed out of the chaise, Charlotte had recovered her poise and was able to thank her escort with tolerable composure.

CHAPTER FIVE

THE Earl was still in his dressing-room the next morning when Miss Ralston's letter was delivered to Clandon House. Chivers, his valet, could not recall when last he had seen his lordship in such an agreeable humour. Though the wagers below stairs had not been entirely laid off Miss Penelope, yet it was held, after the previous evening's dinner, that Lady Warne must now be the prime favourite in the matrimonial stakes unless, of course, as Sefton pointed out, there should be a Dark Horse whose existence the Earl was covering up for reasons of his own.

As he opened Charlotte's letter, Julien was humming a gay waltz tune, but as he read the concisely phrased lines his humming faltered and stopped. She thanked him for his hospitality and assured him how much they had all enjoyed it, then she dwelt briefly on the visit to Vauxhall, but the essence of the letter lay in the last sentences.

'Upon consideration, I have decided to say nothing to Lord Braybridge but to go forward with the marriage, as arranged, in September. I hope you will not take this in bad part for I must assure you that I know myself to have been greatly honoured by your condescension in offering for me. I cannot but feel this to be a needless sacrifice on your part as, I am convinced, there are many ladies of greater consequence than I who would be happy to receive your attentions and who would be better suited to fulfil the obligations and duties attendant upon the position held by your wife than ever I could be.'

To say the Earl was thunderstruck would be to underrate the case. If the ceiling had opened and crashed upon his head, he could not have been more stricken. The world still went on around him, making its customary sounds and movement; he even answered a question Chivers put to him, though he was quite unaware of what was said. Chivers, for his part, was watching him anxiously. That his master had received ill news was plain to be seen, for he was deathly pale and the expression of stunned despair on his face was enough to wring the heart of far more unfeeling persons than his devoted valet.

'My lord,' he ventured at length, 'will you be pleased to sit down?'

'What?' Julien stared at him blankly then, shaking his head as if to clear it, he read Charlotte's letter through again, but no amount of reading could change the unpalatable fact that she had decided to marry Braybridge in preference to himself. This was all the more difficult to understand since he had thought to have detected a partiality in her manner towards him of late. What had he done to turn her against him so? He was saved the trouble of finding the answer to that question by the unceremonious arrival of Colonel FitzJames.

'May I intrude for a moment? I am on my way to call on Sally Warne. What state of health did you leave her in – Sultan! What the devil ails you?'

Chivers slipped out of the room while the Colonel was speaking and, shaking his head darkly, sought out Sefton and advised him to send up the Madeira and brandy to the dressing-room without delay.

The Earl, trying to fob off FitzJames's solicitous enquiries, wished him to the devil. 'A slight malaise, Ned, nothing more. My apologies for deserting you last night, but Sally was looking so green, I thought it best to take her home at once.'

'Not as green as you are looking now, I'll swear!' Julien sensed the suspicion underlying the Colonel's words.

'I imagine you will find her in good health,' he said in as casual a manner as he dared. 'It seems fireworks send her off like that. Once removed from the source of the trouble, she makes a speedy recovery.'

'Indeed?' The Colonel's tone was as cold as his eyes. 'After which you tucked her up in bed and kissed her good-night?'

The accusation struck Julien as being most unreasonably unfair, for it came so close to the truth he could not, in all conscience, deny it, but he was resolved not to allow Ned to pick a quarrel with him over something that had never happened.

'Oh, you are quite out there,' he said, giving his attention to the adjustment of a pearl pin in the folds of his neckcloth. 'If you must know, I ravished her, spent the night with her, and have only just returned home!'

The look of consternation on the Colonel's face changed quickly to one of shame-faced contrition. 'Forgive me, Sultan, I had no right – if you had landed me a facer it would have been no more than I deserved.'

'But you have a right, have you not, Ned?'

'If you mean do I love her,' said the Colonel, reddening painfully, 'yes, I do, but I have no reason to suppose my sentiments are returned.'

'Depend upon it, the only way to find out is to put it to the test.' Julien's interest was now centred on the nice arrangement of his waistcoat. With all his being he longed to be alone to lick his own wounds, but he was not to be granted any immediate relief for a knock on the door heralded the arrival of Sefton with the refreshment advised by Chivers.

Fortifying himself with a large measure of brandy, the Colonel returned to the attack. 'What were you looking so confoundedly peaked about when first I came in?' he asked.

'Did you assume that to have been caused by a sense of guilt at sight of you?' The Earl allowed himself to sound a little amused and FitzJames looked suitably downcast.

'For an absurd moment – yes, I did. But there was no sense in that reasoning. If you had been uneasy in your conscience you would have been more than ready for me. But something has distressed you, Sultan, and do not spin me any tales about a disordered gut!' He nodded towards the Earl's empty glass. 'That brandy went down quicker than ever it was poured out. You had a letter in your hand when I came in, was it bad news?'

'Bad enough.' The Earl picked up Charlotte's missive and slipped it into his pocket. 'I have business to attend to, Ned, and must send you on your way.'

'Not money troubles? You in the clutches of the duns sounds the most unlikely thing.'

'God, no! It – it's a family matter.' The Earl felt that was not too untruthful an explanation but the Colonel was not accepting it.

'The only family you have got is Walter Revel and I cannot imagine you falling into despair over him. I will hazard a guess that it is a woman. Family matters, eh? Have you, too, fallen into the tender trap, Sultan?' The Earl, his face impassive, did not answer, but busied himself with the final details of his dress. 'Well, I can take a hint as well as the next man but – is there aught I can do?'

'Yes, be off to see Sally and leave me to wrestle with my own troubles!'

When, at last, the Colonel was persuaded to leave, Julien drank another glass of brandy and, thus encouraged, set out for South Audley Street in no very tolerant humour. He was fortunate to find Charlotte alone but for Penelope and it was the work of minutes only to convey to that young lady his need for privacy. Having not taken her into his confidence about his arrangement with her sister, she presumed he was about to put her plan into action and, instructing Wiggins to announce no one for the next half-hour, she sped upstairs to Lady Oakley who was having a comfortable lie-in after the evening's exertions, and prepared to engage her in an animated discussion of the latest fashions as portrayed in *La Belle Assemblée*.

Charlotte, whose heart was beating so wildly she felt sure it must be clearly audible, gave all the appearance of being quite indifferent to the Earl's presence. To say that she already regretted writing such a letter to him would be overstating the case. She was out of all reason angry with him, and though common-sense whispered that she had no right to resent his attentions to other ladies when his name was not yet linked to hers, yet the remembrance of where she had last seen him was sufficient to override all other considerations. If he could not keep his hands off his other admirers when he was in theory betrothed to her, what hope could there be of even token fidelity on his part once they were married? Agreed, one could not expect too much from a marriage of convenience but her secret hope of making it a very different sort of marriage had received a rude set-back. No, best to let him marry Sally Warne if that was his wish. No doubt he was heartily regretting having offered for her in any case and would be only too happy to be rid of the Ralston connection.

'May I ask for an explanation of this letter?'

She took it from him as if she had never seen it before. 'My lord, I am touched to think that you treasure my poor missives!'

'I do not treasure that one for poor it is, poor in spirit and in reason!' It was difficult to say which one of them was the more angry.

'My reason, I believe, I made quite plain. If you think me poor-spirited how you must rejoice at being freed from me!'

He controlled himself with a visible effort and spoke more calmly. 'But why, Charlotte, why? I thought all was arranged, that you were better content with me than with Braybridge.' His obvious hurt she misconstrued as injured pride, and chose her words so as to lacerate that pride as far as lay in her power.

'Upon reflection I have concluded that with an older man there is the less likelihood of my being distressed by his actions outside marriage. You, *Sultan*, might pay small regard to the conventions and with a man of your consequence it would not be long before all London knew of your – adventures. This, I declare, I could not countenance however slight a thing our marriage tie might be.' His expression gave her cause for alarm but, resolutely, she plunged on, taking things from bad to worse. 'I have n-no doubt you would be generous enough to allow me a degree of license also as soon as an heir was safely secured, b-but let me tell you, that style of living does not commend itself to me.'

'Nor me!' he ground out between his teeth. ''Fore Heaven,

Charlotte, you have got a pretty notion of me, I must say! Who put such an image into your head – Braybridge?'

'Certainly not!' she flashed back. 'Though I well remember you once called him an ageing roué! Is there so v-vast a difference between that and a – a middle-aged rake?'

It was the word 'middle-aged' that really got under Julien's guard. To be so called when he was not yet thirty was the outside of anything! With a muttered imprecation he strode forward and she, realizing that she had overstepped the mark, thrust out both hands in a futile attempt to hold him away, but his strength was far greater than hers. Struggle as she might, she could not free herself from his imprisoning arms and was forced to submit to his near-savage kiss. She felt engulfed by his anger and her own temper rose to match it. When, at last, because of the necessity to breathe, he relaxed his embrace and lifted his head to look down at her, she was so far gone in rage that she could not recognize how very changed was the look on his face. His first words, too, might have influenced her had she even heard them.

'Charby, my dear, it won't do! I pray you, listen to me!'

For answer he got a stinging blow across the face, delivered with all the force of which she was capable.

'How dared you insult me so! Let me go!' He released her immediately, the mark of her hand showing clearly against his colourless cheek.

'You mistake me. My intention was not to insult you.'

'No? To humiliate me, then? To show me what I was foregoing in turning you down? It must be a new experience for you to be rebuffed, my lord!'

'I love you, Charlotte,' he said simply, but if he had imagined that such a declaration would placate the lady, he had much mistaken the matter.

'As you loved Penny when you offered for her not two months since? As you loved Lady Warne more recently? Love had made you careless last night, had it not? Too careless to observe the carriages that passed you as you strolled home in a – dream of ecstasy?' His look of utter horror merely confirmed her belief that he had escorted Sally Warne not only to her house but into her bed. 'Let me tell you that I would not marry you were you the last man on earth!'

It should have been plain to Julien that such vehemence rarely sprang from indifference, but he was too confounded at the impossible turn of events to reason very clearly.

'That being the case, ma'am, I will remove my unwelcome presence from this house at once. I bid you good-day!'

The slam of the street door behind him brought Wiggins hurrying into the hall and Penelope rushing downstairs.

'His lordship has forgotten his gloves,' Wiggins complained, his face a picture of disapproval.

'Give them to me, I'll return them to him.' Penelope snatched the gloves from him and hurried in to Charlotte to discover what could have made Julien storm out of the house in such fashion. 'Charlotte, you have never quarrelled with him?'

'Yes, I have! I do not wish to see him again – ever!'

'Oh, you blockhead!' Penelope wailed in despair.

'Do not be impertinent, Penelope!' Charlotte was still in a fine rage and anyone within reach was going to feel its effect, but her sister was too anxious to take notice.

'Did he ask you to marry him?'

'No – yes – I will not marry him!'

'Charlotte, you will be the death of me! After all our careful planning!' Charlotte rounded on her.

'What careful planning? What can you mean?'

Penelope, aware that she had said more than was wise, thrust Julien's gloves at Charlotte who took them unthinkingly.

'I mean,' she stumbled on, 'he asked me if I thought you would listen to him and I said I was sure you would – ' She faltered into silence at Charlotte's look of fury.

'How delightful to learn that my sister is plotting against me behind my back!'

Poor Penelope was too dumbfounded by this view of her activities to be able to formulate even a protest before Wiggins ushered in Lord Braybridge. His lordship, having observed

Julien's eruption from the house a few moments before, was filled with curiosity about so interesting a situation.

With a muttered excuse, Penelope fled the room, but he merely looked resigned at the inevitable effect his appearance had upon her. 'My dear Charlotte, you look to be a trifle put out,' he commented mildly. 'Has Clandon said aught to distress you? I could hardly believe it possible after his very obliging attentions yestere'en. I would have been happy of the opportunity to offer my thanks to him but he seemed to be in a great hurry. You were not so indiscreet, I hope, as to mention having seen him as we came home?'

'Yes, I did!' Charlotte was very close to tears and longing for any reasonable excuse to account for them. He shook his head reprovingly at her.

'That was ill-done of you, my dear girl. Young men do not care to be called to account on such matters whether they be influenced merely by the haphazard of selfish passion or are moved by a more worthy sentiment.'

'Selfish!' she exploded. 'Utterly selfish!' Then she recollected that it was her future husband to whom she was talking, and he might well have cause to wonder at her vehemence. But Lord Braybridge, having discovered what he needed to know, was not looking in the least surprised, though the glitter in his cold eyes belied his air of boredom.

'Allow me to relieve you of those gloves,' he offered.

'What? Oh!' She flung Julien's gloves from her as if they were red-hot and turned from him, hands to blazing cheeks. His lordship contented himself with picking them up and putting them in a convenient place where they could easily be found had anyone a mind to look for them.

'I have come from Warne House where I called to enquire for Lady Warne's well-being,' he went on smoothly. 'I am happy to say she appears to be much restored in health. I was ousted by Colonel FitzJames.'

'Ousted?' His use of that particular word caught at her attention as he had intended it should.

'Well, perhaps not quite that,' he amended, 'but I was of the opinion that he and Lady Warne had much to say to each other that could best be said unhindered by the presence of others.' He smiled slightly at her air of astonishment. 'Oh, yes, I think they well might make a match of it, the Colonel and Lady Warne.'

'FitzJames! But he is Ju – Clandon's friend?'

'Just so!' he agreed, giving all his attention to an elegant figurine on the mantelpiece. 'This really is a superb piece of Meissen. I must enquire of your aunt how she came by it.'

'But surely Clandon must be in his friend's confidence?'

'One might suppose so.' Braybridge helped himself to snuff. 'I do believe I have been most unwise to venture out with such a delicate snuff-box, there is quite an Easterly flavour to the wind to-day. I should be advised by Petersham.'

'Poor Colonel FitzJames! That he should be so duped! Oh – oh, treachery!' With that her fortitude quite failed her and, making some excuse about seeking out her aunt, she hurried from the room.

'Thy name is Julien Revel!' murmured his lordship.

When, a few minutes later, a somewhat flustered Lady Oakley entered her drawing-room in response to Charlotte's distracted plea, it was to find Lord Braybridge lost in contemplation of an elegant flower painting by Redouté and, to all outward seeming, quite unconcerned at having been so unceremoniously deserted by his lady.

CHAPTER SIX

PENELOPE was in a fair way to renouncing the world and seeking solace in a nunnery, for Charlotte went about in stony-faced silence, looking like a very Medusa, while of Julien there was no word at all. How her sister could be so bantam-witted as to cast away all the advantages that a match with the Earl of Clandon had to offer was outside Penelope's comprehension and she most earnestly prayed that Charlotte was not going out of her mind, though she entertained the gravest doubts on this head.

In sharp contrast to the aura of gloom that hung over South Audley Street was the gaiety that prevailed elsewhere. The Prince Regent was putting forth every endeavour to ensure that his royal guests were nobly entertained and London breathed a sigh of relief when he removed them to Oxford for a visit, but the respite was short-lived for they were restored to the capital in time for a banquet at Guildhall four days later.

For this splendid occasion Lord Braybridge had engaged a room with windows overlooking the processional route, and had invited the same company to join him as had gathered at Vauxhall a week previously. Penelope sent a note to Clandon House adjuring Julien not to fail to attend, but the footman returned to say that the Earl was out of town. She surmised he had probably gone to Chalice, but a letter arrived from her mother which put all other thoughts from her head.

Melissa seemed to be on the point of winning her naval engagement. At all events, Lady Ralston spoke quite kindly of Mr Philip Vereker as an obliging, pleasant sort of man, with considerably better prospects than she had first been led to believe. The Verekers were a quiet country family of good repute and modest fortune, but there was a nabob of an uncle who spoke of Philip as being the only one of the family to have any rumgumption and who had, it would appear, taken quite a shine to Melissa.

'You may be sure mama has decided that to oppose Melissa would be useless, and so is making the best of things,' Penelope declared.

'Well, you will shortly have the felicity of meeting your future brother-in-law and judging affairs for yourself because they are returning to Heatherstone Hall with your mama this very day and she wishes us to join them there.' Lady Oakley set down her sister's letter at Penelope's exclamation of dismay.

'But the Guildhall procession and Lady Winslow's ball are tomorrow!'

'We will leave the following morning.' Lady Oakley had considered the blighting prospect for Penelope if she could not attend the ball given by Mr Beaumont's aunt. 'I cannot answer for your uncle, but that makes no odds. We will not be gone above a week. Did I hear you say that Clandon was out of town? Is he at Chalice then?' Penelope, stealing a look at her sister's rigid profile, admitted she did not know but rather supposed he was. 'Ah, then, I expect we shall see him there.'

Lady Oakley's sharp glance darted from one to the other of her nieces. She fully comprehended that something was amiss where Julien was concerned but could not, for the life of her, conceive what it could be. Penelope looked quite apprehensive, while as for Charlotte, she might have been struck deaf and dumb for all the response one could get out of her. She admitted to being a little tired and out-of-sorts and even gave the impression of being unwilling to join the following night's festivities when Lord Braybridge called to discuss the event.

His lordship was of the opinion that a short stay in the country would do her a world of good and then went on to mention, as if by chance, that he had called at Clandon House to be informed that the Earl had gone down to Chalice for an indefinite period. Thereafter, Charlotte expressed her willingness to join the party for viewing the procession and even to accompany them on afterwards to Lady Winslow's ball. Life, she recollected, was full of pleasurable entertainment, why should she not savour it to the full? And if there should be no one in particular to look for, no laughing eye to catch across a crowded room, no one with whom to share a secret joke or happy memory – what matter? All that must be forgotten when she married, so the sooner started the better.

The procession to Guildhall proved to be as magnificent as had been anticipated. Lord Braybridge had bespoken a fine room in a wealthy Cit's dwelling, while the owner deemed it his privilege to provide his noble guests with suitable refreshment. Colonel FitzJames, whose superior knowledge of the army gave him the advantage of knowing the regiments taking part in the procession, was only too happy to instruct the ladies but, though Charlotte watched him keenly, he seemed to display no partiality towards Lady Warne, and she concluded that Braybridge must have been mistaken in his notion of there being an attachment between them. Nonetheless, she found she could not feel any kindness for Lady Warne, though there was no doubt that her elegant dress of gossamer net over jonquille satin greatly became her dark beauty. So seductively did the satin cling to her softly rounded curves that Charlotte had every suspicion that it had been damped to provide this effect, and hoped with all her heart that her ladyship might take a chill – preferably a fatal one!

Colonel FitzJames's voice describing the passing spectacle recalled her from her uncharitable daydream. 'Leading all we have the Light Dragoons, and here following are the carriages with the Officers of the Household and the foreign generals – no, Miss Penelope, I do not know who that very handsome young general is – a Russian by his uniform – shall I enquire of the Emperor for you? And here come the Royal Dukes.'

'Each one fatter than the last!' remarked Lady Warne with singular lack of respect.

'And who are all these sedate-looking gentlemen?' Penelope wanted to know.

'The Speaker and with him the members of the Cabinet.'

'Why, yes, there is my lord Castlereagh.' Lady Oakley pointed out the Foreign Secretary and the Colonel continued:

'There go the last of the Officers of State, and these must be the suites of the foreign princes. Following them are the Yeomen of the Guard and the Gentlemen Pensioners – '

'And the heralds. Now please can anyone tell me which herald is which and why is a herald different from a pursuivant?' Miss Branscombe asked, and Lord Braybridge was so obliging as to enlighten her in considerable detail. 'And what of people like Black Rod and Bluemantle?'

'Black Rod is the Staff of Office carried by the Usher of the Order of the Knights of the Garter instead of the mace. He keeps the door while a chapter of the Order is sitting. He also attends the House of Lords during sessions of Parliament and acts as their messenger to the Commons. Bluemantle is one of the Pursuivants – a junior officer of arms – with Portcullis, Rouge Dragon and Rouge Croix.'

Colonel FitzJames interrupted this interesting exposition. 'Finally, the Grand Climax,' he announced, 'the Prince Regent and his illustrious guests!'

After which there was great sighing amongst the ladies over the Emperor's charm and the King of Prussia's striking appearance, while refreshments were partaken of and everyone congratulated Lord Braybridge on his arrangements.

All the party had been invited to Lady Winslow's ball but Lord Oakley, whose tastes did not lie in dancing, excused himself, and Charlotte, who had been considering her future movements, begged to be allowed return to South Audley Street with him on the plea of feeling greatly fatigued. This occasioned much protest, Miss Branscombe offering to accompany her friend and Penelope declaring her evening would be quite spoiled if her dear sister was not by her side. Charlotte, however, was adamant and bade her betrothed farewell very prettily, for it was unlikely they would meet again until she got back from Heatherstone Hall. This, she assured him, was her first consideration in declining to go on to the ball. She feared her mother would be much distressed if she found herself unequal to the journey on the morrow so would go to bed without delay. His lordship appeared to be in complete agreement with her, sent his respectful regards to Lady Ralston, his compliments to the engaged couple, and kissed her hand in the most irreproachable manner though there was that in his demeanour that gave her a sense of unease which, of course, was quite nonsensical, for how should he take exception to her wishing to oblige her mother?

'Tell Julien from me,' begged Colonel FitzJames, as he placed Charlotte's wrap about her shoulders, 'not to bury himself at Chalice for too long, else I will come and bear him off to view my mouldering ruins – that is, when I find some worthy couple to take care of them for me.'

Unfortunately, the mere mention of Julien's name touched off all her angry feelings again so she finished her goodbyes rather hurriedly and allowed Lord Oakley to escort her to his carriage.

* * *

Much about the same time of evening, the Earl of Clandon, having finished a long day with his agent, inspecting estate cottages and his workers' living conditions, was in his office at Chalice, checking over those same workers' wages on his payroll. He paid them well – overmuch, he was informed by one or two neighbouring landowners not so warm in the pocket as he and resentful of it – but who could bring up a family on a few shillings a week, even with a free cottage and piece of garden? He lacked the normal indifference shown by noble proprietors to the people who worked for them; it pained him to think that anyone under his care should be other than comfortable. That he was far ahead of his peers in this way of thinking did not occur to him and he sighed heavily as Sefton came quietly into the room to place brandy and a glass on a tray at his elbow.

'Your pardon, my lord, but here is a letter which was delivered earlier this evening. As James saw fit to place it in the library it has only just come to my notice. From Heatherstone Hall, my lord.'

'Is Lady Ralston at home, then?' Julien picked up the letter and opened it. After a moment he began to smile, and Sefton sighed in relief, for the unhappiness apparent in their young master's face had been the cause of concern to all the household. 'Well, that is one of them off her hands! Miss Melissa is going to tie up with the Navy and they wish me to dine there to-morrow to meet the gentleman. I will pen a note now, would you please see it is delivered the first thing in the morning?'

Sefton bowed and withdrew to inform the household that things appeared to be on the move again now that Lady Ralston was home. Julien, left alone, read her letter again, in particular the latter part of it.

' "I have written to my sister, asking her to bring Charlotte and Penelope down for a few days to meet Mr Vereker, but I cannot imagine it possible for them to arrive before the end of the week, in which case we are likely to be no more than four to dinner, so – very informal, please, Julien, let us not frighten the poor man away!" '

Now why should everyone, including their mother, seem to fear he would frighten away the Ralston girls' suitors? He had not, he reflected bitterly, shown himself to be much of a success at it! 'I would not marry you were you the last man on earth!' Never could he forget the way those words had been flung at him, the passionate conviction in her voice. One day he would have to meet her again, but the farthest off that meeting could be postponed the better. He pulled a piece of writing-paper towards him and with it came some notes he had made for the proposed landscaping of the immediate pleasure grounds around Chalice, with greatly enlarged rose and flower gardens for Charlotte's special delight. Even a pheasantry had been envisaged, and Julien's mouth tightened to a hard line as he crushed the paper in his hand and flung it into the basket at his feet. Let the future Countess of Clandon discuss all that with Mr Repton, or whoever undertook the task. For there was going to be a

Countess of Clandon, on that he had quite made up his mind. This reflection seemed to soothe him and, with every evidence of enjoying his misery to the full, he wrote to Lady Ralston accepting her very gracious invitation.

The next morning confusion reigned at South Audley Street, for Lady Oakley and Penelope were short of sleep owing to their late return from the Winslow ball, and Charlotte could not raise her head from the pillow. She protested it was but a cold, she would be quite recovered in a few days and would follow them to Heatherstone Hall, but Lady Oakley insisted that the doctor should be called and that she must stay behind to look after her niece. At last the whole affair was most sensibly arranged by Miss Branscombe, who had called in to wish the travellers a safe journey.

'I cannot think that Charlotte's indisposition is too grave,' she pronounced, laying a hand on that young lady's remarkably cool brow. 'But it would be wise for her not to travel until she is feeling more the thing. If I may suggest a solution?' She looked at Lady Oakley, who expressed herself as being excessively obliged to her dear Anthea for any helpful notion. 'You, ma'am, must I think, go with Penelope to-day. There can be no merit in all of you denying yourselves the pleasure of this visit. I will undertake to look after Charlotte and if I may beg the loan of your chaise, will convey her this very moment to South Street, for I apprehend you had the intention of releasing your servants for the time you are away as my uncle is going down to Oakley Hall.'

Lady Oakley protested that to risk exposing Charlotte to the outside air could well be the death of her, but Miss Branscombe insisted that, if well wrapped up, she would survive the short journey to South Street, and she pledged her word that the doctor would be called if the patient's condition showed signs of worsening. For this, she got a look of grateful thanks from Charlotte, a stream of objections from her aunt, each one of which was simply disposed of, and a warm hug from Penelope, whose reluctance to forgo Mr Beaumont's company had been overcome by her desire to see what Melissa was bringing into the family. A further inducement to Lady Oakley to accept the plan was that she had received a communication from her dressmaker, explaining that, owing to an unfortunate accident to her foot, she had been quite unable to finish two gowns in time for milady to take them with her.

'Though how her sewing could be affected by such a mishap – had it been her hand which had met with injury – ' Lady Oakley sketched an eloquent gesture in the air indicative of her disbelief in the ability of the lower classes to show resolution in misfortune. 'If you are to follow us, Charlotte, I would be so very obliged if you could collect the gowns for me yourself and bring them with you. Mrs Farley tells me she hopes to have completed them by to-morrow evening, but – ' Her ladyship's hands once again expressed doubt.

Charlotte, who held a high opinion of Mrs Farley, both as a dressmaker and as a diplomat in persuading her aunt to adopt fashions to suit her figure and style, gladly consented to carry out this errand when she should be recovered.

An hour later saw her established in South Street with her surprised hostess, Mrs Fortescue, disclaiming all skill in nursing and wondering that Miss Branscombe should not have advised her beforehand so that she could have made arrangements for the setting-up of a sick room.

'Depend upon it,' Miss Branscombe said briskly, 'a little rest and quiet is all she needs and she will be quite herself in a few days.' Mrs Fortescue did not hold to this opinion and, after a lengthy discourse on the subject of fatal illnesses which had stemmed from no more than a common cold, went to inform her housekeeper of the addition to the household. 'You are not anxious to see a doctor, are you, Charlotte?'

'No, I do not think it at all necessary.' Charlotte snuggled under the bedcovers, keeping a wary eye on her friend.

'I am sure it is not!' nodded Miss Branscombe. 'Now, tell me, why did you not wish to accompany your aunt and sister to Heatherstone Hall?'

There were times, Charlotte considered, when dear Anthea's

perspicacity was a sore trial to her acquaintance. She murmured something vague about feeling a trifle dragged and wishing to be at her best for Melissa's sake when meeting Mr Vereker. Miss Branscombe appeared to be quite satisfied with this explanation and presently went downstairs to soothe Mrs Fortescue's ruffled plumage and wonder how long it would take the Earl to make his way back to Clandon House.

In the event, it did not take him very long, for when he arrived at Heatherstone Hall that evening and was informed by Lady Ralston of the expected advent of her sister and two other daughters on the following day, he at once resolved to take his leave of Chalice and return to London. Melissa was loud in her disapproval when he explained the unfortunate circumstances that necessitated his departure and, as he had only that moment invented them, he was hard put to it to justify them in her eyes.

Melissa, he was relieved to observe, had changed not at all. Neither as beautiful as Penelope nor as taking as Charlotte, she yet contrived to combine a little of both in her pleasant, open countenance and forthright manner. Her hair was a modest brown, her eyes neither blue nor grey but something between, only in her sudden smile was there any clear resemblance to Charlotte, and when she came to greet him with outstretched hands, that gay smile tugged sharply at his sensibilities.

'Julien, my dear! As elegant as ever, but looking a shade pulled down? Too much London gaiety? I hear the place spins like a top!'

'Take my word for it, there is never an easy moment – you, of all people, Melissa, would detest it!' he said, kissing her cheek warmly in the conviction that here, at least, was one Ralston daughter about whom no one need query his attentions. Then he was aware of the steady regard of a pair of searching blue eyes and realized he might have to amend his convictions.

Mr Vereker was a tall, wiry sort of man, whose grace of movement was much hampered by a pronounced limp. By no stretch of imagination could he be deemed handsome, but his bronzed countenance held much character while his smile revealed uncommonly fine teeth and a disarming dimple in either cheek. The Earl, shaking his hand, enquired after his injury.

'Coming along well, so the doctors tell me.' Mr Vereker sounded cheerfully philosophical. 'But I'll not walk even again, I fear.'

'So they'll not have you back in the Navy?'

'They might later, if I pressed it, but Melissa is of no mind to be a sea-widow, so – I'll not press it!'

'Then I am to congratulate you?' Julien looked from one to the other happy face and laughed. 'I had not known precisely how matters stood and your mother never tells me anything!'

'Julien, that is most unfair!' Lady Ralston protested.

'Is it? Then, perhaps, I should say that everything you tell me is not necessarily to be relied upon!'

There was a bite behind his words that silenced her and her distress increased during the evening as the Earl gave them news of the household in London. While speaking of Penelope's prospects, his voice was warm and his manner of presenting Mr Beaumont to their notice could only give satisfaction to a mother's heart, but when Charlotte's name was mentioned he adopted a mask of cool indifference that she knew to be quite foreign to his nature. Clearly he had not succeeded in persuading Charlotte to cast off Braybridge, and it was equally clear that he and Charlotte had fallen out upon the issue.

After dinner, when the betrothed couple were taking a turn in the garden, she broached the subject to him and knew her suspicions confirmed by the curtness of his reply.

'She appears well content with Braybridge and resolved to go through with the marriage. I can do no more.'

'And Penny?' That drew an unwilling smile from him.

'There you were very right, dear aunt! Penny was never the wife for me, but I have no doubt Mr Beaumont will soon offer for her and I am of the opinion you need look no further for her husband.' She thanked him gravely.

'And you, Julien? You, too, had the notion of seeking a wife?' He shrugged.

'I still have the fancy, but fact and fancy can be difficult to match up.'

'Did I not warn you?' she reminded him.

'Oh, have no fear, there are several ladies, any one of whom will doubtless oblige me. It is a matter of – selection.'

'Julien! You sound like the veriest coxcomb! What has happened?' Her very real anxiety penetrated his reserve and he took her hand held out in appeal to him.

'Nothing has happened, dear aunt,' he said gently. 'Since we talked together two months past, very little has taken place – except, of course, for Penny.'

She knew then he was not going to tell her anything and gave up the effort of trying to force his confidence.

When he had gone that evening, Melissa rounded on her. 'Mama, what ails Julien?'

'I wish I knew,' her mother said sadly.

'He has had the most frightful flare-up with Charlotte, that's plain to see.'

'Yes, and I am to blame for that.' Lady Ralston then explained how she had asked the Earl to plead with Charlotte to break off her engagement.

'So that is it. No, Philip, no need for you to withdraw. This is family talk and you are family now. We always used to consult Julien when we needed a man's view, but in this case, we cannot.' Mr Vereker did as he was bid and sat down again. 'I have never met this Braybridge man but you have taken against him, Penny quite loathes him, so she wrote me – she calls him the *eminence gris*, ever dressed in grey and grey of character – and Julien can scarcely utter his name with civility. Mama, if Charlotte was so much in love with that poor soldier why does she have to rush into matrimony so soon after his death?'

'I think she has her reasons,' Lady Ralston managed to say, unwilling to go into them in front of Mr Vereker.

'Yes,' said Melissa thoughtfully, 'I suspect she has. What a capital notion it would be if – ' Her mother eyed her percipient second daughter in some misgiving, but Melissa ended up mildly, 'Well, all this is useless conjecture until we see her,' and Lady Ralston was well content to direct the conversation into other channels.

CHAPTER SEVEN

LADY OAKLEY'S chaise with her head groom and postillion returned to London two days later to hold themselves in readiness to convey Charlotte to her mother's house when she should be sufficiently restored to health. The note accompanying them, advising her of her aunt and sister's safe arrival at Heatherstone Hall, also mentioned the Earl's having dined there prior to his departure for London. Miss Branscombe could not fail to notice that, after this interesting item of news had been absorbed, Charlotte's recovery was little short of miraculous. It was decided that the chaise would take her to join her family on the afternoon of the following day and, in order not to tire the horses before their journey, she would take a hack-carriage in the late morning to Bury Street in the City to collect Lady Oakley's gowns.

The Earl was driving up from Chalice that morning when it occurred to him that he should call upon his bankers to inform them that he did not now wish to use any of the considerable sum of money that had been realized for improvements at Chalice, not at least for the time being. He set down his valet by the Park, bidding him go warn the small staff left at Clandon House that their master would be presently descending upon them and, proceeding by way of the Strand, headed his curricle towards Moorgate. In the narrow mill of streets beyond Cheapside some sort of procession was taking place and, owing to the press of people, he was forced to turn aside and find a more devious and less crowded route. Trotting briskly down a quiet road, he was about to pass a stationary hack-carriage when, out of a side-turning ahead of him, there burst a phaeton and pair, springing at full gallop.

It took Julien a moment to realize that the horses were out of control and unattended, because his attention had been distracted by a lady who had stepped out of a house into the path of the oncoming phaeton. She was carrying a large dressbox and, at sight of her, the hack-carriage driver roused himself and was about to touch up his horse when he, too, became aware of the danger thundering towards them. He shouted a warning at the lady, who looked about her in surprise, and Julien's heart all but stopped beating when he recognized Charlotte whom he had believed to be with her family at Heatherstone Hall. Pulling up his pair, he sprang from the curricle, calling to the hack driver to take the reins, and ran towards the oncoming phaeton.

Charlotte had progressed just too far from the house entrance to retreat in time to avoid the danger. To Julien's horror she was pinned against the wall with small hope of avoiding injury from the frightened beasts. The sharp turn into the street had overset the conveyance, which served as a brake upon the animals but alarmed them even more, for the carriage was crashing over the cobbles on its side, slewing wildly from left to right almost under the horses' hooves.

Julien, aware only that he must somehow prevent her from being trampled upon, flung himself at the nearside horse, putting his body between hers and the animal, forcing it away from her with every ounce of strength he possessed until he feared his muscles must surely burst from the strain imposed upon them. The impetus of the team's advance was so great that he was dragged several yards down the street with them. Behind them the shattered phaeton swung round, a faint cry came from Charlotte and she crumpled to the ground in a pathetic heap. He half turned to look for her and the horse, feeling the slackened grip, reared up and lashed out with its front legs. Julien gasped in pain as a hoof struck him near the groin then welcome hands came to his aid as the owner and groom of the runaway vehicle arrived on the scene and he relinquished his hold, falling back against the wall, shaken and bemused.

'Sir, are you hurt? By God, that was a mad thing to do – they must have checked of themselves with the carriage dragging on them!'

'The lady!' Julien dropped on his knees beside her.

'Lady? Merciful Heaven, I did not see her! Now, I follow your reason – Simpson, take those brutes back to their stable and the next time you let a gander cross their path, 'twill be the last thing you do in my service! Did they strike her, sir?'

'The phaeton did.' Impatiently, Julien flung aside Lady Oakley's gowns which were bestrewing the ground, and gathered Charlotte's limp body into his arms.

People were appearing from nowhere in the erstwhile deserted street and crowding around him, including an odd little woman who kept hopping about on one foot and begging him to carry dear Miss Ralston into her parlour and would someone please gather up milady's gowns?

Laying Charlotte down on Mrs Farley's sofa, the Earl was uncomfortably aware that his left arm and shoulder were fast becoming useless while, aside from the ache where the horse had kicked him, the pain in his left foot was such that he suspected the terrified animal had stamped upon it. The owner of the phaeton, a Mr Miles Ansell, hovered about, uttering apologies and offers of help, for the curricle had been brought to the door and he had been deeply impressed by the dust-covered crest on the panels. Mrs Farley, having inspected Charlotte, gave it as her opinion that she had a broken collarbone and a rising lump on the back of her head, but could find no other apparent injury.

'I'd best take her home.' Even as he spoke, Julien wondered how he was to perform that service in a curricle.

'But she is not at South Audley Street, my lord.' Mrs Farley had been quick to guess his identity from the scraps of conversation she had heard between Penny and Lady Oakley during their frequent visits to her. 'I believe Miss Ralston to be staying with her friend, Miss Branscombe, but I cannot give you her direction.' The Earl turned to Mr Ansell.

'Could I ask you, sir, to be so kind as to procure a chaise so that I may convey this lady to a doctor? And, if you would be so obliging, to take charge of my curricle until I can send for it?'

'With pleasure, sir – my lord.' Mr Ansell, feeling much to blame, was eager to be of service. 'If you'll not mind my saying it, you look to be in need of a doctor yourself.'

Julien was so far in agreement with him that, when the chaise arrived, he directed the driver to proceed at once to Clandon House. He would have taken Mrs Farley with him but for her disability, for Charlotte remained quite insensible, despite every effort to revive her. Covering her with his driving-coat, which had been sadly ripped in the struggle, he laid her down on the seat of the chaise and, instructing the driver to maintain a steady pace, bore her away from a host of well-wishers and a still apologizing Mr Ansell.

Chivers's expression when they arrived at Clandon House he might have found ludicrous had the situation not been so grave.

'My lord, there is no one here! They have all gone out on some junket or other – just a groom left in the stables!'

'Is there a bed made up somewhere?'

'Only yours, my lord.'

'Then that must do. Help me carry Miss Ralston thence.' When she had been disposed as comfortably as possible, looking heartbreakingly fragile in the middle of his great four-poster, with eagles crouching at each corner and the Revel coat-of-arms overhead, he sent Chivers off post-haste to fetch his doctor. 'Then Miss Branscombe or Lady – no! Miss Branscombe it must be, but where – perhaps there is still someone at South Audley Street who could inform you. Take the chaise and do not linger!'

Left alone with his injured love, he did his best for her comfort, easing the rough sling that Mrs Farley had devised and bathing her forehead with vinegar and water, but she remained obdurately insensible. Unbuttoning her spencer, he was alarmed to find that the bodice of her gown was stained with blood. Swiftly he undid the fastenings and pulled down the shoulders of the gown to reveal a jagged tear across the soft flesh. He had dealt with many worse injuries during his service in the army, but none that had caused him more anguish. Searching for something to staunch the bleeding, he found in a drawer several muslin cravats, clean but unstarched which, having bathed the wound, he laid gently upon it and drew up her gown to hold all in place. No sooner done than her eyelashes fluttered and she opened her eyes.

'Don't move, Charby darling,' he implored her, but she appeared neither to hear nor recognize him. His anxiety grew as he felt his own strength ebbing. Where the devil was that doctor? A half-hour must have passed since Chivers went in search of him.

Chivers was, indeed, meeting with mixed fortune. The doctor was out visiting a patient but his wife vowed to despatch him at once to Clandon House on his return. Chivers had no doubt she would be as good as her word for the Earl paid his dues promptly. From thence he drove to South Audley Street and was fortunate enough to encounter Miss Branscombe, who had called to find if there were any letters or messages for her, stepping out of the street door. When apprised of the situation she at once expressed her willingness to accompany him back to Clandon House, but as he had only had the briefest account of the accident from his master, he could not enlighten her further save to inform her that Miss Ralston was laid upon his lordship's bed and he tending to her, which was sufficient to arouse Miss Branscombe's liveliest interest.

She was welcomed by a grey-faced Earl, who told her briefly what had happened.

'She is just conscious but keeps going off again,' he explained. She cast a shrewd glance over his battered person.

'We will have you going off before long,' she promised him. 'Chivers, assist your master into his dressing-room and give him what aid you can while I look at Miss Ralston's hurts.'

While Julien suffered Chivers to lead him away and cut off his boot which was now causing him acute agony, Miss Branscombe made swift examination of Charlotte. Clearly the most serious damage was to her head and that could only be dealt with by a doctor. She then knocked on the dressing-room door and found

Chivers in the act of drawing off the slashed boot. Even removing his stocking caused the Earl such exquisite pain as to make him clamp his lips together and grip the arm of his chair with his one good hand in order to suppress a groan. Miss Branscombe was on her knees, studying his swollen foot.

'Broken bone there, I shouldn't wonder,' she said bracingly. 'A cold compress, Chivers – and stay in that chair, my lord, until the doctor sees you. Are there no other servants here?'

'They appear to have taken themselves off for the day.' She looked round the dressing-room.

'You had better have the bed made up in here. I feel it most likely that the doctor will not allow Charlotte to be moved from where she is for a time.' He made to move in his chair but was arrested by a stab of pain down his left arm. 'What troubles your arm?'

'I think I have wrenched it.' He fell back in the chair, looking so drawn that, without hesitation, she undid his neckcloth and laid bare his shoulder.

'Not wrenched, dislocated, though you may well have wrenched the muscles.' Her cool fingers explored the damage. 'May we have this shirt off? The other sleeve first – that's it.' Julien, who had suffered tortures while Chivers had removed his coat, was astonished to discover how painlessly his shirt slid away from him. 'Those pantaloons,' she was eyeing his nether integuments thoughtfully, 'may have to be split to get them over that foot, and if it has to be splinted – '

'Do you wish to strip me naked, ma'am?' The twinkle in his eye, defying his pain, made her want to hug him.

'No, Chivers can do that! Ah, here he comes with the compress.' At that moment there sounded a great banging on the street door. 'Please God, that will be the doctor. No, my lord, stay where you are. I can tell him what he needs to know and when he has seen Charlotte he will come in to you.' She laid the compress on his foot while Chivers hurried downstairs. 'There, that should give you some ease, and now I must attend Charlotte.'

She rose and returned to the bedroom, wondering why it was that the sight of strength humbled to helplessness had such a lowering effect upon one's morals.

Dr Bolton showed himself to be in complete agreement with Miss Branscombe that Charlotte was not to be moved until it was plain how much damage had been done to her head. She was still in a very dazed condition and complained of shooting pains through her temples, but suffered him to re-bandage her injuries without protest, only once murmuring: 'Where am I?'

'In a friend's house,' interposed Anthea quickly, taking the blood-stained cloths from the doctor and handing him fresh linen that she had found in the housekeeper's room. 'And I am here to look after you.'

'And that, ma'am, will necessitate constant care until we are assured of no lasting harm,' the doctor warned her. 'Have you got others to help you?'

'I trust I shall have,' she replied cheerfully. 'Now, sir, if you would be so good as to step in to see his lordship who, I fear, is in little better case.'

Dr Bolton made no attempt to disguise his anxiety about the Earl's condition. 'Broken bone and crushed left foot,' he told her. 'I have put back the dislocated shoulder but the arm is badly bruised and, in rearing up, the animal kicked him on the upper right thigh, near to the groin. He is suffering a deal of pain and I have instructed his valet to give him several drops of laudanum in his wine to-night, else he'll get little sleep. He will have to keep to his bed – you, ma'am, are going to be excessively busy.'

'Yes,' agreed Miss Branscombe. 'I am, indeed.'

When the doctor had left, promising to call back later that evening, she had Chivers and the groom place a bed for her in Charlotte's room, then that and the bed in the Earl's dressing-room had to be made up. He protested that he would remove himself to a room across the passage and leave the dressing-room free to be used as a medical post.

'No, thank you!' she retorted. 'There will only be either Chivers or I on duty during the night. How much more sensible for our invalids to be in adjoining rooms with a door between left ajar? I cannot be for ever running across the passage to see if you have broken out in a fever or – or something.'

'Miss Branscombe, you must require Dr Bolton to get a nurse, you cannot undertake all this yourself. And Lady Ralston will have to be informed, and my staff – Sefton and the others, must be got from Chalice.'

'Don't fret yourself into a fever!' she soothed him. 'To-morrow, when we are more assured of Charlotte's condition, I will send Lady Oakley's chaise to Heatherstone Hall and to Chalice. No sense in alarming them unduly.'

'They could help you if they were here.'

'Hmm!' she said. 'Lady Ralston could, I doubt not, but can you fancy my Aunt Oakley in a sickroom? And Penny's enthusiasm for nursing would, I feel, wane very speedily under the influence of other attractions! As for nurses, they are mostly filthy, drunken women who visit a house for the pickings.'

She was sitting beside him in the dressing-room as Chivers made up the bed. The strain of the doctor's attentions had greatly tired him and he was clearly in pain, but his concern was all for her and Charlotte.

'How is she? Has she regained consciousness?'

'Yes, but she is still very dazed and her head aches dreadfully. She does recall the accident but not your part in it. She may not have recognized you.'

'Then don't tell her,' he said swiftly. 'Does she know where she is?'

'No, she supposes herself to be in South Street if she thinks of it at all.'

'Then leave it so. To have her feel obliged to me – ' He stopped, remembering Chivers's presence. Miss Branscombe, looking around the room's handsome appointments, the toilet-table with its silver-topped, crested bottles, the silver basin and ewer, the French flock wallpaper, the rich damask hangings and fine Brussels carpet, thought Charlotte would have to be quite addled in the head not to appreciate that her surroundings were rather more magnificent than might be expected in the house of a junior diplomat, however well-breeched he might be.

'That is very well for the moment,' she agreed, 'but what tale am I to tell her later, for she surely will ask?'

'Merely that I chanced by just after her accident and, not knowing if there was anyone in residence at Audley Street, brought her here.'

'And how did you come by your injury?'

'Oh, that! The horses were still rampaging and, in trying to steady them, I got trampled on for my pains. That's near enough the truth.'

Miss Branscombe promised herself a long cose with Mrs Farley in the near future in order to discover what precisely had taken place. The Earl had been deliberately vague about his part in the incident, but his injuries and the fact that even his hands were bruised and cut, convinced her that he must have put his person at considerable risk for Charlotte's sake. She rose, smoothing down her crisp cotton skirt, and picked up her long suede gloves.

'I leave you in command, Chivers, for an hour or so while I return to South Street to gather together some clothes and acquaint my hostess of the situation. No,' she added, catching the unspoken question in Julien's eye, 'she would be quite useless here, most like to have the vapours and add to my worries. I only wish your servants would return – do you realize we have not eaten since breakfast and it is near three o'clock?'

'I cannot conceive what they can be about,' he sighed, hand to head.

'Taking advantage of their master's absence. How many are there of them?'

'There will be but a couple of footmen and housemaids, miss,' interposed Chivers, 'another groom and the porter, the rest having gone with us to Chalice.'

'In that case, Mrs Tremlett must come up with Sefton. I will write a note – ' began the Earl.

'You will get to bed!' said Miss Branscombe firmly. 'Chivers, take his other arm.'

She departed for South Street a few minutes later, praying fervently that neither of her patients would take an acute turn for the worse in her absence. Fortunately, no such calamity occurred, and when she returned to Clandon House in Lady Oakley's chaise with her own and Charlotte's clothing, having spent more than an hour in soothing Mrs Fortescue's nervous forebodings, she found the missing household staff in attendance and in a decidedly chastened mood, having had the benefit of Chivers's opinion of their conduct.

Charlotte had fallen into an uneasy doze so she left her undisturbed. The Earl, she was concerned to see, was somewhat flushed and disinclined for food, so she set one of the housemaids to make him some gruel while she and Chivers shared out some cold viands she had filched from Mrs Fortescue's larder. A quick review of the stock of food in Clandon House assured her they were not going to starve for some days if only they had someone to cook it. Then another thought occurred to her, and she dashed off a note and gave it to one of the footmen, requiring him to deliver it to Lord Braybridge's residence and await a reply if his lordship should be at home.

Dr Bolton expressed himself as well enough satisfied with Charlotte's condition when he returned that evening. 'She is suffering from a severe concussion but there is no sign of fever so I do not think it necessary to bleed her. I will be better able to give a definite opinion in the morning.' About the Earl he was not so pleased. 'Although I believe his over-heated condition to be more of the mind than the body. Is there something that troubles him?'

Miss Branscombe, seeing with Julien's eye a picture of Charlotte lying in his bed, said there might be but was not prepared to disclose anything further. The doctor departed, promising an early call in the morning, and the footman she had sent to Lord Braybridge came to inform her that his lordship was gone to attend a cockfight at Highgate and was not expected home until late that evening. After a little thought, she warned the housemaids that she would require three bedrooms prepared on the morrow – no, on second thoughts she amended that to five, because Lady Ralston could hardly leave Melissa and Mr Vereker at Heatherstone Hall and Lady Oakley's staff would not be returning for at least another three days – then she persuaded Charlotte, who had awakened and appeared to be in a vastly more perceptive condition, to partake of some gruel and warm milk into which she introduced the laudanum prescribed by the doctor. This had the desired effect of sending Charlotte to sleep again before she could ask too many questions. After which, she undressed and slipped into her bed, instructing Chivers to arouse her at one o'clock, when she would take over the vigil.

This he faithfully did and she, seeing how weary he looked, despatched him to his room. 'I'll want you fresh in the morning,' she warned him, observing his hesitation. 'How is his lordship?'

'Well, miss, he's sleeping like a babe now, but I did add something to the doctor's potion. I hope I haven't done wrong, but he was in such pain I could not bear to see it.' Miss Branscombe eyed him in some apprehension. Chivers, she knew, had been valet to the Earl's father and had taken care of the orphaned boy from a very early age and, while she had no doubt of his devotion to Julien, his discretion might well be in question. 'His lordship brought back a distillation of poppies or some such from Spain, which he vowed was a potent pain-killer and much used during the late wars to reduce the agony of wounds or for those undergoing the surgeon's knife. I added a few drops of that to his wine.'

'What? As well as the laudanum?'

'Yes, it isn't a sleeping draught, you see, miss. He gave me a drop or two when I had the toothache a while back. It is a wonderful thing, lifts you above yourself and above all pain.'

'But you said he was asleep?'

'Well, that's the laudanum, miss, or maybe both together. I gave him a good measure of that, too.'

'Great Heavens! I hope he wakes before Dr Bolton comes at

nine o'clock or you will have a deal of explaining to do! Now, off you go, Chivers, and get some rest.'

The cool winds that had tempered the June sunshine had dropped away and the evening became increasingly hot and humid. Anthea threw open the windows of Charlotte's room though the air that came in was no fresher than that already in the house.

She put on a yellow muslin robe-de-chambre, and was brushing out her heavy brown hair when a slight sound from the dressing-room attracted her notice. Moving to the half-open door, she saw by the light of the candle left by Chivers, that the Earl was tossing and muttering in his sleep. He had flung most of the bedcovers off, but one look at his flushed cheek persuaded her to leave them and just draw a sheet up over him. His forehead was hot and dry to her touch and, as she stroked back the thick wave of his hair, he spoke again, half-aloud, and she bent down to try to hear what he said.

'Darling, oh, my darling!' he murmured drowsily, his arms stretching out towards her. With great presence of mind, Miss Branscombe extinguished the candle and, avoiding his clasp, stood in the darkened room for several minutes, knowing full well that the endearments he was uttering, part in Spanish, part in English, were never intended for her ears.

She did not dare to move until his restless turning had ceased and he was breathing quietly again. Then, stealing upon tip-toe, she returned to the other room where the sight of Charlotte's copper curls on the pillow caused her to smile fondly at her sleeping friend.

'It was you he was loving, not me,' she declared, shaking her head. 'You are all his desire and you deny him.'

Startlingly, Charlotte's eyes opened wide and stared at her. 'What are you talking about, Anthea?' she asked in a perfectly rational voice.

'N-nothing! Go to sleep, dear!' said the surprised Miss Branscombe.

Obediently, Charlotte turned over and closed her eyes while a thoughtful Miss Branscombe, surrounded by books and magazines to help keep her awake, and propped up against a mound of pillows, made herself comfortable in bed. All cats were grey in the dark, she reflected, and the Earl was most unlikely to remember anything of what had occurred or, if he did, would put it down to a touch of fever.

CHAPTER EIGHT

THE following morning dawned bright and sunny, giving promise of greater heat as the day advanced. So heavily humid it had been in the night that Miss Branscombe, in spite of her firm resolution to stay awake and watch over her invalids, had drifted into an uneasy doze when a gentle tapping on the door aroused her at eight o'clock.

'Great Heavens! The time! Yes, who is it?' The scared face of the more intelligent of the housemaids peered round the door.

'Should I call Mr Chivers, miss?'

'Yes, yes, at once, please. And bring me up chocolate or tea or something.'

'I can make tea, miss.'

'Good, but be sure the water is boiling.'

'I would dearly love a cup of tea,' came Charlotte's voice from the big bed.

'Charlotte! How is it with you?'

'Very full of aches but much clearer in the head, I thank you.'

'Good, then plenty of tea as soon as you may,' Miss Branscombe commanded the waiting housemaid, praying that Charlotte's mental clarity did not date from too early an hour. 'But make haste, for the doctor is due at nine o'clock.'

'My poor Anthea, you have been awake half the night.'

'Yes, Julien was restless.' Miss Branscombe was busily splashing water from the ewer into the basin.

'Julien?' Now the moment had arrived and Miss Branscombe prayed that her sleepy brain would give a good account of itself.

'Yes, by the greatest good chance, he saw the accident and came to render what help he could. Mrs Farley informed him that South Audley Street was shut up and, as he was not sure of just where I might be found, he thought it best to bring you here to Clandon House. His valet discovered me most fortunately and conveyed me hither within a very short time.'

'Then,' Charlotte looked about her in disbelief, 'this is his bedroom – his b-bed?'

The application of cold water had done much to restore Miss Branscombe's powers of thought. 'Yes, indeed it was the only one prepared for occupation since most of his staff are at Chalice and those remaining – well!' She rubbed her face briskly with a fine linen towel. 'You know what happens when there is no mistress to oversee a household. However, I have sent them scuttling about their business, I can tell you! Now, I must look in on Julien to see if he has awakened.'

'Why, is he hurt, too?'

'Yes, he was forced to check the rampaging horses before he could get to you and, in so doing, received injuries to his foot and person. Or so I understand the case.' She came to adjust the sling for Charlotte's arm and, seeing her patent anxiety, added more kindly, 'Oh, nothing too grave, we trust, but he'll not put foot to the ground for a time. There, is that more comfortable? Does the bone ache greatly?'

'Yes, it does, much more than before.' Charlotte was very quiet and downcast.

'That is perhaps because you are more aware of it.' Miss Branscombe was seeking her bedroom slippers which seemed, after the fashion of such things, to have taken themselves into the most far distant spot under the bed.

'Is he in great pain?'

'He was yesterday, we will hope for less to-day.'

'I seem to remember a gentleman thrusting the horses away from me. Was that Julien?' Miss Branscombe got up off her hands and knees, having retrieved the two errant slippers.

'To be truthful, I cannot tell you all the ins and outs of it until I have spoken with Mrs Farley.'

'Mrs Farley? Anthea, Aunt Oakley's gowns!'

'Safe with Mrs Farley, I have no doubt. I will go and collect them when your mother and the rest of the Heatherstone Hall party arrive – now I must write to her. I have ordered the chaise to be standing ready at nine o'clock and they must be off immediately I have had the doctor's opinion of you.'

She peeped round the door to discover the Earl still asleep with the covers in imminent danger of once more descending to the floor. Replacing them carefully, she was relieved to find his cheek and forehead but slightly warm to the touch. 'No more of that potion for you, my lad, whether you wish for it or no!' she whispered, making a mental note so to instruct Chivers.

The housemaid's tea might not have met with a connoisseur's approval but both ladies drank it gratefully, Miss Branscombe the while writing to Lady Ralston in such wise as to convey the gravity of the situation without spreading undue alarm. Charlotte was very silent and, when questioned, admitted to feeling thoroughly out-of-sorts. Voices from the dressing-room and the tactful closing of the door gave warning of the Earl's having wakened and Chivers being with him. A moment later, Dr Bolton was announced.

The doctor spent a short time talking quietly to Charlotte and noting her replies, then he looked at Miss Branscombe.

'You are sending for Lady Ralston?'

'Yes, I am but awaiting your final word before closing the letter.'

'Her condition is much as one might expect after such an experience, but the next day or two could be exacting. She must rest here in the utmost quiet.'

'Oh, may I not go back to South Audley Street?' Charlotte's eyes were directed in supplication at Miss Branscombe but that damsel shook her head firmly.

'Impossible, my dear, there are no servants there, save only a porter. Now, sir, if you will attend his lordship I will complete this letter and despatch it away at once.'

As the dressing-room door closed behind the doctor and Miss Branscombe sat down at a secretary table to finish her note, a small voice whispered from the bed: 'Anthea, I cannot remain here – I cannot!'

'You can and you will!' Even to her own ears, Miss Branscombe sounded uncommonly curt. 'What do you fear? Julien? 'Pon my word, Charlotte, when I think – as I do think – that he hazarded his person, even his life, for your safety, I am out of all patience with you!'

'Anthea, I beseech you!' Charlotte's scarlet cheeks and trembling hands reminded Miss Branscombe that she was in no case for such reprimand and, instantly contrite, she came to the bedside to comfort her friend.

'What is it, my dear? What has fallen out between you?'

'The things I said to him – but I trusted him – ' The broken confession was barely audible.

'And you cannot trust him now?'

'How could I after – for all they named him Sultan, I never dreamed that Julien could be like that – '

'You mean other women?' The sobbed assent caused Miss Branscombe to marvel at how the Earl had contrived to remain on a pedestal for at least two of the Ralston girls for so long.

'My dear,' she said gently, 'he is not tied to you in any way nor, to my knowledge, to any other woman. May he not take a mistress if he so pleases?'

' 'Tis no Cyprian I complain of!' Charlotte burst out bitterly. 'At least not one that would describe herself as such! And I had a right – I – ' She dissolved into tears and Miss Branscombe's further contribution to this interesting conversation was curtailed by a knocking on the door and a footman to say that the horses had been kept standing these twenty minutes and the coachman was wishful to know if he was to stay or to go.

She sealed her letter with a wafer and handed it to him as another caller was ushered into the hall below. Going on to the landing she looked down into Lord Braybridge's upturned face.

'My dear Miss Branscombe,' he said, coming up the stairs to her, 'it was so late last night when I received your message I dared not call. Tell me the whole.' This she did as fully as was in her power and wondered at the look of resentful fury that passed over his face. 'Clandon allowed himself to be so damaged by a fractious horse? I cannot credit this.'

'Nor I,' she agreed, 'but it is all he will admit to. Ah, here is Dr Bolton.'

The doctor and his lordship were already acquainted and, while Miss Branscombe went to inform Charlotte of her betrothed's arrival, they discussed the injured pair.

'I have little fear that Miss Ralston will make a good recovery, but I am concerned for my lord – oh, not his foot, that is painful but I have no doubt of its mending perfectly in time – but the kick he received is another matter. He tells me the horse was maddened by fright – in which case, why approach the beast? Better far to have one's curricle smashed to pieces, as he informs me would have happened, than one's body.'

Braybridge shrugged slightly. 'These impetuous young men,' he drawled in such a manner that Miss Branscombe, returning to conduct him to Charlotte's bedside, was tempted to remind him that, but for Julien's impetuosity, his betrothed might well be in far worse case. Dr Bolton glanced from one to the other in question, but his patients' welfare was his first concern and he set about instructing Chivers in the application of a hot fomentation to the Earl's bruised body.

'This you must do faithfully every hour,' he declared. 'However my lord may protest against it.'

Julien, lying back on his pillows, not a little exhausted from Chivers' ministrations, managed a wry smile. 'And be sure I shall protest against such Turkish treatment!' he promised.

'Then I must make it clear to Miss Branscombe, my lord, that in this you are not the master here!' With an admonishing shake of the finger, the good doctor departed, declaring his intention of calling again later in the day.

Chivers was busying himself with clothing the Earl in a fine cambric nightgown and knotting a dark blue silk scarf loosely about his throat, when Miss Branscombe called to know if she might enter.

'I will not enquire how you are, my lord. You have been put to the torture, I can see – a little brandy perhaps?' She turned to a side-table to pour out the brandy and carried the glass to the bedside. 'You look quite dragged down, what has the doctor been doing with you? No, rest easy until Chivers brings more pillows, then we can lift you up and make you more comfortable.' She put an arm under his head and held the glass to his lips.

'Hot fomentations, miss, every hour,' Chivers put in. 'How many pillows, miss?'

'Three or four, I should think,' replied Miss Branscombe, concentrating on her patient. 'But the fomentations are designed to help the bruising and ease the pain so, however unpleasant, we must persevere with them.' Julien all but choked over the brandy that was being relentlessly poured down his throat but Miss Branscombe continued talking blithely. 'There, that's enough. We don't require you to be quite foxed.'

Just then the sound of voices rose up from the hall and, before the Earl could make reply, Chivers returned with an armful of pillows.

'Colonel FitzJames, my lord, and another gentleman.'

' 'Pon my soul, this place is like a posting-house. Best go down and warn him of what has happened, he's not likely to have heard.'

'The pillows, my lord?'

'I'll take them,' nodded Miss Branscombe. 'Ask the Colonel to step up for a moment, Chivers.'

Julien glanced in the direction of his bedroom. 'You have left them alone together?'

'They will come to no harm. Can you sit up a little? There, that's easier for you.'

She leaned over to pack the pillows behind him and, as she straightened up, she found her wrist imprisoned in his clasp.

'Had I a fever last night?'

'Yes, at least – ' She hesitated. 'You were very restless.'

'And kept throwing off the covers?' The slight quiver in his voice was too much for her, she ventured a glance at him and, in an instant, they were both laughing.

'I must tell you, my lord,' she said, 'that Chivers saw fit, without asking my advice, to give you a potion which he said you had brought back from Spain – ' His look of consternation checked her.

'Not that! I beg of you to forgive me if I did or said anything to offend you.'

'No, no, of course you did not. Now, here, by the sound of it, is Colonel FitzJames. I will go back to Charlotte.'

'Where you ought to have been all this while,' he reminded her.

'Yes, my lord. Good-morning, Colonel FitzJames.'

'Miss Branscombe, what are you doing here?'

'I am chief sick-room attendant!' she said with dignity, and removed herself into the bedroom. The Colonel stared after her, open-mouthed, before turning his attention to Julien.

'What the devil's to do here? Your man informs me you are half-dead, and there is an odd fellow downstairs who says he has brought back your curricle.'

'Who? Oh, it must be Ansell, I suppose. Could somebody – oh, God, if I could but move!'

'That you cannot do!' Miss Branscombe, who had been standing just inside the half-open door, shot back into the room. 'Who is Mr Ansell?'

'He is the owner of the runaway phaeton. Perhaps I ought to see him.'

'You have seen quite enough people for one morning,' said Miss Branscombe with some severity.

'Clandon, I am desolated to find you in so sorry a state.' Braybridge had come in from the bedroom behind her and, despite his air of sympathetic commiseration, she was put in mind of nothing so much as some feline flexing its claws before springing upon its prey.

'Perhaps you would speak to this gentleman, my lord,' she suggested quickly, and the Earl seconded her request.

'I'd be obliged if you would. He holds himself responsible for the accident – which, in truth, partly he was, but it was an unfortunate thing, the horses were frightened and his groom not standing to their heads. Please assure him that Char – Miss Ralston and I will survive. How do you find her?'

'Tolerably well – in better case than you, I'd say. Where is this fellow?'

'Will some kindly disposed person,' said Colonel FitzJames, dropping on to a convenient conversation chair after Braybridge had gone out and Miss Branscombe returned to Charlotte, 'be so obliging as to tell me precisely what has occurred?' The Earl deftly changed the subject.

'What brings you here so early in the day, Ned?' The Colonel grinned sheepishly.

'To ask you to dance at my wedding – which, it would seem, will be quite beyond your powers!'

'What – to Sally? Ned, this is the best of news!'

'And I am confoundedly grateful to you! No, don't look bashful, Sultan, 'twas your doing! Oh, we would have come to it, I don't doubt, but in a roundabout way. Yes,' he nodded, seeing the Earl's enquiring look, 'she told me it all. No wonder you were a bit taken aback when I descended upon you the next morning!' Julien thought gratefully that Sally, wise girl, had most certainly not told it all! 'God, Sultan, but she's a gorgeous creature, I am the luckiest devil on earth!' The Earl let him run on for a few minutes, reflecting that never had he expected to see Ned FitzJames so floored by love, then Miss Branscombe came in again to suggest that her patient needed rest and FitzJames realized he had not yet been told of what had happened. 'I have been so full of my own affairs, but what mishap has befallen you?'

'I can give you the best account of that!' Braybridge's voice as he entered the room was so unlike his customary lazy drawl that they all stared at him, surprised. 'I collect I have to thank you for Charlotte's life, Clandon.' He then gave them Mr Ansell's version of the accident while Julien silently cursed that gentleman for his loquacity.

'All this is a very highly-coloured tale,' he said when

Braybridge had finished. 'I protest I did no more than any other man near to hand would have done. Mr Ansell was in no position to judge of what took place.'

'Possibly not, but the dressmaker was, and he has had it all from her.' Braybridge stepped forward, hand outstretched. 'I am deeply obliged to you, Clandon.'

The last thing the Earl wanted was to be thanked for saving Charlotte's life, which he considered to be a gross overstatement in any event, and certainly not by the man she was going to marry. As their eyes met, he experienced a firm conviction that Braybridge was neither as blind nor as indifferent to what had been going on between himself and Charlotte as he had believed him to be, but courtesy compelled him to accept the Viscount's hand with at least a show of complaisance.

'Well, Sultan, you would seem to be a general benefactor this morning!' FitzJames remarked cheerfully.

'Yes, and he is going to be quite worn down if he is not allowed some peace and rest,' Miss Branscombe declared.

'How much sleep did you get last night?' Julien accused her.

'I will send Sally round to relieve you for a time, how would that serve?' asked the Colonel. Miss Branscombe's eyes opened very wide.

'You will send Lady Warne round?' she asked in gentle enquiry. He laughed.

'May as well admit it now as later. She's agreed to marry me, but it is meant to be kept secret until she breaks it to her family, so I must rely upon you not to spread it abroad.'

When the congratulations had died down, Miss Branscombe said there would be no need to trouble Sally though, of course, she would be glad to see her if she called later in the day.

'I am tolerably sure that the Heatherstone Hall party cannot arrive here much before seven o'clock this evening, and no one of them will be in great shape to assume my duties on the instant, so I must rest a little now,' she pointed out, and so cleared the house of visitors in a very short time. Then, having adjured Chivers not to neglect the hourly fomentations in spite of what the Earl might protest to the contrary, she lay down on her bed to sleep soundly for several hours.

She had reason to be grateful for those snatched hours of rest when Lady Warne was announced that afternoon and she went down to the drawing-room to receive her. To her surprise, her ladyship was not alone. A tall dark young man, who had been examining the collection of porcelain set out in a richly japanned and veneered cabinet, turned to make his bow to her as she entered. The general cast of his features and his fine brown eyes proclaimed his kinship with Sally even before she presented him.

'My brother, Wychfield, just home from the Americas.'

Miss Branscombe looked at Lord Wychfield with lively interest as he shook her hand. 'How do we fare in that field, my lord?'

'The battle wages with increasing fervour.' She liked his deep quiet voice and accompanying smile that held much of his sister's charm. 'But now that Napoleon is beat and we can turn our Peninsula veterans' attention westwards, the issue cannot be long in doubt.'

Lady Warne brushed aside the American wars. 'Pray tell us how we can be of service to this stricken household. Colonel FitzJames relayed to us a horrifying tale of disaster.'

'Not too disastrous, it is to be hoped, though Clandon is in none too good a case.' Miss Branscombe hesitated. 'Should I – may I offer my felicitations?'

'And they say women can never keep a secret!' Sally pretended to be displeased but failed to look other than delighted.

'I think he is too proud and happy to resist sharing his joy with his friends,' said Miss Branscombe simply.

'Thank you, Anthea.' Sally swooped upon her and kissed her warmly. 'How do you go on here? Are you not run ragged?'

'Nearing that, but they are very good, both of them. I have them in adjoining rooms for my convenience – '

'With a connecting door, of course!'

'Of course!'

'And you have left them alone? My dear Anthea!'

'Neither can move out of bed!' protested the laughing Miss Branscombe. Lady Warne was bubbling over with mischief and her brother directed a reproving look at her.

'Adam, you go up and talk to Julien,' she commanded him. 'And no peeping in on Charlotte! I have a matter to discuss with Anthea.' Miss Branscombe led Lord Wychfield into the hall and directed him to Julien's bedroom.

'You will find him somewhat weary and pulled down,' she warned him.

'I'll not stay long,' he promised her.

She watched him go up the stairs with the oddest feeling of pleasure which she was quite at a loss to explain, and when he paused at the top to smile down at her she had to turn away quickly and rejoin Lady Warne lest her face should reveal her feelings too clearly.

Sally grasped her hand and drew her down beside her on to a sofa. 'Anthea, did Julien really save Charlotte's life? How incurably romantic! Surely this must melt her heart towards him for I am quite assured that she loves him.'

'I am not so confident on that head.' Miss Branscombe looked troubled. 'I collect there is something or someone that has come between them.'

'A woman?' Lady Warne rose and began to pace to and fro while Miss Branscombe admired her handsome walking dress of dark green silk, set off by a fall of lace at throat and wrist. 'Ned said something of that to me to-day. It appears that when he called upon Julien the morning after our visit to Vauxhall he found him most distressed about a letter he had received – a family matter, he termed it, but would not elaborate further. Ned is convinced it is to do with a woman.' She stopped in mid-stride and clapped her hands together. 'Anthea, I have the most famous notion! You have been tending him and I have heard that gentlemen have a great partiality for those who oblige them in such a way. Could you not work upon him to offer for you?'

Miss Branscombe stared at her in amazement. 'Work upon

him to offer for me?' she repeated as if she could not quite believe her ears. 'How could I do such a thing? Charlotte is my dear friend. No, no, indeed I could not!' In her agitation she had risen and had joined her ladyship in pacing the floor.

'Why not? You can terminate the engagement at will by saying you feel you will not suit.'

'Jilt him? Oh, no, that would be unmannerly of me.' Miss Branscombe eyed her friend in some curiosity. 'Besides, what is the object of all this?'

'To make Charlotte jealous, of course. While he is free she imagines she can play fast and loose with him, but once he is hand-tied, too, it puts a very different complexion upon the matter.'

'What of Braybridge?' Lady Warne's eyebrows shot up.

'Would it break his heart to have to give up Charlotte?'

'I doubt he has a heart,' said Miss Branscombe thoughtfully. 'But he is proud and avaricious. And I think he hates Julien.'

'Pooh! What can he do if Charlotte says she has changed her mind? He need never know the true story.'

'Depend upon it, he knows now!' declared Miss Branscombe. 'I tell you, Sally, he is a man to hold in respect for I am persuaded he is of a vengeful disposition.'

'Then would it not allay his suspicions if you and Julien were to pretend to make a match of it?'

'No, Sally, I cannot undertake it.' Miss Branscombe shook her head decisively. 'I could not carry it off.'

'Do you fear that you would fall in love with Julien?'

'Are we not all a little in love with him?' countered Miss Branscombe.

'True,' mused Lady Warne. 'And to be betrothed to him, to be the object of his attention, why it would be difficult to resist his attraction.' She glanced slyly at Anthea. 'Would it bear so hard upon you to be his countess?'

'Yes, if he loved Charlotte.'

'Charlotte has had her chance and can still win him from you if she has a mind to it. Think on it, Anthea! Now, shall we go upstairs and intrude upon the old comrades' convention?'

'They were old comrades, then?' Miss Branscombe asked, grateful for a new topic of conversation.

'Yes, when my brother was so tragically widowed seven years and more ago – his wife was thrown from her horse and died in the second month of their marriage – he went with Julien to the Peninsula, but I doubt they have seen each other since Julien came home.'

'He must have been married very young.'

'Yes, but in my opinion it would not have done in later years, so maybe it was not such a tragedy after all. That sounds a monstrous cruel thing to say, but it is the truth.'

As Miss Branscombe followed Lady Warne up to the Earl's room she wondered why the sun appeared of a sudden to be shining brighter and the difficulties with which she was surrounded to have subsided to the importance of mere trivia.

She was proved to be right in her prognostications both about the numbers and time of arrival of Lady Ralston and her party, but there was one circumstance which she could not have foreseen. Lady Oakley had received a letter that very day from her spouse at Oakley Hall, telling of a robbery that had taken place there and requesting her immediate presence, together with an inventory of the silver, since no one could be quite certain of what exactly had been stolen. So, no sooner had Lady Oakley eaten and looked in upon Charlotte, than she was off, escorted by Mr Vereker, to South Audley Street, to search for the silver lists.

'Though dear knows where they may be. I am convinced that Oakley has them in his keeping. Oh, what a tiresome circumstance! And I must be away to St Albans in the morning when I would liefer far rest upon the nearest bed with drawn drapes and my hartshorn!'

Soothing her agitated sensibilities occupied the combined efforts of all, but at last the missing lists were found and she was persuaded to bed. Both Melissa and Penelope were eager to take over the night watch from Miss Branscombe, but she would have none of it.

'To be truthful, I cannot think it very necessary, but if either should need anything then I shall be in Charlotte's room to render assistance and can rouse Chivers in a moment.'

Lady Ralston had been horrified by the makeshift domestic arrangements, but realized that the urgency of the situation had allowed of none but the most convenient improvisation. She was also concerned for Miss Branscombe, who looked weary and was, at times, quite distrait and unlike her usual collected self, but improved greatly in spirits when the Earl of Wychfield called to enquire if there was anything he could do, like talking Julien to tatters as she roundly accused him of doing that afternoon.

'To tell truth, I felt so confoundedly de trop at Warne House, with Ned and Sally holding hands and gazing lovelorn at each other, that I took myself out for a walk only it came on to mizzle, so I found myself here.'

Sefton, who had arrived with Mrs Tremlett and other members of the Chalice staff in Lady Ralston's wake, took his lordship's coat to be dried, while Miss Branscombe led him to the saloon to join the other members of a now numerous household.

'When does Sally leave for Leicestershire?'

'In the morning. She feels the sooner the news of their new father is broken to her children the easier she will be!'

'Then they are not marrying at once?'

'No, but she'll not be away above a se'ennight, and Ned particularly wishes Julien to stand with him. How is he to-night?'

'In less pain, but the doctor is still concerned for him.'

'He is the most courageous fellow, you know, and would have us all believe that he has done nothing out of the way.'

The Earl had been very quiet and withdrawn while everything shook itself into place around him. Only once during the evening had he permitted his composure to be ruffled and that was when Lady Ralston had come to put her arms around him and thank him in broken accents for saving her daughter's life. He answered her nothing, just held her until she should be calm again, then teased her gently on her lack of fortitude.

'You, Julien, that you should be so hurt – oh, my dearest boy, to risk your life for her.'

'Aunt Emmelina, you know well there is nothing I would stop at to succour a daughter of yours! At least you have not offered to warm my backside for me!'

At that she had to laugh, remembering the far-off occasion when a nine-year-old Julien, engrossed in his favourite game of knights and dragons, had rescued his lady, the infant Charlotte, from one of these fearsome beasts and ridden off with her upon his saddle-bow, to the consternation of her nurse who had fled to pour out the tale to her mother. When, at length, he had safely brought back his tiny charge, he was highly outraged to be ordered to attend Lady Ralston in her sanctum and there bidden bend over a chair while she administered to him a beating sufficient to make him very thoughtful when he mounted his pony to ride back to Chalice.

'My dear, it was the only time that ever I was angry with you, and I should not have done it. I should have sent you to your uncle.'

'Thank God you did not! His was a heavy hand!'

'I know, that is why I did not. Oh, Julien, if only – '

'If only what?'

She longed to reply: 'If only you would run off with her again!' but did not quite dare.

He, sensing her troubled spirits, put up a hand to stroke her soft brown hair, scarcely touched by grey, and covered by a saucy little lace cap.

'Pretty auntie!' he murmured mischievously.

'You always used to call me that then you wished to turn me round your finger!'

'No less true now than it was then!' he pointed out.

'You were such a dear little boy.'

'A pity dear little boys have to grow up!'

'Not in your case, you grew up just as I would have wished.'

'Dearest Aunt Emmelina, if I could I would make you the lowest of bows for such an obliging compliment!'

'Make me a bow, indeed! You can scarce keep your eyes from closing! Ah, here is Chivers with – not another fomentation?'

'The last one to-night, my lady.'

'I have had the last one,' the Earl said firmly. 'You can take that away, Chivers.'

'Miss Branscombe said, my lord – '

'I care not a reed for what Miss Branscombe said. I am not having another fomentation to-night.'

'Are you not indeed?' Miss Branscombe's calm voice interrupted the argument. A sharp look was exchanged between her and Lady Ralston and, with one accord, they took hold of Julien's wrists and each pinioned an arm above his head.

'Now, Chivers, you can strip him and proceed!' Lady Ralston ordered. 'Anthea, look to the wall, if you please!'

'Chivers, if you dare, it is the last thing you'll do for me!' The Earl, in his weakened state, was quite helpless against two determined ladies.

'The doctor did order it, my lord, until you were prepared for sleep.' Chivers, knowing himself to be quite safe with Lady Ralston's support, drew back the covers and made as if to lift his lordship's bedgown.

'I capitulate! Begone, for pity's sake, and let me suffer it in peace!' The roughness in his voice made both ladies realize how exhausted he was and instantly they released him.

'Be as quick as you may, Chivers.' Lady Ralston laid a hand on the valet's shoulder as she went out of the room and he nodded in understanding. In the bedroom, she turned to Miss Branscombe. 'I hope Dr Bolton knows what he is about. Despite his cheerfulness, that poor boy is near the end of everything.'

Miss Branscombe could only shake her head and agree, while Charlotte looked from one to the other troubled face and wished with all her heart that she had not been the unwitting cause of the Earl's injuries.

The night promised to pass without event, for Dr Bolton had instructed Chivers to give the Earl a double measure of laudanum and this the valet had done. He had not, however, stayed to watch it drunk down so did not know that the Earl had tipped up the glass into a convenient receptacle. Miss Branscombe, very tired but her mind spinning with new thoughts and images, managed to stay alert until well after midnight. Then, seeing that Charlotte was asleep, she thought she had better look in on the Earl. After a moment's hesitation she picked out the yellow robe-de-chambre from her wardrobe.

'You silly goose, he's going to be sleeping soundly, and you would never have the courage to carry it off in any case!' she told herself scornfully.

Julien looking, she was of the opinion, rather like a black-haired angel, if such beings existed, was lying with closed eyes, the covers as ever, half off him. One of his window curtains had been drawn back and a ray of moonlight lit up part of the room, so she stole to his bedside to put out the candle that was burning down to its socket. Before she knew what was happening, she was grasped firmly while the Earl said in a remarkably wide-awake voice: 'Now, my lady in yellow, explain yourself away if you can!'

'Of course I can!' she retorted indignantly. 'I am merely seeing to your comfort!'

'As you did last night? In God's name, what took place? That draught that Chivers gave me – well, it has more qualities than those of numbing pain and inducing sleep!'

'N-nothing happened that you need concern yourself about,' she stammered.

'If I have done ought to displease you, may I offer you the protection of my name?'

'It is vastly obliging of you, my lord, but I believe quite unnecessary.'

There was a lengthy silence before he said quietly: 'I put myself in your hands, Miss Branscombe.'

'I shall not betray your trust, my lord.' She hardly knew how to get away but he made no effort to detain her. At the door, she said: 'I fancy you did not take your laudanum. I will fetch you some now and you will please to drink it.' She came back a few minutes later with the laudanum. 'All of it, my lord.'

'Thank you.' He handed her back the empty wine-glass. She studied his white face and heavily-shadowed eyes.

'You are worn to the bone. Does – does it hurt a lot?'

'Not so much now. Stay for a little, please – Anthea.'

Without a word she sat beside him, watching his eyelids droop as the laudanum had swift effect. Sally Warne might call her the greatest chucklehead in the world but to accept the Earl's proposal under such circumstances was something she could not do. When she was sure that he slept she stole back to her bed, congratulating herself that things had passed off very easily. Which, as she was later to admit, was an excessively rash presumption on her part.

CHAPTER NINE

RICHARD, third Viscount Braybridge was, as Miss Branscombe had observed, a man possessed of a vengeful disposition.

Wed at an early age to a lady for whom he could pretend neither affection nor respect and whose only claim to superiority lay in her impressive fortune, he had speedily withdrawn into the more rarefied atmosphere of the collector's world. Everything that was exquisite or difficult to obtain became a prime object with him, and when he suffered an accident driving his curricle at speed, during the course of which his wife was hurled from the vehicle and killed, it was whispered by the malicious that it had come about because she had not measured up to either of these requirements. These whispers had at no time assumed the magnitude of accusations and he had easily been able to ignore them, but the fact that he was a notable whip and his wife not at all in favour of fast travel made it the more difficult to explain just why he had been springing his horses on a poorly-surfaced road that bordered a disused quarry on the bounds of his estate. His wife's brother, a contentious fellow, had ever made it clear that he held Braybridge responsible for her death, but as he mostly lived retired in the country his blusterings were scarcely heard in the fashionable saloons and clubs of London.

The Viscount continued to enjoy to the full the pleasures available to any well-breeched gentleman of rank which, for him, included making many additions to his impressive collection of china and *objets d'art*. Then his eye had chanced upon the eldest Miss Ralston and he had at once appreciated that she was possessed of a quality rarer than beauty, a fineness of feature and form, allied to sensitivity and a quick understanding, that excited his connoisseur's taste.

There were other factors, too, that aroused his interest and made him passably certain of securing the lady's hand, but he had to confess himself surprised when she accepted his offer without any undue persuasion on his part, and at once set himself to discover the reason for her ready capitulation.

Now he was tolerably sure that he had the whole picture in clear prospective. Her heart had long been given to Julien Revel who, with so many pressing for his attention, hardly spared a thought for the girl he had known all of her life. So she had accepted Braybridge's offer – though whether out of desperation or with the set intent of alerting the Earl to an awareness of what he was losing, the Viscount could not be perfectly certain, but that she had succeeded in the latter object was beyond dispute.

Braybridge's thin lips curled in a sardonic smile as he surveyed his reflection in a tall cheval mirror. A pity, he thought, that powdered wigs had gone out of fashion for they had set off his aristocratic lineaments to a nicety. His valet, observing that smile, made haste to remove himself, but thought it only fair to warn his wife who acted as housekeeper to the establishment, that His Nibs was in a fine humour which boded ill for somebody.

As he stood in the hall, drawing on his gloves, Braybridge debated whether or not to continue in his present rôle of gullible fiancé and to prolong the game of cat and mouse a little longer. On the whole he thought it might be diverting to discover how Charlotte would conduct herself towards her deliverer. Should gratitude outweigh her condemnation of the Earl's character, then there would be nothing for it but to step in and put a stop to the affair before it got out of hand. His lordship's eyes narrowed thoughtfully as he considered the possibilities. He knew himself to be a fine swordsman and a reliable shot, but he was under no illusions about the Earl's capabilities in these fields. No, other means would have to be employed to make the lady see reason, much as he regretted having to put a period to so delightful a source of entertainment. He was still smiling as he stepped up into his carriage and gave directions to be driven to Clandon House.

At that establishment a certain amount of confusion existed, for despatching Lady Oakley off to St Albans would have exhausted the ingenuity of the household had not her sister taken a firm line with her and pointed out that it was no less than her duty to be at her husband's side in such a situation.

No sooner had her weeping and expostulating form been bundled off in the chaise than there was Dr Bolton come to see his charges. He expressed himself to be satisfied at their condition, though still troubled for the Earl.

'All would appear to be well,' he said to Lady Ralston. 'Though one cannot be sure how far the internal bruising may have penetrated. The fomentations must be continued, they will do more than anything to relieve his discomfort.'

After that, with the doctor's consent, Charlotte was moved into a room next to her mother, the Earl's bedroom was put to rights and he was installed in his own bed, while Chivers prepared to settle into the dressing-room. Lady Ralston then called upon Julien to see how he fared but no sooner had she seated herself beside him than there was a frantic scratching on the door and Penelope's voice demanded instant admittance.

'Julien – mama, forgive my intrusion!' Her mother cast a critical eye over her daughter's sketchy toilette.

'Penelope, what can have given you the notion that, because we are a house of sickness, you can be going about looking like a rag-bag?'

'I have but woken up!' protested Penelope, in the clear conviction that that explained all. 'And I must ask Julien if I may send a footman at once to bear a message for me.'

'At once?' echoed her mother, being deliberately obtuse, 'Now, what in the world could be the reason for such urgency?'

'Well, you see, I am back in town before – anyone looked to expect me.'

Penelope was getting more and more confused and Julien, in pity, put her out of her difficulty.

'I think it an excellent idea to acquaint Mr Beaumont of your return,' he said with admirable gravity. 'I am confident we can rely upon him to take you off your mother's hands when she has so much to occupy her.'

'Thank you, Julien!' The stars were back in Penelope's eyes. 'Oh, I nearly forgot – *The Gentleman's Magazine*, the *Gazette*, and the *New Monthly Magazine*, all just arrived!' She tossed them down on the bed with such abandon that Julien visibly winced, and was gone, skipping out of the room, singing a lilting air with such fervour that Melissa, encountering her on the stairs, had to hush her to silence lest she disturb Miss Branscombe, who was trying to snatch some rest.

Her fleeting visit and the reason for it had given much amusement to her mother and the Earl. 'Though, to be sure, we are such a ramshackle household here, I cannot imagine what Mr Beaumont's aunt will be thinking of us!' sighed Lady Ralston.

'Is something not to your liking, ma'am? But tell me and I will have it set right at once.'

'No, no, Julien, I am not complaining – how ungrateful that would be! But it is such an imposition on you – all the Ralston family, to say nothing of Mr Vereker and Miss Branscombe.'

'I would think it very ill-done of you to desert me when I lie stricken here!' he quizzed her.

'But Mr Vereker – '

'Philip,' said the Earl, 'is hardly an old friend, I allow, but if only for Melissa's sake, let us not banish him! To Miss Branscombe I owe more than I can say. There can be no question of her leaving us unless she so wishes.'

'She is indeed a delightful and capable young lady. I am most grateful to her for her care of Charlotte.'

'Then that is agreed? There will be no further talk of transplanting this ramshackle household?' He took her hand and kissed it, smiling at her so sweetly that she could do no other than smile back her acceptance of his wishes.

Colonel FitzJames and Lord Wychfield were then announced, followed closely by Lord Braybridge, and Julien's bedroom began to assume all the appearance of a morning reception. As it was such a fine day, the gentlemen were discussing the relative merits of a visit to Mr Thomas Lord's ground to view a cricket match, or a drive out to Barnet where a promising mill was due to take place.

'In either case you will need food.' Lady Ralston rose. 'I really must have a word with Mrs Tremlett, for I have no notion of what there may be to eat in the house.'

She descended to the housekeeper's room to find Sefton there informing Mrs Tremlett that, in his opinion, the best course she could pursue would be to purchase a whole ox because, if the present rate of increase in the household was maintained, that would scarcely be sufficient to feed them above a day or two.

In spite of these gloomy forebodings, Mrs Tremlett produced a very creditable meal. Cold beef, chicken and tongue flanked a great brawn brought from Chalice which, with a game pâté and pigeon pie, formed the first course, followed by syllabubs and peaches, ripe to perfection, from the Earl's glasshouses, all washed down with more of the hock that had met with Colonel FitzJames's approval on a previous occasion.

Lady Ralston carved off a delicate portion of meat and fowl to be carried up to the Earl and Charlotte while Melissa and the Colonel insisted on being her waiters.

'And, I beg of you, stand over them and make them eat. Julien, in particular, has hardly touched food since he was laid upon his bed.'

'Then, I think,' said Melissa to her fellow servitor as they went upstairs, 'that we will change over – I to Julien, and you to Charlotte. I'll force it down his throat!'

'If you have any trouble, call me,' said the Colonel, knocking on Charlotte's open door. 'Now, ma'am, every mouthful of this is to be devoured, or so I am instructed, and when I tell you that not one crumb has passed my own lips and that I am nigh fainting from hunger, you will understand that the case is desperate.'

'Colonel FitzJames,' said Charlotte shyly, 'I understand I have to wish you happy and I do, believe me, sincerely I do.'

'I must thank you, Miss Ralston.' The Colonel set his tray on a table beside her. 'But from your style of expression I cannot but feel that your wish is rather a devout hope than because you anticipate our future bliss.' He spoke in jest, but when he saw her alarmed unease the smile faded from his lips. 'So? Have you cause to think that we shall not suit, Sally and I?'

'I – I have no d-doubt you will!' Charlotte was covered with confusion and wished herself at the ends of the earth rather than trapped in a chair, facing this agreeable big man whose happiness she feared she could shatter by a few words. Desperately she feigned ignorance of his meaning, her words had been a mere commonplace, he had read into them something not intended, but he was not to be deterred. Finally, forced to speak, she said hesitantly: 'Lady Warne has such great charms, sir, we all did wonder upon whom her choice might fall.'

'If you mean, did she appear to favour Sultan,' said the Colonel, calmly setting out her food convenient to her hand, 'I will confess to having endured some moments of doubt, even of green-eyed jealousy, for he would have been no mean rival. But all has resolved itself and I am the fortunate being she has chosen.'

'Well, then, indeed you are right to be happy and I am talking the greatest fudge,' she said warmly, much relieved to be able to drop the subject. Colonel FitzJames, however, a recent conversation with Lady Warne on the subject of Julien and Charlotte sharp in his mind, pressed on a further point.

'But, after all, there must have been some reason for you to have entertained such a notion,' he commented idly. 'I do counsel your attempting a morsel of this pâté. I am assured it is quite out of the ordinary.'

'I d-do not quite know,' stammered Charlotte, feeling she was mismanaging the whole business sadly. 'Possibly it was that evening at Vauxhall w-when Lady Warne was taken ill – '

'And Sultan escorted her back to Warne House and had to

break in because she had forgotten her key – quite a Gothic tale, I assure you!'

He thereupon regaled her with a spirited account of that fatal night's doings, and watched with sympathetic interest the play of emotion on her expressive face. From disbelief through surprise and, finally, to utter horror as she realized her incredible foolishness in condemning the Earl unheard, every shade of feeling was reflected in the wide grey eyes fixed so earnestly upon him.

'If only he had told me!' The words were out before she could prevent them, but he wisely paid no heed. He had seen and heard enough to tell him the whole story, and what he would have to say to Sally on the subject of her indiscretions was going to be strictly between themselves.

Just then Melissa called from across the landing. 'How do you two go on?'

'Famously!' asserted the Colonel. 'My subject is proving perfectly docile.'

'Well, mine is not!' Melissa returned tartly. 'It would please me if you would come and lend weight to my entreaties.'

'That is easily done.' The Colonel put a peach in his pocket and rose. 'Now, Miss Ralston, if I give you my support, do you think you could walk across the landing?'

'To Julien's room? I c-cannot – I h-haven't seen him since – ' Words quite failed her.

'No, neither you have. So, in your opinion, is it not high time you offered your thanks to him for doing what he did? May I remove this?' He took the rug off her knees and assisted her to rise. She was trembling so that he feared he was asking too much of her and, taking her sound arm, he pressed it warmly to his side. 'Courage, my dear girl!' he whispered.

'Oh, what have I done?' she breathed.

'Nothing, I imagine, that cannot be undone. Come along now, steady does it!'

'Well, you have been a time!' Melissa was trying to coax the Earl to taste a piece of chicken, and her head was turned away from the door, but he had a clear view of Charlotte, walking in on the Colonel's arm. The fleeting expression of joy on his face did not escape Melissa, nor did the fact that his mouth had dropped slightly open in his amazement, and she seized the opportunity to thrust the piece of chicken in before turning round. 'Charlotte! Come and sit down, sister dear, and see if you can be more adept than I at feeding this creature – oh, Julien, please do not choke!'

When the Earl, red-faced and with streaming eyes, had got his breath back, he was obliged to drink an amount of wine before being capable of greeting his unexpected visitor.

'I am delighted to see you so improved in health,' he got out at last.

'Take it quietly, old fellow,' the Colonel counselled. 'Miss Melissa, allow me to instruct you in the art of feeding the sick. You simply do not cram the food down the throat. You take it delicately so – though why, Sultan, you should have to be fed when you have two perfectly good hands is beyond my comprehension.'

'Because he will not feed himself!' sighed Melissa. 'There is a saying about fetching a horse to the water and then being unable to induce him to drink which I believe to be peculiarly applicable in this case. Julien, please peel this peach for Charlotte. Colonel, I am assured you are quite set down from lack of food. Can I prevail upon you to go downstairs and partake of some refreshment?' Talking volubly, she urged him to the door and out on to the landing. 'Leave them together for a few minutes!'

'But what of Braybridge?'

'What of him? I am here. Now go, and do not permit anyone to come up for any reason just yet.' She gave him a push towards the stairs and went back to Charlotte's room.

Meanwhile that young lady, left unprotected by the Earl's bedside, ventured to enquire how he did.

'Exceeding well, I thank you. But for this wretched foot I should be as active as yourself.'

Charlotte, who felt far from active and on whose sensibilities the Earl's coolly courteous manner was having a very lowering effect, bravely struggled to express her gratitude.

'I am so excessively obliged to you – to have no consideration for your own safety – I cannot ever adequately express my thanks – ' she managed to get out, but he turned aside all her protestations.

'I can only say that whatever I did was most ill-done. To look at you now, your head, your arm, depend upon it, my intervention was of small value.'

'Indeed, that is not so,' she said earnestly. 'If that beast had struck me well you know I would not be sitting here to-day.' The Earl had finished preparing her peach and placed it on a plate, near to her.

'Can you contrive with one hand?' She raised her eyes, bright with tears, to his impassive face.

'Julien, forgive me for the dreadful things I said to you. I never meant them. I was out of all reason angry.'

'Truth often will out in moments of anger,' he replied lightly. 'Think no more of it. Come, will not even a peach from Chalice tempt you?' Obediently, she tried to swallow some of the fruit, but it almost stuck in her throat.

'Julien,' she said again, desperately. 'Please l-listen to me. I know how wrong I was, how wrong to p-presume what I did.'

'Do you? Who can have been your informant, I wonder?' He sounded so disinterested she could have boxed his ears.

'Colonel FitzJames told me,' she confessed miserably.

'I see. But I was of the opinion – and pray correct me if I am in error – that if I had protested my innocence you would not have believed me.'

'No,' said Charlotte, making her most catastrophic blunder, 'I would not. N-not then, anyway.'

'Thank you. I must confess I had thought our friendship to have meant rather more to you than it obviously did.' Gone was his assumption of cool disinterest, he was white to the lips with anger and, at sight of it, she flung out her hand in supplication towards him while the slices of peach spilled, unheeded, over the bedcover. 'Your trust in me was scarce worthy of the name. Did you imagine I could – ' His rage had so worked on his physical weakness that he was quite unable to continue and she caught at the opportunity to plead with him once more.

'Julien, cannot we forget that dreadful day? Cannot we go back to – to that evening at Vauxhall, to our – '

'To our arrangement, you mean?' He had control of himself again. 'To our marriage of convenience? Hardly that, my dear!' The cynical note in his voice hurt her more than anything he could have said. 'I cannot but feel that this excess of remorse is prompted by a misguided notion of gratitude. You have nothing to be grateful to me for, Charlotte, now or ever.'

'I would do my utmost to be a good wife to you,' she whispered.

'That I do not doubt, but there is no need for you to be putting yourself to such inconvenience. Nor, to be honest, do I wish for a wife who offers herself in atonement for past faults because she considers such to be my due.'

That was the end, even if it meant losing him forever, there was no more she could do.

'I can but offer you my thanks for my life, and my regrets for any distress I may have caused you,' she said with commendable dignity. 'N-now I will leave you.' This she did, only pausing at the door to say with awful politeness. 'Forgive me, my lord, for having so troubled you. Rest assured I shall never do so again.'

A little later Colonel FitzJames came upstairs in search of Melissa and found her on the landing, unashamedly crying.

'What to do with them?' she sobbed. 'They tear each other to pieces in their fury!'

'Have patience, Miss Melissa,' he advised, 'they will do the same in their love when they confess it to each other.'

'It will be too late!' she wailed. 'She will be wed to Braybridge and he to some – some atrocious female!'

'This we must prevent at any cost. Given time, I feel, all will resolve itself.'

'We have so little time.'

'Therefore we must use what we have to the best advantage. Come, dry your eyes and join us downstairs. They can break their hearts up here very nicely without our assistance.'

CHAPTER TEN

As the days went by, Lady Ralston confessed to a growing concern for Charlotte and Julien.

'We are into July now and they should be in the country, away from this town heat. I only await Dr Bolton's permission and I will remove the entire household to Chalice and Heatherstone Hall,' she declared as she sat, enjoying a dish of tea one afternoon with Miss Branscombe. 'My sister returns to town to-morrow and, I believe, may be persuaded to join us. I am given to understand by Colonel FitzJames that Lady Warne will be delayed for some days owing to the unfortunate circumstance of her children having contracted the measles, so he can go with Julien to Chalice and visit his estate from there. If Mr Vereker and Mr Beaumont wish to join us, they could go to Chalice too, I have no doubt.'

'And I have no doubt that Mr Beaumont will so wish!' Miss Branscombe gave vent to one of her delightful chuckles.

'Well, he did ask me last night for my permission to pay his addresses to Penelope.' Lady Ralston's voice was carefully devoid of expression, but Miss Branscombe made not the least attempt to conceal her merriment.

'I should have thought he had been doing that for some time!' she remarked.

'He is a very correct young man and, I am in full agreement with Julien, in every respect suitable for Penelope.' Lady Ralston set down her teacup. 'And what of you, my dear? It would please me greatly if you could accompany us. You have been quite pulled down by all this sickroom attendance.'

'Well,' admitted Miss Branscombe, 'I feel I have fulfilled my engagement in South Street, since Mrs Fortescue is in strong anticipation of her spouse's early return. But, if I add to it, will you not be too large a party?'

'No, no, for if my sister can be with us she could act as chaperone at Chalice and you, perhaps, and Melissa could go there with her, while – but there is no point in making plans until we are assured of her inclinations.'

Lady Oakley having expressed her delight and readiness to accompany the party, the cavalcade that set forth three days later was sufficiently impressive to cause an appreciative small crowd and several stray mongrels to gather outside Clandon House, and Colonel FitzJames to remark that they really ought to be charging a viewing fee for nothing better could be seen at Astley's Ampitheatre. There was Lady Ralston's chaise, the Earl's chaise, and two curricles, Lord Braybridge's and the Colonel's together with the carriages for the Chalice staff and the baggage coach. Lord Wychfield, who had still some business to attend to in London, had elected to remain at Warne House until Sally should return when he proposed to escort her to Chalice.

Despite the journey being broken by the partaking of a light nuncheon in a pleasant woodland setting, the necessarily steady pace that had to be maintained for the invalids' comfort and to allow for the heavier carriages to keep up with the rest, proved irksome for the speedier curricles which kept dashing off on small forays to left and right and exchanging their passengers to relieve the tedium. On one of these exchanges towards the end of the journey, Miss Branscombe found herself alone with the Earl in his chaise. He was half-reclining with his injured foot supported on the opposite seat but, despite his cheerful manner and the superb springing of the vehicle, his weariness was plain to be seen.

'How this slow progression must gall you when you can do the journey in less than three hours in your curricle.'

'As I am chiefly the cause for the slow progression, the blame must rest on me.' He leaned back in his corner and turned his head a little against the squabs behind it to look at her. 'One thing must be understood, ma'am,' he continued with mock severity. 'You are, at no time, to resume your occupation as sickroom attendant! We are very stout in health now, Miss Ralston and I, and must be looking to ourselves.'

'I take leave to doubt that!' she retorted. 'You cannot put your foot to ground while, as for Charlotte, she bears such an appearance of fragility that, I dare swear, one ill-intentioned puff of wind would sweep her away.'

'Yes.' There was such a world of feeling in the single word that Miss Branscombe judged it prudent to say no more, and presently the Earl began to speak of how he proposed to have the estate carpenter at Chalice make him a pair of crutches. 'And then, I promise you, I shall be in and out of everything!'

She sighed. 'Yes, like a child that has not yet fully learned to walk, you will be falling about and getting yourself overtired so that I shall be forced to take over the handling of you again.'

'Which, of course, you do with consummate ease!' He picked up her hand which rested on the seat between them and carried it to his lips. To her annoyance, Miss Branscombe felt a blush rising to her cheeks, and wished with all her heart that the Earl would not look at her in quite that way which seemed to portend that he might not be so docile to hand as she had supposed. 'Why do you imagine our two dear dragons have left us together unguarded?' he asked, all seeming innocence.

'I can only suppose it is because they have not fully considered who is with who,' replied Miss Branscombe confidently if ungrammatically, for she, too had been wondering at such laxity, particularly on the part of Lady Oakley, who could be a high stickler on matters of propriety.

'Shall you lean out of the window and call for help?' enquired the Earl in an interested way.

'I think not,' said Miss Branscombe upon reflection. 'I am persuaded that I may rely upon you to behave at all times in a most gentlemanlike manner. And – oh, we are stopping!'

'There, you see! They have been counting their chickens and realize there is mischief afoot!' he teased her.

But nothing of so alarming a nature had occurred; they had merely arrived at the parting of the ways of the two estates. Lady Oakley's expression, however, when she left her sister's chaise to join the Earl and found him tête-à-tête with Miss Branscombe, caused him to direct such a mischievous glance at that young lady as seriously to threaten her composure.

On arrival at Chalice, willing arms lifted the Earl and carried him up the sweep of steps into the great hall, where he was seated in a chair, with a stool for his foot and a glass of brandy set in his hand by the resourceful FitzJames.

Miss Branscombe, following him, was suitably overawed by her first sight of the great house and he, amused at her wondering eyes, promised her that Melissa would show her over it since he could not. She thanked him but begged him not to trouble himself about such things for the moment.

'Indeed not, my lord!' Lady Oakley, for once not at all overset by the rigours of the journey, was in brisk command and, ignoring his protests, ordered two footmen to bear him up the massive oak staircase to his room.

'If you feel sufficiently rested, my lord,' said Miss Branscombe from the doorway on her way to her own room, 'I will come and resume our backgammon struggle after dinner – oh, I forgot to pack the board!'

'There are several here,' he assured her. 'Sefton will find you one.'

After an early meal, the Colonel and Mr Vereker repaired to the billiard-room, taking with them a protesting Melissa to act as marker. Miss Branscombe waited until Lady Oakley's regular breathing proclaimed her to be soundly asleep then she carried the backgammon board upstairs and set it out on a bed-table convenient to the Earl's hand.

'Quite alone, Miss Branscombe?' he enquired.

'I have set the door wide open,' she pointed out. 'But I doubt Lady Oakley will waken before tea is brought in!'

'Such an excess of propriety is surely a little behind the fair in our case?' he suggested and then laughed softly. 'I vow I uttered that impertinence only that I might see you blush, you do it so enchantingly!'

'You are very gallant to-night, my lord!' she reproved him. 'Is it being king of your own castle again that has put you in such high spirits?'

'I own I am happier at Chalice than anywhere,' he said. 'It is more than my home, it is the greater part of my life.'

'I know,' she answered him quietly. 'Shall we play?'

They wrought for some time in silence. Miss Branscombe was an eager student of the game, but the Earl had learned in a sterner school than she and when, triumphantly, she cried out: 'Bearing off!' he only smiled and tossed the dice again, 'Oh, not a four!' she wailed, too late aware of her danger.

'A double four!' he reminded her.

'Oh, you abominable creature!' In despair, she threw up her hands and, accidentally flicking the edge of the light board, suitable for sickroom use, overturned it.

'Well played indeed! When in difficulty tip up the table!' The Earl was shaking with laughter.

'How clumsy can I be?' She was picking up the pieces and dice which had scattered all over the bed. 'The game is yours! I yield!'

'Do you, Anthea?' he said softly. 'Do you?' He was looking at her in so searching a manner that Miss Branscombe, of a sudden, experienced a sharp sense of alarm. However, she was well aware that one had to humour the fancies of the sick so she contented herself with saying:

'My lord, I d-don't know what you mean.'

The Earl, for his part, still smarting in spirit from his last encounter with Charlotte, had come to a decision. Instead of behaving like a love-sick boy whose lady would have none of him, he would get himself a wife without delay. And who could be more suited to that high position than Miss Branscombe? She was pretty, intelligent, conversable and, he suspected, not altogether indifferent to him. Such a reaction was understandable in one of his temperament once he had made up his mind to renounce Charlotte. He had been prepared to offer her everything in his power and ask for nothing in return that she could not readily give, and his offer had been flung back at him with scorn. Her later capitulation and attempt to make amends he attributed to belated remorse and not to any real understanding of his feelings. Nonetheless, his tone was not entirely steady when he said:

'Anthea, will you do me the honour of becoming my wife?'

'My lord,' protested Miss Branscombe, playing for time, 'let us not proceed at too rapid a pace! From sickroom attendant to – to countess is a breathtaking elevation!'

That diverted him, as she had hoped it might. 'What, then, should be the procedure, ma'am?' he enquired politely.

'We-ell!' She pursed her lips and wrinkled her brow in thought. 'You understand I must be assured that you can support me in the state to which I am accustomed. After all, I have not yet seen over Chalice!'

To her relief, he laughed outright. 'Am I to understand, ma'am, that you will, at least, consider my offer, and may I, perhaps, hope for a favourable reply when you have – ah, assessed the situation?'

Dear Heaven, what to do? thought the distracted Miss Branscombe. He does not love me but feels that, if he cannot have Charlotte, I would make as good a wife as any. Aloud, she said: 'I am very sensible of the great honour you do me, my lord, and, believe me, would be very happy to oblige you but – '

'Then oblige me by calling me Julien,' he interrupted swiftly. 'What is it, my dear? Have you formed an attachment for some other gentleman?'

'Oh, no, it's not that,' protested Miss Branscombe in what she felt to be not at all a sensible manner, and wishing she could ignore her heart that kept performing the most odd antics, 'I – you – do you wish for another game of backgammon?'

'If we are to be betrothed, ma'am, I must remind you that we may play countless games of backgammon, unattended, without the least impropriety!' She, thinking of Lady Oakley, peacefully snoring below, could not withhold a small chuckle. 'Yes,' he went on in a musing sort of way. 'I am hopeful that we shall deal uncommon well together.' She looked at him then, his dark head thrown back against the heap of lacy pillows, his countenance, though pale and tired, alive with what might be fairly termed amused affection, and the magnificence of him struck her like a blow – who he was, what he was, what she would be undertaking if she married him, and her courage began to fail her. Quick to sense her distress, he asked: 'What is it? What troubles you?'

'It won't do, Julien,' she managed to get out. 'You – you don't love me.'

'Love? What has love to do with marriage? Affection, trust, a pleasure in the same interests, these are the durable qualities. Passions may flare but they die away and leave nothing but burnt-out embers.'

'But love has to be – overcome, Julien,' she said very steadily. He did not pretend to misunderstand her.

'I promise you it will be, with your help. It is unfortunate, I grant you, but I believe, mistaken.' The puzzled question in her eyes moved him to great gentleness. 'I give you my word never to do anything to reduce your standing or consequence. And if you tire of my attentions – '

'What then?' she enquired.

'I don't know,' he admitted. 'I do not fancy myself wearing a pair of horns with any good grace!'

'That you will not have to,' she promised him.

'Anthea,' he said, almost shyly. 'Do not permit yourself to become too attached to me. I am an unworthy fellow – '

'And would detest to be shackled to a doting wife!' she agreed. 'Besides, consider how unmodish it would be for me to appear besotted about you!'

'Why you might even want to sit upon my knee in public like what's-her-name did to her horrified spouse!'

'Quite odious!' she shuddered.

'We will agree to reserve our transports for the privacy of our bedroom,' he murmured, watching the fiery colour rush into her cheeks. 'Or, if you don't care for that, you have but to say.'

'You need an heir for Chalice,' she pointed out resolutely.

'If you would be so obliging.' His mouth hardened momentarily as he recalled another all too similar discussion.

'Yes, well.' She was at her most matter-of-fact again. 'That is all in the future. I have my father to consider. You must know I cannot desert him entirely for he is an old gentleman of decided habits and he does not go on at all smoothly with my elder brother's wife, so there is no fobbing him off on to her. We have a good housekeeper, but whether she will be content to remain when I am not there to bolster her from his uncertain tempers I will best discover when I go home after this long stay. It is the greatest time I have been away from him since my mother died.'

'There is room and to spare for him in Chalice, if he had a mind to join our establishment.'

'I make no doubt he would,' she said frankly. 'Because it would greatly add to his consequence to be your pensioner, but I'd not have him a drag on your patience.'

'Are you already guarding my comfort, oh attendant-in-chief?' he teased her, but there was that in his eyes that made her heart ache in pity for him.

'Julien, there must be some other way!' she cried, casting reserve to the winds. 'Cannot she be brought to understand what she is doing?'

'Not by me!' His tone was so harsh as to forbid further discussion, but she went resolutely on.

'Is this in some sort your revenge upon her?'

That shaft went home and he looked at her in dismay. 'Dear God, can I be so far sunk in malice?' he wondered.

'Not malice,' she said swiftly, 'but an instinctive wish to hurt as you have been hurt.'

'And, without thought, hurting you, too.' Humbly he took her hands and kissed them. 'Forgive me, Anthea, but had there not been Charlotte – ' He stopped in rare confusion.

'I might have done very well?' she finished for him, with a

rueful little smile. 'But, Julien, there *is* Charlotte, which makes it difficult for me.'

'Yes, impossibly difficult,' he agreed, looking so contrite that she longed to take him in her arms and comfort him. Thrusting away that impulse, she continued briskly.

'As I said before, to become betrothed is the first step and not totally irrevocable, more particularly if we make it a private engagement until my father's future is assured. That should give us a little time.'

'Time for what? he asked suspiciously.

'To see whether Charlotte cares for the idea of your marrying me,' she replied coolly.

'Why should she care? She appears content with Braybridge.' Miss Branscombe, observing the spark of anger in his eye, tactfully reminded him that the arrival of the tea-tray must be imminent belowstairs. 'And that of Lady Oakley upstairs, no doubt! So let us come to a decision. Having utterly compromised me, ma'am, how do you intend to make reparation?'

'I daresay, my lord, I should make an honest man of you!' she replied demurely.

His face was very grave as he replied, 'I am more than willing for you to make the attempt.' Miss Branscombe realizing that she had gone too far to retreat without offence, resolved to make the best of the situation.

'It will be my pleasure and my duty, my lord,' she said, and was about to elaborate on the conditions attached to such an undertaking when she was interrupted.

'Indeed, it would appear that pleasure and duty are inextricably combined, or perhaps backgammon is played in other ways than I remember!'

Melissa's voice, exuding tart disapproval, startled Miss Branscombe and she made to move away from Julien, but he maintained his clasp of her hands addressing Melissa over her head.

'Be the first to wish us happy, Melissa. Anthea has consented to be my wife.'

'Then, indeed, you have my felicitations.' She did not move

from the doorway, nor did her tone bear out the meaning of her words. 'I am come to tell you that tea has been brought in. Do you wish to join us, Anthea?'

Seeing her hesitation, Julien answered for her. 'Do so, Anthea. I am confident that tea could not be other than beneficial. We will reserve the champagne for to-morrow when, with your consent, we may announce our betrothal more formally.'

It was clear that Melissa's antagonism had stirred his temper and Anthea, after bidding him a rather nervous good-night, followed the second Miss Ralston out of the room. At the head of the stairs Melissa swung round to face her.

'How could you – when you know he loves Charlotte and she him?'

'Melissa,' replied Miss Branscombe with commendable restraint, 'while I make every allowance for your sisterly concern, I beg leave to inform you that here is an affair that has to be played out by the principals. If Charlotte has in mind to become the Countess of Clandon then she must first disengage herself from Viscount Braybridge. Meantime, the Earl is at liberty to seek a wife where and as he pleases.' Having delivered herself of this declaration, she walked confidently downstairs, followed by a deflated and open-mouthed Melissa.

The entire Heatherstone Hall party had been invited to Chalice for dinner on the following evening and had, by then, had sufficient time to compose themselves. Charlotte had accepted the news of Julien's betrothal to Anthea with a sort of fatalistic despair. Melissa, who had carried the tale post-haste to Heatherstone Hall, had been so up in her high trees about it that she was out of all patience with anyone who had a good word to say for Miss Branscombe. It was Charlotte who gently reproached her by pointing out with commendable magnanimity that Anthea had quite as much claim as anyone to become the Countess of Clandon, nor could there be any reason why Julien should not offer for her other than in Melissa's own lively imagination. This little homily, delivered with a sidelong glance to where Lord Braybridge stood drinking a glass of sherry with

Mr Beaumont, put a curb on Melissa's impetuous tongue, though Penelope, as distressed as she by the unexpected turn of events, revealed her sentiments all too clearly by bursting into tears and hastening from the room.

Charlotte, maintaining her air of calm resignation, even contrived to put on a show of good spirits during nuncheon. Her conduct was so much that of a sensible woman surprised, but nonetheless pleased, at her friend's good fortune, that not even Braybridge's keen observation could fault her performance. But when, at last, she could be alone in her bedroom, the story was a very different one. The bravely stemmed tears flowed freely while she was at liberty to point out to herself that it was utterly unreasonable of her ever to have expected that Julien should stay single, Julien who had so much to offer to the lady of his choice, Julien to whom she might now be betrothed had she not been such an unthinking ninny, so eaten up by jealousy as to abuse his trust and betray the friendship that had ever formed such a bond between them.

When calmer reflections prevailed, she came to the opinion that the only course open to her was to release Braybridge from his obligations and resign herself to a life of devotion to her mother as became an eldest unmarried daughter. Her sisters' futures were secured, and if she and her mother had to retrench somewhat and go to live quietly in Bath, what better excuse could there be for removing from the vicinity of Chalice where she could not, in all courtesy, be excused from attending upon the newly-married couple and seeing Anthea enjoy the felicity and consequence she had hoped would be hers.

Once resolved, it only remained for her to put her decision into effect so, composing herself for the forthcoming ordeal, she went in search of Lord Braybridge. She found him alone, reading in the book-room. He rose as she entered, setting down his book, to enquire how he might be of service to her, and his cool formality of manner gave her courage to say what she had to say in as few words as possible. His lordship weighed the great diamond ring thoughtfully in his hand while she stumbled for words to express her regret, her regard for him and the reasons for her casting him off. He let her run on until she faltered into silence, then he spoke, and the scorn in his voice lashed at her like a whip.

'My good girl, all your excuses are expressible in two words – Julien Revel. Is that not true?'

To her dismay, she felt the hot tears pricking at her eyelids and though she answered him in as light a manner as she could contrive she was uneasily aware that her treacherous emotions were likely to betray her. 'I beg, my lord, that you will not put me to the blush by forcing me to confess to a childish tendre for Clandon – '

He cut her short by taking her hand and thrusting the ring back upon her finger. 'Nor do *I* intend to be put to the blush by your throwing me over for whatever reason. Be pleased to be seated, Charlotte. I have that to say to you which may take some time and can only hope that the others of this household are too concerned with their own affairs to trouble us until I have finished.'

His words and the livid aspect of his countenance were of a sufficiently alarming nature to distract even Charlotte's overwrought mind. She had seen him bored, intrigued, intolerant, but never before had she seen him angry, and his anger was of a piece with the rest of him, cold and passionless. She allowed him to hand her to a chair and sat trembling, not a little apprehensive of what further troubles she might not have unleashed upon herself. He took a turn about the room as if ordering his mind for what he had to say, then came to stand in front of her so that she was forced to meet his regard.

'You will have observed, I daresay, that I am a collector of beautiful or unusual trifles. My display of china at Meudon Hall is generally held to be one of the finest in England, while my collection of snuff-boxes is, I am led to believe, only bettered by that of Lord Petersham. When I first had the honour of being presented to you, my dear Charlotte, now close on a year ago, I recognized at once that you had something of that rare quality which I am for ever seeking in less animate objects. To be blunt, while you are not precisely an accepted beauty, you have a delicacy of form and understanding that is not often to be met with in so youthful a lady. I determined then that no other man should have the moulding of your character. Oh, yes, I observed what you are pleased to call your "childish tendre" for Clandon and deplored it. Love, I declare to be the most commonplace of emotions, rarely does it rise above physical desire, and once that is satisfied – ' He shrugged slightly and, folding his arms, leaned his shoulders back against the bookshelves, watching her closely.

'D-did you not then love your wife?'

'I married my wife for her fortune. She was a worthy, good woman but dull, and when she – er, died, I promised myself to be more particular in my next choice. You, my dear, are that choice.'

Charlotte began to doubt her own sanity. In her experience, which was admittedly small, a gentleman when informed by a lady on whom he had pressed his attentions that, under no circumstances could she favour his suit, was expected to accept his dismissal with a good grace. She started to protest uncertainly.

'My lord, I do not understand you – '

'Oh, yes, I think you do. Clandon, for reasons best known to himself, has contracted to marry Miss Branscombe. His motive, I suspect, must be pique, because you have remained resolutely contracted to me in spite of his efforts to attach you. He is a young man, too easily swayed by his passions and too accustomed to having every whim fulfilled, every need gratified, to be able to support such a situation with any show of complaisance.'

To be sure, such accusations or something like them, had been levelled by Charlotte herself at Julien but, womanlike, she quite overlooked that and sprang to the Earl's defence.

'He is a man of honour which, 'pon my soul, my lord, I begin to doubt you are!' she flashed. 'Or do I have to make myself more plain? I do not wish to marry you! What my lord of Clandon does with his life is his concern, I am sure I wish him happy, but it has nothing to say to our affairs!'

In her agitation she had risen and was pacing to and fro while he eyed her in a coolly appraising manner that quite set her teeth on edge.

'Pray do not wear yourself out in futile protest, my poor child!' he mocked her. 'For futile it is. You shall marry me.'

'You sound very confident, my lord,' she retorted.

'I have reason to be, and if you would cease your perambulations and hear me out, I will tell you on what base I rest my confidence.'

Charlotte, who had been strongly tempted to walk out of the room, leaving him to make what he could of the situation was, in spite of her defiant words, deeply impressed by his whole demeanour. It could hardly be spoken of as being threatening or insulting, yet his very choice of phrase held a hint of each and she felt her own assurance ebbing as she confronted this man to whom she had been betrothed for close on four months and of whom, she was now brought to realize, she knew no more than when first they had met. She paused beside a chair, holding on to the back of it to steady herself.

'Very well, my lord. Tell me what you must and have done with it.'

He bowed his head in acknowledgement. 'It concerns your father,' he began, and she stared at him, amazed. 'Most likely you were not aware that I knew him, our acquaintance was not of an intimate nature, we met at our clubs and at gaming houses. Though not to such a degree as my own parent, your father was something of a gamester.' Charlotte said nothing, for though Lady Ralston had never uttered a word of reproach against Sir Greville, Lady Oakley had not felt obliged to be so reticent and had, on more than one occasion, been heard to declare that, had not their father been so spendthrift, his daughters' expectations must have been very much greater. 'One evening he joined a small party at my house in Berkeley Square. We were playing faro and the luck was with the bank, held by a young cub named Cotterell. We were all of us badly dipped and when the evening broke up there was a veritable mountain of vowels in front of Cotterell.'

'You mean – promises from people who could not pay?' she ventured to ask.

'I mean promises from people of their intention to pay,' he corrected her. 'At the end, most of us were punting on tick, in especial your father, who had lost heavily.' Dear God, thought Charlotte, can it be that this man paid my father's debts and now expects that I should pay him? A faint smile touched Braybridge's lips and he went on as if she had spoken aloud. 'No, Charlotte, while to be unable to meet one's debts of honour is social ruin, murder is quite another thing.'

'Murder?' she gasped. 'Explain yourself, my lord!'

'Simply this,' he said. 'Before we had settled at faro, your father had been boasting of a particularly fine pair of duelling pistols that were in his possession. My collector's instinct was aroused and, as he had them in his carriage, he consented to allow me to inspect them. They were outstanding specimens and I was prepared to make him an offer for them when the rest of the party arrived and so they were set aside. At the end there was only your father, young Cotterell, myself and one other gentleman. My servants I had sent to bed long before. Cotterell was in prime and plummy order, excited at his success, thumbing through the vowels and exclaiming on the amount of money your father had lost to him until Sir Greville fell out of all patience with him and told him to hold his tongue, he would get his money. Then Cotterell saw the duelling pistols and said something unforgiveable about blowing out one's brains if nothing else would answer. Your father retorted that he had as lief blow Cotterell's brains out, for which remark I, for one, could not hold him to blame, but the young fool had to take him up on it and question his resolution to do any such thing. Whereupon your father snatched up one of the pistols and shot him through the head.'

Charlotte stared at him, horrorstruck. 'Oh, no!' she protested. 'He could not have – to shoot a man down so! I confess he was hasty, hot-tempered to a fault, but he would never do such a thing! I cannot believe it!'

Braybridge helped himself to snuff and brushed his fingers on his fine, lace-edged handkerchief. 'I daresay you cannot. Your father did protest that he had no notion of the pistol being loaded and that his intention was merely to scare young Cotterell into a semblance of good manners, but – ' He sighed, as one weary of the whole subject, and put away his snuff-box.

'You say you inspected the pistols before you started play. Were they loaded then?' His eyebrows rose in faint surprise.

' 'Pon my word, I do not remember,' he said idly. 'I must suppose they were not. But that is hardly to the point. Sir Greville shot the boy and by so doing saved himself a vast amount of money for, by his death, the whole evening's play was wiped out. Lord – the other gentleman and I agreed to say it had been an accident. Cotterell had been examining the pistol and it had gone off and so the matter stood. Nor would I have thought more of it had I not chanced to meet you, for within a month of this unhappy event your father met his end in the hunting-field – opportune, perhaps?'

The tone of his voice inflamed Charlotte to helpless fury. Not content with branding her father as a murderer, he would add the stigma of suicide to his account. 'Yours is the most despicable character it has ever been my misfortune to encounter!' she choked. He walked over to stand beside her.

'You would not wish your mother to be distressed by this sorry tale, would you, my dear? Nor, indeed, for the world to learn of your father's infamy? The whole wretched business does not rest on my word alone, I would remind you, there was another witness.' Lightly he kissed her fingers, and the very touch of his lips sent a shudder through her whole body. 'Forgive me,' he said softly. 'I had hoped that this would never be necessary, but though I claim to despise the gentler emotions, I have to confess that I have become vastly attached to you, my dear Charlotte, and find the prospect of sharing a marriage bed with you not at all repugnant, nor do I intend to relinquish it to another.' He paused significantly. 'One thing more. Do not play me false with Clandon or I promise you I will divulge the whole of this unsavoury affair.'

When the door had closed behind him Charlotte fell into a chair and sat staring, unseeing, out of the window, her mind twisting and turning like a fox trapped in his earth and with as little chance of winning free.

'Oh, God!' she whispered. 'What shall I do? What *shall* I do?'

To that question there was but one answer. She must wed Richard Braybridge with every appearance of cheerful consent. None must guess at her inner turmoil. An odd sound, half-laugh, half-sob, escaped her. How, indeed, had she been paid in her own coin! The whole fantasy she had woven about Harry Taverner, her being obliged to make a good marriage, her betrothal to Braybridge, sprang less from the desire to restore her family's fortunes than from the hope of making the Earl aware of what was slipping from his grasp. To her the most astonishing facet of the situation was to learn that Braybridge had a partiality for her. She could more readily believe him when he declared love to be a commonplace emotion, for she could not conceive of his ever losing his self-possession so as to succumb to the dictates of passion. But there was little point in refining upon her misfortunes. She had thought to use his lordship for her own ends and had found that she had mistaken her man. Well, she had made her bed and so must lie on it, but the literal implications of that reflection so overcame her new-found resolution that she was forced to retire quickly to the privacy of her bedroom, there to compose her feelings before it should be time for her to make ready to dine at Chalice.

Here, to their surprise, the party found the Earl on his feet, with the assistance of a pair of crutches fashioned by his carpenter, his uncertain steps being guided by Miss Branscombe and Colonel FitzJames.

Lady Ralston expressed her good wishes in a calm and sensible fashion, quite devoid of sentiment, and Julien was grateful to her, but Penelope's reproachful look was hard to meet and when Charlotte stepped up to the newly affianced couple to wish them well he had to force himself to accept her carefully worded congratulations with at least an appearance of gratification. Braybridge, at her elbow, contrived to pass the difficult moment off by a graceful compliment to Anthea and a light quip to the Earl, but there was an expression of sardonic amusement on his face that Julien could not like. The Earl reminded himself that his announced intention of wedding Anthea must assure Braybridge that he had no cause for jealousy, but he suspected that the Viscount was not deceived and warned himself to step warily.

'Our betrothal,' he felt obliged to stress, 'must remain private for the time, since I have not yet asked my lady's father's permission to wed her.'

As no one present could think it at all likely that Mr Branscombe would put forward the slightest opposition to the proposal, his daughter considered she ought to enlarge upon the difficulties that might delay the engagement.

'My father being an elderly gentleman and not in the best of health, arrangements will have to be made for his care,' she explained. 'Perhaps any announcement was a trifle precipitate, but – ' Her eyes met Melissa's and that young woman had the grace to blush. Lady Oakley stepped into the breach.

'Nonsense, why should it be?' she said bracingly. 'If your intention is to marry then the sooner it can be arranged, the better.'

Lady Ralston looked at her as one who had been harbouring a snake in her bosom unaware but then, to be sure, Anthea was Oakley's own niece. It was not to be expected that her sister could be other than overjoyed at the unexpected brilliance of the match.

Charlotte, standing behind them, clenched her hands so tightly upon her fan that one of the delicate ivory sticks snapped between her fingers. The tiny sound carried to Braybridge's ears, and gently he removed the fan from her clasp.

'Unfortunate,' he mused. 'It was a pretty thing. Grant me the pleasure of giving you another in its place.'

'You are too kind, my lord,' she faltered. 'But do not be

troubling yourself, it is n-nothing. I have many such.'

'But none, I believe, from me.'

The low-spoken words were implicit with menace but then, to her relief, Sefton came to announce that dinner awaited them and, in a rustle of silken skirts and softly murmured conversation, they moved into the dining-room.

CHAPTER ELEVEN

THE proposed expedition to Fairleigh House to view the Colonel's 'mouldering ruins' took place two days later. The Earl had become quite proficient on his crutches and Miss Branscombe reluctantly allowed that it might be possible for him to undertake the ten-mile journey, provided he travelled in the chaise with Chivers to attend him. Julien, who very much wished to get away from care and cosseting for a while, had perforce to agree, and the Colonel declared he would go ahead in the curricle to forewarn the staff.

'Though Heaven knows what we shall find,' he said. 'I have written to bid them expect us but cannot say if they could even read my letter.'

Fairleigh House, set in pleasant parkland, presented an orderly and well-kept appearance, and the reception accorded them by the husband and wife who were in charge of the house left nothing to be desired in willingness and civility. What remained of the day was spent in looking over the buildings, which proved a pleasant surprise, for the place was in good shape, despite shabby furnishings, and there was little amiss with it that could not be put to rights by the laying-out of a sum of money and some housewifely skill.

'Leave all that to Sally,' Julien advised as they lingered over a dinner which had earned their approval, both for the number and variety of dishes that had been dressed and for the presentation of them. Mrs Dankers was an accomplished cook and her husband, a powerfully built, silent-moving man, clearly no stranger to serving at a first-rate table. 'A house, after all, is a woman's affair. When shall she be with us, I wonder?'

'Before too long, else my patience will surely be at an end! Which puts me in mind of something I would ask you, Sultan – a favour, no less!'

Julien drained his glass of Burgundy and pushed it towards the Colonel to be refilled. 'Ask your favour, Ned. I am well disposed towards all the world to-day!'

'Towards *all* the world?' The gentle inflection in the Colonel's voice won a sharp response from the Earl.

'It is your affairs we are speaking of, I believe. What is it you wish of me?'

'Your permission for Sally and I to be wed at Chalice, if you would be so obliging. There is no living in my gift here nor do I wish to visit what she calls "Warne Country" until we are firmly shackled. Your Reverend Hattersley is a good sort of man and a bruising rider to hounds – what the devil amuses you, may I ask?'

'The thought that my chaplain's seat on a horse could have any bearing on his religious capability! Gladly do I grant your request, Ned. It is an age since Chalice had a wedding to make merry over.'

'We may be setting a fashion,' the Colonel warned him. 'Apart from yourself, there are three Misses Ralston to be arranged for and it would be a mighty puff to their importance if you made them free of your chapel and house.' Then he wished he had held his tongue for all the laughter had died from Julien's face and when he answered there was no warmth in his voice.

'As to that, they are very welcome if they so wish, though Lady Ralston's cousin holds a living near by. Had you and Sally thought upon a date?'

'That's another thing,' stated the Colonel warmly. 'She leaves me here, hanging in the boughs, while she panders to her wretched brats! Such treatment is not at all to my taste, I can tell you! I am of a mind to beat her for it!'

This palpable piece of nonsense brought the smile back to the Earl's eyes and the Colonel was careful not to touch upon the delicate subject of the Misses Ralstons' nuptials again.

The next morning, the weather giving every promise of

continuing fair, Julien set out with the Colonel in the curricle to inspect the Fairleigh estate, while Chivers and the groom were directed back to Chalice in the household gig with baskets of soft fruits, of which there were a profusion in the gardens, far more, declared Mrs Dankers, than she could possibly put to good use at Fairleigh.

'This is a tight little estate, Ned, and one that, with care and small expenditure, can profit you handsomely. The ornamental grounds, too, are well laid out, though the lake needs draining and clearing of weeds.'

The Earl, absorbed in his favourite subject, quite failed to recollect that his strength was not equal to his enthusiasm, and looked so fine-drawn when they sat down to a late nuncheon that the Colonel would not hear of his going out again that day.

'No, there are many small things I need to look over and can do easily by myself,' he declared. 'Besides the heat is growing oppressive. I'll not have you knock yourself up for Miss Anthea would never forgive me. Lie on your bed until Chivers returns. I'll not be long away.'

At length, Julien agreed to rest in the book-room on a deep sofa, with Fidela, his spaniel, by his side, and there Mrs Dankers came to him with a tisane that she had prepared.

'You are doubtless overtired, my lord. This infusion, I promise you, is most soothing and may help you to sleep awhile.' But as he thanked her with his usual courtesy for her care of him, the Earl was puzzled anew by her air of authority, her cultured voice and appearance of being other than a housekeeper to a small and somewhat run-down estate. He wondered also what was delaying Chivers and the groom for they had set out before ten o'clock that morning and it was already close on two o'clock. Mrs Dankers, talking away easily, re-assured him. 'They will have stayed for some food, no doubt, and maybe will let the greatest heat of the day pass before setting out to return. May I place a cushion thus, my lord, under your foot? Is not that more comfortable?'

Julien protested, laughing. 'Mrs Dankers, I pray you, no more cosseting! I have had a surfeit of it!'

'And why should you not? Your Mr Chivers has explained how you came by your hurts, but I will not put you to the blush by praise of your gallantry. Is my tisane to your liking, my lord?'

In all politeness, Julien had to confess it to be the finest infusion he had ever tasted, and submit to being poured another cup. For a moment it seemed to him that the sunlit room became shadowy and her dark intelligent face bending over him blurred and receded, but the mist cleared almost at once and he put it down to a passing faintness due to over-exertion and the heat, for the day had become excessively humid, giving promise of thunder. He drank of the tisane quickly, its piquant flavour refreshing to his mouth, yet behind it there was another taste that eluded him.

'Is there – have you put brandy in this?' he asked as she took the cup from him.

'No, my lord, no brandy. Are you quite comfortable?'

Her voice sounded distant, as if coming from afar off, his eyelids were as lead, and such a powerful desire for sleep overcame him that he could do no other than submit to it.

When he awoke Fidela had her paws on the edge of the sofa and was politely intimating to him that she had been shut up for rather longer than was agreeable and wished to be released. Somewhere in the silent house a clock struck four and, in response to Fidela's now somewhat urgent pleading, he sat up slowly, rubbing his eyes.

'By Jupiter,' he muttered drowsily, 'that was a powerful infusion she gave me! My head feels as light as a dandelion clock!' Fidela uttered a short bark to recall his attention to her needs. 'Yes, yes, girl, I am coming.'

With the aid of his crutches, he weaved an unsteady course towards the French windows and, after a little fumbling with the latch, contrived to fling them open for the spaniel to rush out gleefully. The sun was still strong but the air was a great deal fresher than it had been earlier in the day and, feeling the need to blow the cobwebs from his brain, the Earl cautiously descended the few steps into a delightful little herb garden, fragrant with perfume and loud with the sound of bees. Here, seated on a moss-covered staddle-stone, he enjoyed the sunshine until accosted by a dripping Fidela, who came to inform him that she had found the lake and wished him to share her discovery.

At first he could discern no way through the thick hedge of sweet-briar and honeysuckle that surrounded the little garden, but Fidela led him to a narrow gap through which, with some difficulty, he managed to edge his way. He glimpsed the lake, heavily overhung with trees, not twenty yards distant and, in an effort to shake off his persistent lassitude, he hobbled towards it in the wake of the excitedly barking dog. The path by the edge of the water was overgrown with weeds and rendered perilous by tree-roots and, despite his careful progression, a crutch caught in one of these so sharply that it was jerked from his grasp and fell to the ground. Slowly and with difficulty he lowered himself to retrieve it, while Fidela, swimming about in the water beside him, uttered encouraging barks. He was endeavouring to draw himself upright again when her barking changed in tone from encouragement to warning. Aware of a rustling in the bushes behind him, he tried to turn but, the next moment, found himself plunged into the water on top of the startled dog.

Instinctively he struck out away from the path and the danger that threatened him, but was unable to avoid a stunning blow below his right ear delivered, he correctly surmised, with one of his crutches. As he slid into insensibility he was dimly conscious of Fidela's furious protest ending in a yelp of pain and somewhere, a voice calling his name.

The next thing he knew, he was lying face downwards on the path, coughing and choking, as he expelled the lake-water from his lungs. Cautiously, he tried to raise his head, and was rewarded by so acute a stab of pain through neck and shoulders that he at once gave up the attempt. Then Chivers' voice spoke close to his ear.

'What in God's Name happened to you, my lord? Were you taken faint? 'Twas a miracle I chanced to hear the dog barking and came in search of her to find you in the water, your chin mercifully supported by one of your crutches. Another moment and you would have slid under and drowned. Your other crutch is snapped clean in two. Did you trip on the path?'

'Yes,' said the Earl, trying to marshal his thoughts into some sort of order and not succeeding any too well. Chivers carefully assisted him to a sitting position and he found that by keeping his head and neck quite rigid he suffered no further discomfort than that of a powerful sensation of nausea. Fidela, apparently little the worse for her experiences, endeavoured to lick his face in an excess of sympathy and he ran a hand over her lightly. 'Good girl! You are not hurt, then? Oh, the devil! My head!'

'Did you strike it, my lord, when you fell?'

The Earl made no reply for, though he now recollected perfectly what had taken place, yet he needed time to consider all the implications of it. Someone had deliberately attempted to drown him, therefore his assailant was no casual vagrant. His hand, stroking Fidela's head, touched on a sore spot for the dog winced and drew away from him. So he had not imagined her yelp of pain. Then he was aware that Chivers was regarding him in some unease, and managed to summon up a rather crooked smile.

'I caught a crutch on a tree-root and, in attempting to pick it up, I fell in on top of Fidela,' he explained tiredly.

Chivers looked politely incredulous but realized that this was hardly the moment to dispute his master's statement. 'Be so good as to stay where you are, my lord, while I fetch aid to have you carried to the house.'

The Earl, conscious of what might still be lurking in the bushes, caught at his sleeve. 'No, give me a few moments then, with you to support me, I shall do very well.'

He did not precisely live up to his boast, but he did achieve the sanctuary of the book-room where he sat in a widely spreading pool of water while Chivers aroused the household.

'It was that tisane that made you so drowsy, my lord,' declared Mrs Dankers, all anxious contrition. 'What with that, and the heat, and your bodily weakness, it was no wonder you fell, for water has the most bewitching effect upon eyes not clearly focused. I blame myself, my lord, and what the Colonel will say, I dread to think!'

The Colonel, returning shortly afterwards, had plenty to say, but a few words aside with Chivers brought him to the Earl's bedside in a very thoughtful frame of mind.

'I understand you to have a mighty bruise coming up behind your ear, Sultan,' he began. 'Difficult to account for since Chivers tells me there were no low-hanging branches in your near vicinity.'

The Earl opened eyes that showed startlingly blue against the pallor of his cheeks. 'Someone broke a crutch over my head when I was in the water,' he said.

The Colonel nodded, as if satisfied. 'I suspected it to be no accident,' he remarked. 'Weak and unsteady though you may be, I cannot see you falling to your death in a few feet of water without outside assistance.'

'I was confoundedly sleepy,' confessed the Earl. 'That tisane was infused with sufficient of some sleep-inducing drug to render me less than usually alert, and the blow on the head could well be put down to my having struck it against a branch – not everyone is as acute of perception as Chivers. I was pushed face down into the water and was in no condition to judge of what had struck me, or so it could be supposed.'

'You say you were pushed?'

The Earl attempted to shrug but found the effort too painful and desisted. 'A touch was all that was necessary for I was precariously ill-balanced on one foot. It could be argued that, in my addled state, I had imagined it.'

'But you did not imagine it, did you?' The Colonel's face was very grim. 'And it happened on my land, when you were my guest. There is also the tisane. If that was drugged then Mrs Dankers must have known of it.'

'Not of necessity. Tisane takes a little time to brew. Anyone might have – added to it while it stood, infusing.'

'There are only besides ourselves in the house, Chivers, your groom Brereton, and the Dankerses. I may add that Dankers has a brother staying with them but he, I can assure you, was with me for all of the afternoon, having offered himself as a guide and then contrived to get us both thoroughly lost! Left to myself, I should have been back here long since.'

'What do you know of the Dankerses?'

The Colonel grimaced. 'They came to me on Braybridge's recommendation when the old couple who had looked after my aunt gave up the post. I spoke quite freely of my predicament and he told me of their having been in his service at one time and now, being desirous of removing to a country situation, having applied to him in hope of being taken on at Meudon Hall – which was not possible, his staff there being sufficient for his needs.' He paused and then continued in a disbelieving way. 'He knew, too, that you were to visit me here, where you would be less closely watched over than at Chalice, but to attempt your life, Sultan! It is beyond reason!'

'My lord must do me the honour of thinking me to be more of a menace to his peace of mind than is the case!' The bitterness in Julien's voice moved the Colonel to protest.

'Sally and I are of the opinion, and we are not alone in this, that Miss Charlotte is by no means indifferent to you.'

'The facts do not bear out your beliefs.' The Earl closed his eyes wearily. 'If such is the case, why does she not rid herself of the fellow?'

'Could there be something,' the Colonel hinted delicately, 'something a shade indiscreet that he has got wind of? If – ' But he got no further for the Earl, despite his hurts and weakness, looked to be on the point of springing out of bed to choke his friend's words down his throat.

'How dare you suggest that she could be guilty of any misdemeanour! That – that – '

Words quite failed him and the Colonel, taking him by the shoulders, gently pressed him back against the pillows.

'Softly, Sir Galahad!' he quizzed him. 'I am suggesting

nothing of the sort, only that Miss Charlotte would be no match for Braybridge's cunning. But that he should proceed to such an extreme against you is beyond anything.'

'He would appear to have a talent for arranging seeming accidents,' mused the Earl.

'You mean his wife? Yes, I had forgotten that. What if another attempt is made upon you?'

'It will need to be a deal more skilful in execution,' the Earl pointed out, 'because I am forewarned. It would be best if that was not generally known,' he added, raising a hand to check the Colonel's protest. 'No, let it rest, Ned. The attempt was unsuccessful. Allow whoever set it in motion to believe that I accept it as an accident, caused by my own muddled condition.'

'As you wish,' said FitzJames. 'But to-night Chivers will sleep in this room with you. I am having no more "accidents" while you are in my care. To-morrow morning Brereton will go to Chalice and acquaint them with the sad tale of your near drowning, then, as soon as you feel stout enough, we – Chivers, Brereton and I – will convey you back to Chalice.'

'Let us not be too hasty in our judgement, Ned. I suppose there could be another explanation.'

The Colonel snorted. 'It would make interesting hearing – did it exist! Now get some rest, Sultan, while I have a word with Chivers.'

That observant retainer had no need to be informed of the necessity for watchfulness. 'You ought to know, sir, that Brereton and I had a mishap on our way to Chalice this morning. Lost a wheel, and fortunate that we had less than two miles to go when it happened.'

'*Not* an accident?' suggested the Colonel.

'Oh, it could be put down to carelessness or neglect, but it delayed our return by several hours. One thing more, sir,' he added as the Colonel was about to leave him, 'when I got back to the house with his lordship I noticed that Dankers, who came to our aid, though wearing dry house-slippers, had dark patches at the ends of his trousers as if they were damp.'

'Hmm!' said the Colonel. 'The sooner his lordship is back at Chalice, the easier I shall be in my mind.'

Chivers owned himself to be in full agreement with this expression of opinion and, secure in each other's understanding of the matter, they parted.

Meanwhile at Chalice Miss Branscombe, who claimed to be suffering from the headache and had excused herself on that score from attending at Heatherstone Hall for dinner, was about to sit down to a lonely meal, thoughtfully set for her in the breakfast parlour by Sefton, when two guests were announced, Lady Warne and Lord Wychfield. While entertaining none but the warmest feelings of delight at their arrival, she felt herself quite unable to reveal the secret of her betrothal until after they had eaten and she and Sally were alone in the drawing-room. That young woman did not seem to be as pleased at her news as she had anticipated.

'I will confess to you that I had a long prose with Adam on the journey down here which has somewhat reversed my opinion. I am persuaded that he is in a fair way to falling in love with you, and if you could possibly return his regard then nothing would please me better, for you are just the one to suit him.' This blunt confession quite overset Miss Branscombe and her eyes filled with tears.

'Oh, dear!' she sighed. 'If only I had known!'

'Then it is not a case between you and Julien, but only designed to tease Charlotte?'

'It is not a case on his part – how could it be? – but he seems to have given up all hope of her and to be bent only on seeking a wife. Love is all very fine, but not in marriage, or so he informs me.'

Sally smiled indulgently. 'Foolish boy! Nothing could betray him more than such a declaration. How did Charlotte receive your news?'

'With great composure,' Miss Branscombe had to admit. 'It was as if she had expected something of the sort and was, after a fashion, resigned to it. But I could not go there to-night for, behind this seeming calmness, I suspect a deep distress. There are moments when her guard slips and her eyes rest upon Julien and it is then, if one looks for it, that the heartbreak shows through. Braybridge, too, watches her as close as a cat would a mouse.'

Lady Warne pulled a face. 'What a coil! But upon reflection, Anthea, could you not be the answer to Julien's difficulties? He knows you to be a reasonable sort of woman, one not likely to lower his consequence in any way.'

'And I love Chalice,' added Miss Branscombe, as if that settled the matter but, collected though she might sound, her fingers were knotting and re-knotting the fringe of her handsome Norwich shawl in a frenzied sort of way.

'Oh, my poor Anthea!' Lady Warne got up and went to sit beside her friend, putting her arm around her. 'How ill have I counselled you! Is it only Chalice you love?'

'If you mean do I love Julien, the answer is no, I do not, not yet,' averred Miss Branscombe stoutly. 'But, as you once did warn me, to be the sole recipient of his attentions, to be aware that all that charm, all that – that – oh, I cannot put a word to it! – could be one's own wedded husband, does arouse emotions that are difficult to control.'

'That I can well believe! But – ssh! Here is Adam. Not a word to him now, we will concoct a tale later. How is this, brother? Cannot Sefton tempt your palate for longer than ten minutes?'

'It is poor sport drinking alone,' Lord Wychfield replied, but the look he directed at Miss Branscombe gave the lie to that excuse for his early descent upon the ladies.

'Well, I am glad you have come for I was trying to recall what you told me last night of that American – what was his name? Paul something who rode somewhere – oh, you know what a poor memory I have for such things.'

'Paul Revere,' he said, seating himself on a low stool beside Anthea. 'His was a ride that must go down in history.'

'In American history for the poor souls have not a deal of it as yet, have they?' The scorn in Lady Warne's voice drew an amused glance from her brother.

'Do not belittle them, Sally. One day they will be a great nation, make no doubt of that.'

'"One day" is a long way away!' she teased him. 'Now continue your tale for Anthea's enlightenment.'

Adam looked up at Anthea and there was that in his expression that gave her further cause to regret her hasty action in attaching herself to Julien. 'It is a tale of the American Revolution,' he explained, 'and relates how an ordinary citizen – he was a silversmith and, I believe, a tooth doctor – made a night ride to warn his countrymen that the English were coming upon them. He rowed across the river to Charleston, oars muffled with a petticoat – '

'Whose petticoat?' asked his irrepressible sister.

'That of a "fair daughter of Liberty"!' Adam frowned reprovingly upon her while Miss Branscombe thought how very attractive was the manner in which his dark hair grew into a peak on his forehead. She was not destined, however, to learn more of the fortunes of Paul Revere for the early return of Lady Oakley, with Philip and Melissa, from Heatherstone Hall, interrupted the narrative.

Their pleasure at meeting Sally and Adam again was so great and so many questions had to be asked that Miss Branscombe's unusual preoccupation escaped observation until Lady Oakley exclaimed archly: 'And I make no doubt that you have been told of our most famous bit of news!'

'Ah, you mean Anthea and Julien?' Sally tried to carry off the situation. 'But we are not to speak of it as yet, are we, except in whispers?'

'Not quite that.' Anthea rallied nobly to her assistance. 'But there is my father to be considered and – and other things,' she ended rather lamely. She dared not look at Lord Wychfield who was staring at her in horrified disbelief but Sally was rattling on in the most addlepated way and, somehow, the difficult moment slid by. Later, when the ladies were retiring to bed, Adam came to hand her her candle and utter some formal phrases of congratulation.

'It is most kind of you, my lord,' said she, feeling a very Jezebel. 'But the thing is not at all – settled.'

'I see,' he said, but it was clear from his pained expression that he did not and she longed to utter something that would not be disloyal to Julien but, understandably, could find no words to do so.

CHAPTER TWELVE

WHEN Colonel FitzJames took Lady Warne to wife only their close friends attended the ceremony. The following day the newly-wed pair left for London, where they were to remain at Warne House for a few days before departing for Leicestershire, so as to view the great celebrations that were to take place at the beginning of August in Hyde Park. A mimic naval battle had been proposed for the Serpentine, with the added attractions of balloon ascents and fireworks, and it was rumoured that Sir William Congreve had contrived a grand transformation scene wherein a Castle of Discord was to be set on fire and obscured by smoke, which would then thin away to reveal a delightful Temple of Concord. This elegant fantasy, the Colonel declared he had to see, since his wife's inconsiderate choice of wedding date had put it quite out of the question for him to attend the fête which had been held at Carlton House in honour of the Duke of Wellington's return to England.

Melissa and Philip had decided to be married in mid-August. At first it had been thought likely that they would make a double occasion of it with Penelope and Robert, but the elder Miss Ralston had refused to contemplate any such suggestion.

'I am not going to be shone down on my wedding day by my younger sister!' she declared roundly. 'And if that is not sufficient objection, there are the guests to consider. I cannot imagine that the Vereker and Beaumont connections will blend at all smoothly and, as there are a considerable number of the latter who must be invited, I feel the magnitude of the assembly may overstrain the resources of Heatherstone Hall.' The Earl, to whom she was addressing herself, at once offered to put Chalice at her disposal, but she insisted that it would not do. 'Can you conceive of Philip's uncle, the Nabob, hob-nobbing with Robert's grandmother, the Duchess? Not that Uncle Edmond is not well-bred, the Verekers are a sound established old family, you understand!' She scowled severely at Julien as if he had dared to question the good standing of the Verekers. 'But he has indulged much in business and is, perhaps, not fully alive to – ah – ' She was lost for words so the Earl supplied them for her.

'To all the niceties of social behaviour that might be expected of one – er, hob-nobbing with a Duchess?' he suggested.

'That's it!' Melissa agreed, much relieved, then, 'Julien, are you quizzing me?'

'Only a very little!' he promised her. 'But, you see, I have met this Duchess, and I can promise you she is a fearsome old witch, with less manners than her serving maids, so that I doubt she would find much amiss with any mode of address employed by Philip's Uncle Edmond!'

'Julien! What a way to describe a noble lady, and Robert's grandmother at that!'

'He has all my sympathy,' confessed the Earl. 'But for the fact that she is so oppressively wealthy and, apparently, resolved to make him her heir, I feel sure he would cut the connection, grandmama or no!'

'How well do you know her, then?'

'Through my uncle for whom, I believe, she had a certain fondness. Her Grace lives very retired now, I understand.'

Melissa grinned. 'Would Her Grace, by any chance, be susceptible to handsome young noblemen of good address?'

'I will do my best!' he promised gravely.

'Coxcomb!' she teased him. 'We are such a trial to you, all we Ralstons, are we not?'

'Such a trial,' he admitted, 'that when you are set up in your own establishments with husbands to order your affairs, my life will be very empty.'

'You will presently be setting up your own establishment here with Anthea,' she reminded him. A curious expression, as if she had touched on something he would have preferred to forget, crossed his face.

'As you say,' he replied evenly. 'Now, since you are resolved that there shall be two weddings – and I must own that I think you wise, though not at all for the same reasons as you have just declared – when do Penny and Robert intend to forge the link?'

'Robert believes late September to be the most convenient for Her Grace, and that, of course, must be the first consideration. What are you reading, Julien?' She picked up the book he had laid down at her approach and inspected it. '*Waverley*? Walter Scott? But I had thought him to be a poet, never a writer of novels.'

'I admit this to be the first of his novels that I have read, and I must confess that I like it very well.'

Melissa was glancing through the pages with interest. 'It does appear to me to be a work that would appeal to a gentleman rather more than the moral tales of Miss Edgeworth or even our dear Miss Austen.' She handed him back his book and stood, looking about her. They had been sitting on the southern terrace at Chalice, which was Italian in construction, complete with balustrades, vases and statuary. From this terrace a flight of steps led down to a lower one which was laid out as an elaborate flower garden and beyond this lay the lawns, broken here and there by groups of evergreen shrubs and deciduous trees to where, on the one side, they were bounded by dense woods of beech, acacia and silver-leafed abele and, on the other, by a merry stream along the banks of which flourished many varieties of aquatic plants. On the farther side of the stream, crossed by a rustic bridge, lay a fair prospect of hills and woods as far as the eye could behold. 'I do love this situation, I believe, more than any other Chalice has to offer, though I am of a mind with Charlotte when she claims that more colour is needed, beds of bright flowers here and there throughout the lawns, to enliven the scene.'

'I had not supposed you to be an ardent gardener, Melissa.'

She chuckled. 'That I am not, I promise you! But mama and Charlotte are for ever discussing flowers and exclaiming over

Loddiges' catalogues so that even I, who can scarce tell the difference between a daisy and a dandelion, am learning to speak knowledgeably of peonies and phlox, and how delphiniums show to best advantage against a background of rhododendrons!'

The Earl cleared his throat and spoke rather hesitantly.

'When do – have Charlotte and Braybridge agreed on their wedding day?'

'Charlotte declares she will see Penny and I settled first, so all depends on the Duchess. And what of you and Anthea? Are you any further forward in your arrangements?'

'These must depend on her father's convenience and she will surely have to return to him before too long to acquaint herself with his wishes.'

If it occurred to Melissa that Anthea was being remarkably dilatory in forwarding her affairs, she said nothing of what was in her mind but went on chatting in her normal, bright way until they were joined by Philip, when the trend of the conversation turned to boxing and like subjects of common interest to the gentlemen.

Despite the unfortunate circumstances of Lady Ralston's cousin having contracted the mumps two days before so that it was deemed wise to remove the entire ceremony to Chalice and the Reverend Hattersley's care, it was freely conceded by all that the first Ralston wedding was an admirably conducted affair. Philip and Melissa had few relations on either side, and Uncle Edmond proved to be a loquacious, but perfectly presentable old gentleman who was greatly to the Earl's liking.

Lord Braybridge, too, was most correct, coming to enquire punctiliously after the Earl's health. Julien, not to be outdone in civility, protested that there was no cause for anyone to be concerned about his physical well-being, though he freely admitted that allowing himself to become bosky on an infusion of tisane might well reflect upon his mental powers. After a further exchange of pleasantries, they parted, the Earl reasonably assured of having convinced his lordship that he regarded the affair as a stupid rather than a sinister accident, but he failed to observe the speculative expression on the Viscount's face as his eyes dwelt for a moment on Charlotte, deep in conversation with her mother, and then slid back to Julien.

'Mind you, my lord,' said the elder Mr Vereker as he stood, taking a glass of wine with the Earl while waiting for the carriages to bear them off to Heatherstone Hall, 'I am not saying that Philip is not a good lad, he is all that, but he is a sailor and no business man.' His bright observant eyes were taking in every detail of the great saloon in which they were standing. 'You, for all that you are an Earl and born to the ermine, are a great deal more shrewd than he. Take this place of yours, I have never seen one in better shape and Philip tells me you attend to it all yourself. There is but one thing lacking that I can see, a wife to share it with you – and do not tell me you have not the power to drop your glove where you will and not have it snatched up before it touches ground! Have I offended you, my lord?'

The Earl turned away to set down his glass. 'No, Mr Vereker, but such things do not always fall out as one might wish.'

Mr Vereker, glancing at him, surprised a look on his face that caused that astute old gentleman to, as he would have phrased it, take a tuck in his lip. Then Julien suggested that they went out to the waiting carriage and Mr Vereker was tempted to wonder if he had not, after all, imagined that fleeting expression of hopeless yearning that was now dispelled by the Earl's usual pleasant smile.

Penelope's wedding was quite another story. The Duchess had decided that London was as far as she was prepared to travel, so the ceremony was held at St James's and, as above two hundred guests were to be expected, Lady Ralston gratefully accepted Julien's offer of the use of Clandon House.

Penelope had insisted that no one but Julien would hand her over to Robert and no one but Charlotte would attend her. A shimmering vision in white Brussels lace over white satin, she floated down the aisle on the Earl's arm. A dainty bonnet of the same lace, trimmed with white ostrich feathers, adorned her shining golden head, and from this depended a fine gauze veil, also lace trimmed. The church was filled with a distinguished throng and the regard of more than one pair of eyes was drawn from the attractive young couple to the tall figure of the Earl on the one side and that of Charlotte, in celestial blue silk, with a ravishing bonnet trimmed to match, framing her copper curls, on the other.

Just once, as Robert slid the ring on to Penelope's finger, did Julien's eyes meet those of Charlotte and timidly she smiled, but drew no response from him other than a slight lift of the eyebrows. Truth to tell, he was vastly preoccupied for, that very morning, he had received a letter from Miss Branscombe who, in response to an urgent message from her father to the effect that he was in need of her counsel, was now re-united with him in Yorkshire.

It was evident from her letter that the old gentleman had conceived it to be his duty to offer marriage to his housekeeper, or she had put it into his head that such was his duty, and Anthea, while admitting that it might be a very good notion, found herself being required to make the decision for him. Such a course would leave her free, but she earnestly trusted that this consideration would not weigh upon her judgement unduly. In any event, she wished the Earl to know that she had no intention of holding him to their rather nebulous engagement.

'"Whether or not papa does marry Mrs Chapman,"' she had written, '"I am increasingly of the opinion that to proceed with our betrothal would not be in the best interest of either. Pray do not press me for further explanation, my lord. You know the deep regard in which I hold you and that I would not willingly do anything to prejudice your future happiness. As there has been no formal announcement of our betrothal and the prime object for its initiation does not appear to have been achieved, I suggest that we allow it to be understood that we have had second thoughts upon the matter, but I shall be entirely guided by your opinion and, believe me, will remain always your devoted friend, etc. etc."'

So he was free again, mused the Earl ruefully. He looked

across at Charlotte, and if she had chanced to catch his eye at that moment she could not have mistaken his feelings. But Charlotte, set down by the lack of response to her smile and all too aware of Braybridge's watchful regard, was devoting her attention to the wedding service, and hoping that the sparkle of tears in her eyes would be put down to the sentiments proper to such a joyful occasion.

The gathering at Clandon House after the ceremony was of such a nature as to fill any mother's heart with understandable pride. The Duchess, to whom Julien had paid assiduous court, declared him to be a very pretty-behaved young man, and his friendly familiarity with her grandson's wife, she regarded with tolerant amusement.

'No doubt you could have had her from under his nose if you'd had a mind to it,' she observed, rapping him over the knuckles archly with the fan she carried to help her support the heat of the day, 'but she's not to your style, I fancy, not as a wife – though, mark my words, Clandon, it is time and enough that you settled upon some fortunate lady. All this,' a gesture of the fan embraced Clandon House, 'needs your Countess, and you,' she looked him up and down in so frankly appraising a manner that he felt like a horse having its points displayed in Tattersall's Yard, 'you need a woman for your bodily comfort. Oh, I make no doubt that you have mounted many a mistress in your time, but a wife is the thing for you now, less demanding and a deal less expensive.' Her Grace retained the forthright speech of her younger days and believed in calling a spade a spade. Julien, rather entertained by her bluntness, said he was keeping marriage very much to the forefront of his mind. 'Hmm!' she commented, 'can't say I have ever heard of your name being linked with any girl in that way. You should come up to town more often and view the fillies on parade, though I'd not counsel you to marry a chit out of the schoolroom, you would find yourself bored in a month.'

At that point, to Julien's relief, Robert came up to speak to his grandmama, and he was able to make his excuses and leave her to join Colonel FitzJames.

'God, Sultan, are you not worn down by these never-ending nuptials?' enquired the Colonel, touching a handkerchief delicately to his overheated brow. 'I hear you have been sporting your buff at Jackson's. How is the foot holding up?'

'It is not as sure as I would like,' admitted the Earl. 'A sharp turn can undo me when least expected.'

'So I can insult you without fear of being called to account? All right, I know the foot is not employed when discharging a pistol, so I shall still take care! By-the-by, it may interest you to know that the Dankerses have left my employ, saying they found Fairleigh too secluded for their taste, and are gone to a situation in London. Since their prime reason given for coming to Fairleigh was its remoteness from the bustle of town life, I find this *volte-face* a shade incomprehensible.'

'They have served their turn,' said the Earl quietly. 'Any further "accidents" might bring them into suspicion.'

'Yes,' agreed the Colonel, then raising his voice a trifle, he went on, 'what of your new cabriolet? Is it come?'

'Yesterday, which puts me in mind of what I would ask you. I have no animal suitable for such a carriage, but I learn that Mountfitchet is selling up and there should be some sound cattle to be had.'

'Tatts have the sale of them, I suppose?'

The Earl shook his head. 'If you remember, Mountfitchet near came to cuffs with Richard Tattersall over a certain light-fleshed, spindly filly which my lord had hoped to pass off as a prime 'un. No, Aldridge's have the auction. Do you care to join me there to-morrow?'

'Just so long as I may be away before three o'clock, for Sally is insistent that we return to Fairleigh without loss of time to greet some aged female relative of hers who is coming to make a stay with us. Depend upon it, Sultan, when you marry a wife you take not one woman but a host! Devil take it! Is not that "King" Allen speaking with Braybridge? I vow I've not laid eyes on him since Talavera.'

Julien, who had not met Lord Braybridge since the first

Ralston wedding and had little wish for such an encounter, was nonetheless eager for a word with Viscount Allen, an old friend of the Peninsular campaign. Standing with him was a tall, fair young man whose face was vaguely familiar to the Earl, but it was not until Braybridge made a slight gesture, murmuring: 'You, I am persuaded, are acquainted with Captain Sir Francis Bellingham,' that the memory slipped into place.

'I can scarce suppose that you'll remember me, my lord,' began Sir Francis, but Julien held out his hand, smiling.

'A hot-headed cornet, if I recall aright!'

'To whom you gave at least one good set-down!'

Bellingham had all the assurance that good looks and noble birth could bestow on a high-spirited young man of twenty-five years of age. His career in the Peninsula had been somewhat meteoric before he had been snatched away to join Wellington's staff and, urged on by Allen and FitzJames, he displayed the utmost willingness to recount some lively tales of that exalted existence. Then Sally was with them, upbraiding her husband for desertion and greeting Julien with all her customary warm affection.

'I see you are walking without a stick, yet perhaps not as sprightly as I could have hoped for. Lady Ralston informs me that Anthea has been summoned to her father's side. Does this mean your wedding will be delayed?'

For answer, he guided her away from the press of people and drew Miss Branscombe's letter from his pocket.

'Our wedding is not to be, Sally,' he said. 'I am assured that Anthea would be happy for you to read this and make the melancholy story generally known amongst our friends.'

Her eyes questioned him, but she read nothing in his impassive countenance so bent her attention on the closely written page. 'So, Julien,' she said slowly when she had made an end, 'you are unleashed once more upon womankind!'

'A prey to every female vulture!' he corrected her, but with a twist to his smile that quite wrung her heart. She was about to go into further detail about the advantages that might accrue from his freedom when, reflected in the pier-glass behind him, she saw Braybridge, standing not a yard from them, with head downbent in the attitude of one listening intently to everything that was being said. As if warned by her silence that his presence had been observed, he strolled away slowly, pausing by Bellingham's elbow in passing as if to check that young gentleman's flow of reminiscence.

'That is an unlikely friendship, to be sure,' she remarked, handing the Earl back his letter.

'What is?' Julien had drifted into an abstraction and had no notion of what was going on around him.

'Braybridge and Bellingham. Sir Francis is a guest of my lord's in Berkeley Square, which would seem to provide the sole reason for his attendance here to-day. Where lies the connection between so ill-assorted a couple?'

'The gaming-table, I have no doubt. Bellingham is known to play deep, while Braybridge – '

'Has ever had a reputation of being on hand when young gentlemen are wantonly hazarding their fortunes upon a cast!'

'Bellingham is no Johnny Raw, he can look to himself.'

'I daresay he can, but there are others who cannot!' she rapped out. 'What of Charlotte, Julien? It is as plain as the nose on your face that she is in the lowest possible spirits. Her association with that – that man has so wrought upon her that she is all to pieces.'

The Earl, who had not failed to take note of his loved one's pallor and the deep shadows under her eyes, replied as levelly as was in his power. 'Her mother informs me that she is to marry "that man" a week from to-day.'

This intelligence so alarmed Sally that she roundly abused the Earl for permitting such an absurdity to be even spoken of, but he silenced her with the curt reminder that Charlotte was of an age to conduct her own affairs and the remedy, if such was needed, lay in her own hands. But even as he uttered the words he knew he could not wholly believe them. Charlotte's obvious mental distress was apparent to all who knew her well but how could one offer to assist a lady who would not accept that she was in need of assistance? Sally, knowing nothing of what was going on in the Earl's mind, thought dark thoughts about the astonishing stupidity of otherwise blameless gentlemen where female sensibilities were concerned and resolved to lose no time in seeking out Miss Ralston and informing her of Anthea's defection.

On the farther side of the saloon Charlotte was striving to sustain a conversation with Mrs Drummond Burrell, but her eyes and attention were so centred on snatching a glimpse of Julien as he moved about, greeting his friends, that her top-lofty companion had occasion to remark later to Lady Hertford: 'I am sure I don't know what anyone can see in Miss Ralston that is above the ordinary. She is scarce able to piece two words together. I had thought her wit to be of a very different order.'

'Charlotte?' said her ladyship in surprise. 'Clementina, I must inform you that you are far and wide there! She is a most intelligent young woman – indeed, at one time, I had the greatest hope of her attaching Clandon.'

'Clandon? Pooh! He is far above her touch. She has done very well for herself, let me tell you, in securing Braybridge.'

Lady Hertford, who missed little of what went on around her, contented herself by saying: 'I wonder if you are right?' which mild comment only served to convince her friend of the truth of her opinion.

Sally's admirable intention of securing Charlotte to herself was denied fulfilment for, after the reception, Braybridge swept his betrothed and Lady Ralston off to dine with him and Sir Francis and thereafter to visit the theatre. Consoling herself by the reflection that another day could scarcely affect the issue, Lady FitzJames promised herself a call upon Miss Ralston on the following morning.

The Earl, finding himself alone in his great house with only the disorder of the day's festivities to remind him of the noisy, brilliant throng that had so lately surrounded him, desired Sefton to serve him a tray of refreshments in the book-room, where he ensconsed himself in a deep chair, by a fire that the sudden chill of the September evening made very welcome, with Fidela by his feet and *The Corsair* to exercise his mind. But not even Lord Byron could exert sufficient fascination over him to the exclusion of all else, and he laid the book upon his knee, gazing into the flames and gently drawing Fidela's long ears through his fingers, which attention reduced her to a state of drooling delight.

'What can I do in such a situation?' he pondered half-aloud. 'No one could hold her to blame for changing her mind, so it is to be presumed that she is content with things as they are. But with two daughters comfortably established, can Aunt Emmelina be so behindhand with the world that Charlotte must needs yield herself to the highest bidder?' Fidela stirred her tail and nudged him to continue with pulling her ears. 'Not the highest bidder, either.' The Earl was mentally comparing his financial resources to those of Braybridge to his considerable advantage. 'Was I, perhaps, too intolerant, would you say? But I could not accept her on the score of misplaced gratitude. Then on what terms could I accept her?' Fidela, not fully understanding the problem but willing to offer all the assistance possible, gently licked her master's hand. 'Only if she could bring herself to love me and that, it would appear, she cannot do. No, nor trust me either! Oh, Charby, my dear, dear girl!'

This last *cri de cœur* was too much for Fidela. She struggled to her feet to place her forepaws on the Earl's satin-clad knee and utter a muffled yelp of sympathy.

'Indeed, you have the right of it, my old friend,' said the Earl, taking her muzzle in his hand and shaking it kindly. 'How, indeed, have the tables been turned if it is I who now require love to be a necessary ingredient for marriage!'

Sighing, he poured himself a comforting glass of brandy while Fidela, assured of his inattention, positioned herself as close to the fire as she dared and lay, head on paws, with eyes fixed watchfully upon her beloved master.

CHAPTER THIRTEEN

THE Earl, having dissipated an amount of understandable irritation by an hour's hard riding, joined Lady Ralston who, for convenience was in residence at Clandon House, in his breakfast parlour the following morning to find her in a somewhat troubled frame of mind.

'I must tell you that, as we were about to leave the theatre last evening, a message was delivered to my Lord Braybridge informing him that his mother, the Dowager, was taken ill at Meudon Hall, and requesting his attendance there,' she explained. 'This put us all about as you may imagine, though my lord made no great matter of having to drive off into the country at such an hour. His chief concern was for Charlotte whom he had engaged to escort to Mitcham this morning in order to view the physic gardens, but Sir Francis quickly set his mind at rest by vowing it would be the greatest pleasure to him to accompany her there.'

'Most obliging of him,' commented the Earl dryly, helping himself from a dish of braised sweetbreads. 'And did Braybridge give his consent to the expedition?'

'Willingly, which perplexes me not a little, I can tell you, for of late he has given every appearance of resentment should Charlotte so much as suffer her hand to be kissed by another gentleman, and Bellingham has made no secret of his admiration for her.'

'How long has he known her?' The glint in the Earl's eye belied his mild manner.

'Not above a week or two, I believe, just so long as he has been staying with Braybridge and she at South Audley Street, giving what assistance she could to Penny.'

'Captain Sir Francis Bellingham is a very eligible parti. He is also a notorious flirt,' remarked the Earl thoughtfully.

'You cannot be thinking that he is attempting to fix his interest with her? And she to be wed next week! Come, Julien, confess that to be an unlikely story!' She waved an admonishing finger at him. 'No, the truth of it is that Charlotte has ever had a great wish to visit these gardens and she would have been sadly disappointed if the expedition had to be put off for there is small chance of coming at it again until the spring.' Seeing his preoccupation, she went on quickly. 'The gardens are quite out of the ordinary, you know. She tells me that as much as two hundred and fifty acres are occupied there by the gardeners in cultivating lavender, wormwood, camomile and I do not recall how many other medicinal plants, but principally peppermint, of which there are a hundred acres. I have commissioned her to visit Mr James Moore's establishment and purchase me some oil of lavender.'

'And does Bellingham share this interest in medicinal plants?' asked he with biting sarcasm.

'Julien, you are not in doubt as to his – well, his conduct?'

'Even if I was, I would place every reliance in Charlotte's good sense,' he assured her.

She glanced at the near-by bracket clock which obliged her by striking the hour. 'Ten o'clock. Should I forbid her to go? But why, when Braybridge has agreed to it? And she was so looking forward to the visit – you know how deep her interest is in herbs and simples – I would not take so slight a pleasure from her, she for whom the future holds so little.'

'What can you mean, Aunt Emmelina?' Gone was the Earl's air of indifference. 'Is she not to be the Viscountess Braybridge, mistress of Meudon Hall, with a house in Berkeley Square, and God knows what besides?'

'And, I suspect, cares nothing for any of it. Oh, I have attempted to reason with her, but always she turns aside my questions and speaks of something else. She conducts herself as if living in a sort of dream – a nightmare rather, and I dread her awakening to find herself wed to a man whom, I am perfectly sure, she cannot like.'

'Perhaps Bellingham's attentions may bring her to her senses.' The Earl did not sound as if he enjoyed any such expectation. 'What feelings does she entertain for him, do you know?'

'She thinks him a pleasant enough young man but – Julien, I cannot be comfortable about her!' He leaned over to cover her nervously clasped hands with his own.

'You must not be fretting yourself to shreds, dearest aunt,' he comforted her. 'I am assured it would be more than even Bellingham's undoubted talents could encompass to commit any impropriety in the physic garden!' That was not precisely what Lady Ralston had in mind, but she allowed herself to be teased out of her forebodings and continued to eat her breakfast with at least an appearance of calm.

'What shall you be doing to-day, Julien?'

'Going to Aldridge's with Ned to choose a likely animal for my cabriolet. I may be away for much of the day, can you occupy yourself?'

'Indeed there will scarce be enough hours in the twenty-four to do all there is to be done. Julien, there is no reason now for me to abuse your hospitality further, for Philip and Melissa are engaged to visit his brother for a few days, so Oakley is driving them there this morning, their destination being not above eight miles from Oakley Hall, and my brother-in-law feels the need to breathe some country air! So my poor sister is left quite alone, save of course for Charlotte – and, by-the-by, she would like us both for dinner this evening if that suits your convenience.'

How well it would suit his convenience, thought the Earl ruefully, to be again with Charlotte had the circumstances been different, but he hastened to assure Lady Ralston that there was no need for her to remove herself from Clandon House.

'Come, confess, you have been tolerably comfortable here, Aunt Emmelina!' he quizzed her.

'More than comfortable as well you know, which I could not have hoped for in so overladen a household as was to be found in South Audley Street this last week.' She hesitated. 'There is one thing more I would ask of you. I do not know if it is your intention to remain in London for our next wedding, but as my brother-in-law Warner is in poor health and Oakley refuses to attend another wedding, could you, of your kindness, do the same service for Charlotte as you did for Penny?'

'You mean give her away? To Braybridge? My God, Aunt Emmelina, you ask rather too much!'

'Do I, Julien?' she said innocently. 'Would it be so difficult an undertaking?'

'It would be perfectly damnable!' he said, rising. 'I hope to be back here no later than five o'clock.' With that he left her, but Lady Ralston did not appear to be in the least put out by his hasty departure. Sefton, coming in to enquire if there was anything she needed, surprised her ladyship smiling, as if well-pleased by some turn of events.

The Earl was still in an agitated frame of mind when he returned to Clandon House, having first put his new purchase through his paces. Brutus was a sound, if not lively, animal, admittedly no high-flyer, but with a good easy action and, so Julien was informed by his previous owner, possessed of exceptional powers of endurance. The Colonel had been against the purchase, favouring a showy chestnut, but Julien would have none of it, remarking that, as he was unaccustomed to driving one-horse carriages, he had better have a horse that knew how to conduct himself. He found Lady Ralston in the small drawing-room, with Sefton setting the teapoy by her side so that she could infuse as many dishes of her own sort as she chose. She eyed him closely as he sat down with a sigh of relief.

'You have been standing too long on that foot,' she chided him. 'After yesterday's exertions, it is not to be wondered at that it gives you pain. I must confess I shall be very happy to see my bed to-night.'

'At what time are we bid to Lady Oakley's?'

'At any time past seven o'clock, and quite informal, just we four.' The Earl set down his cup.

'Her ladyship will scarce welcome me, smelling of horses and leather. I am in no case to be drinking tea with you, let alone dine in Audley Street.'

'Fastidious creature! It must be the French half of you, I do declare!' She smiled at him indulgently. 'Off with you to bath and make yourself elegant – I promise you I can be ready in half the time!'

The Earl had just finished dressing when Sefton appeared at the door of his room to request that he attend Lady Ralston as soon as was possible as she had received a disturbing missive from Audley Street.

She came forward as he entered the drawing-room, holding out a letter for him to read. One look at her face precluded him from asking any questions. The note, which came from Lady Oakley, was admirable for its brevity.

'Charlotte and Bellingham have not returned. Is she with you? If not, what shall we do?'

'What, indeed?' reflected the Earl. 'For it is now near dark and raining heavily. What was he driving, do you know?'

'He spoke of a yellow phaeton, drawn by a pair of chestnuts, I believe.'

'Hmm. Not an ideal carriage for this weather. They may well have checked somewhere, hoping the rain would cease.'

'Julien, it is close on seven o'clock! Charlotte had every expectation of being home by four.'

'Then, depend upon it, some trifling accident has served to delay them.' Julien, wishful of allaying her anxiety, was treating the matter lightly, but she would not be turned from her purpose.

'If there has been an accident the groom could have been sent back with a message. No, Julien, I must hold myself responsible to Lord Braybridge for Charlotte's conduct, and who can I turn to, save you? Had Philip been here or Oakley – ' The appeal in her eyes was more than he could withstand.

'If it will please you, I will go in search of them. There will not be many on the road on such a night, so they will not be hard to find. Do you, if you please, go now to South Audley Street and support Lady Oakley. I will order the chaise to be made ready.'

'But you, Julien, you cannot take your curricle in such weather?'

'No, I will take my new toy!' He smiled reassuringly at her as he tugged the bell-pull for Sefton. 'It has a hood that can be raised and Brutus seems a sturdy sort of animal who will think nothing of a wetting. Do not be troubling yourself, dearest aunt. Mitcham is not in far Cathay. I have small doubt I shall discover them before too long.'

'I trust so,' she said quietly. 'At least in time to lend an air of propriety to the escapade.'

The Earl wasted no time in setting out on his quest. The rain gave no indication of easing, if anything it intensified in vigour, and a stiffish south-westerly breeze had arisen which added little to his comfort. At Kennington he hesitated between taking the Brighton Road through Brixton and Streatham or bearing right to proceed through Clapham and Tooting. The obvious advantages of the fast well-surfaced Brighton Road might well be minimized, he considered, by having to bear across country from Streatham to Mitcham, so he decided in favour of the Tooting highway, and could only hope that the heavy rain would not have reduced it to mud, for the land about Tooting was principally arable and much used for growing potatoes.

At Tooting it was blowing half a gale, and the Earl was beginning to entertain grave doubts of his ever coming up with the errant pair. He learned that the rain had commenced to fall there before three o'clock in the afternoon, and as it was coming from a southerly direction, it could well have reached Mitcham even earlier.

'Please God it did!' he prayed silently, as he urged the reluctant Brutus forward, 'and I will discover them snugly ensconced in the White Hart or the King's Head, for if he has attempted to drive home in this it could be the death of her.'

Mine host of the White Hart at Mitcham plainly considered

the dripping wet young gentleman who alighted from the mud-splashed cabriolet to be quite out of his mind.

'Indeed, yes, sir, the lady and gentleman left here just past two o'clock as the weather looked like turning shuckish.' Julien, a true countryman, rightly translated this as meaning 'showery', but refrained from commenting upon so profound an under-statement. 'He had the notion, I collect, of crossing the Common and joining the Brighton Road and so on to Streatham.'

The Earl groaned inwardly. It would seem that, by taking the other road, he had missed them and they were, no doubt, now safely back in London, for Bellingham would have had little difficulty in exchanging his open phaeton for a covered chaise at any of the posting-houses on the Brighton Road. The landlord's next words re-aroused his anxiety. 'I was in full expectation of their returning here, sir, for the heavens fairly opened within a short time of their leaving. They would not have had time to cross the Common before the deluge descended. That road is none too good in fair weather and becomes middling foundrous on such a night as this.'

'Could they have pushed on to Streatham, do you suppose?'

' 'Twould be their most likely course, I would say, sir.' As Julien stood, considering what best to do, the landlord offered to dry his sodden driving coat. 'I have just prepared a bowl of "bishop" for any distressed travellers. Could I prevail upon you to take a glass, sir?'

As the Earl gratefully sipped the steaming port, flavoured with roasted lemons, the ostler came in to enquire if he should unharness Brutus. 'You'll not be venturing further on such a night, sir?'

'I think I must go on to Streatham.' Julien had come to the conclusion that if Charlotte and Bellingham had broken their journey anywhere, it must be there, or at least he could get news of them at the Greyhound or one of the other inns in the town should they have changed carriages. Then the ostler made a remark which, for the first time, caused him to wonder if other than bad weather and unlucky circumstances had prevented

Bellingham from returning Charlotte to her anxious family before nightfall.

'Even did they meet with mishap over the Common, sir, and that's likely enough with the pot-holes and looses, the gentleman's groom who rode on ahead of them did say to me as how he was a-visiting his wife who was biding in a cottage some three miles from there. 'Tis likely the lady and gentleman would take refuge there, hoping the storm would ease.'

'Where is this cottage?'

'As well as I could make out, sir, 'tis on a track off to the south on the way to Gilpin's Farm.'

'Three miles, you say? But could they not return – ?' He stopped, remembering that the reason for his having come on this quest unattended was to avoid giving rise to any possible gossip, such as even the best of servants delighted in, but the old ostler merely said:

'If there had been an accident to the phaeton, sir, you could not expect the lady to ride back here, not in this storm. Depend upon't, if they be not at the cottage, they will have pressed on to Streatham.' Julien set down his glass.

'I must find this cottage, for if the groom's wife is there surely she will know of their movements.'

'You cannot go to-night, sir,' protested the landlord. 'You'll never discover the place in the dark.'

Julien looked at the ostler. 'Could you find it?'

'Nay, sir, I know it not. But if you are bent on a-going in search of it to-night, I beg that you leave your horse here and take our old Meg. She is no elegant tit, but she was bred on the Common, and if you get lost she will carry you back here. Should you go on to Streatham, leave her at the Greyhound, sir, for I'll be thataway come Monday and can drop your bit of blood in her place.'

The Earl thanked him and, his pocket the heavier by a guinea, the ostler went out to put Meg to, reflecting that the ways of the gentry were powerful strange. 'A tall, dark, devilish handsome figure of a man he will be,' had said the first gentleman. 'See that he knows where I may be found and how to follow me, but do not be telling him overmuch nor give him the notion that I am laying a trail. There's a guinea for you now, and I make no doubt that if you play your cards well, you will get the same from him.'

And so he had and was well content with his night's work, though he could not help but feel a sympathy with this second gentleman who was plainly concerned about the lady – and rightly so, the ostler judged, for a sweeter-faced young lass he had seldom set eyes on. Not at all the sort to be holed up in a cottage all night with a gentleman who was not her husband. Then he wondered if the second gentleman, maybe, *was* her husband but, if so, why should the first gentleman wish him to know where they were hid? The ostler shook his head and started in to work on the unhappy Brutus, reflecting that maybe he would never learn the answer to this interesting problem as to so many others.

The Earl's passage across the Common was not improved by the advent of a violent thunderstorm. Thanking his good fortune that Meg appeared to be impervious to the elements and that the almost continuous flashes of lightning illumed the track ahead, his anxiety was now only equalled by his degree of saturation. He prayed that Charlotte was safe and dry, no matter where, out of this inferno, for he well remembered her horror of lightning. Of course, she could be safe back at South Audley Street, in which case he hoped she would spare a thought for her would-be rescuer, getting wetter and more ill-tempered by the second.

Just then, a particularly vicious flash showed him the track, if track it could be termed, bearing off to the south and Meg, obedient to his touch on the rein, ploughed steadily down it for more than a mile. The storm had intensified in fury and the Earl was beginning to wonder what he should do if he found no one at the cottage, for it was clearly impossible for him to continue his nightmare journey for much longer, when a gleam of light showed on his left and the next flash outlined sharply a small building set back from the path, with candles alight in several windows. Turning Meg smartly in between the gateless entrance posts, he drove to the side of the cottage where there was a rough, lean-to stable. There his doubts were set at rest for, occupying more than half the stable space, were a couple of nervous chestnuts, a nondescript grey and a yellow phaeton. Quickly freeing Meg from the pole and securing her by the head-stall, he splashed around in the searing rain to knock imperatively on the front door. A woman's voice answered him and asked his business.

'I am the Earl of Clandon and I wish to speak with Sir Francis Bellingham. Is he within?'

There was a muttered colloquy, then the sound of bolts being drawn and the door was flung open to reveal Bellingham in shirt and buckskins, holding out a welcoming hand.

'Come in, come in, my lord. Good God, was there ever such villainous weather? Harper, take my lord's coat and dry it off.'

Another man, whom Julien presumed to be the groom, stepped forward to assist him while Bellingham forced the door shut again in the face of the gale. The small room in which they stood was quite unfurnished save for two chairs, but a bright fire blazed in the hearth. Mrs Harper, a respectable-looking, middle-aged woman, bobbed to the Earl and asked if there was anything she could offer him.

'If that bowl of punch is ready, I'll warrant his lordship would be glad to try it. Come to the fire, Clandon – the devil, but you are wet through! What possessed you to venture out in such dress in this storm?'

'It was not a storm when I left London,' replied the Earl shortly. He was finding it difficult to account for his friendly reception. Indeed, Sir Francis appeared to welcome his arrival, the contrary to what might have been expected from a would-be ravisher. Doubtless the whole thing had been an unfortunate mishap, but one which could reflect seriously upon Charlotte if not handled with delicacy. 'May I ask why you essayed the crossing of the Common in such weather?'

He kept his tone light but his eyes watchful, for there was no doubt that Sir Francis was not as completely at his ease as might be expected of a gentleman whose conduct had been above reproach.

'Well, again, it was not raining when we left Mitcham. I had allowed Harper come on here to spend a few hours with his wife while Miss Ralston and I inspected the physic gardens and she made some purchases. Then we had a nuncheon and set out. It only came on to rain as we turned down here to collect Harper. Believing it to be no more than a heavy shower, we remained until it should be over but, as you are very well aware, it has turned into a truly shocking storm. I was just about to set out with Harper for Mitcham, leaving the two women here for, I do not have to tell you, it is a ticklish situation.'

'Where is Miss Ralston?'

'Er – she has locked herself in the bedroom, having conceived some notion that this whole unfortunate affair was prearranged and nothing I can say will convince her that it was not! I ask you, my lord, would one take one's groom and his wife on such an expedition?'

Mrs Harper appearing with the punch-bowl, which she set down on the hearth, the Earl was unable to reply to this interesting question. 'I beg you will excuse our lack of furniture, my lord,' she said primly, 'but we do not use this place except in full summer, it being difficult of access during bad weather, and so have not troubled to leave more in it than is necessary for our wants.'

Her husband, following her in, ladled out generous measures of the steaming punch. The Earl, studying them covertly, came to the conclusion that a more respectable couple could not be found, and Bellingham's explanation must be accepted as perfectly reasonable, while his declaration that he was about to set out for Mitcham, if true, would be what any man of honour must hold to be his duty in such circumstances. But why had Charlotte locked herself in the bedroom? She was no missish girl, on the contrary as game as a cock, and most unlikely to lose her head. He swallowed his punch, wondering how it would fare atop of the landlord's 'bishop', and when Harper had refilled the glasses and withdrawn to the kitchen, he said quietly to Bellingham: 'Might I attempt a word with Miss Ralston? You must understand that her mother and aunt were greatly alarmed when you did not return before dark and I am here as their emissary.'

'I quite understand and I am much obliged to you, my lord, for who is to confirm my story save my own groom and his wife, and perhaps the landlord and ostler at the White Hart, all of whom could be persuaded, or so it might be held, by the exchange of a few guineas, to say what I chose. With your word to support me, no one can question the truth of it.' The Earl had, perforce, to agree to the sense of this argument and Bellingham indicated a door in the corner of the room. 'Miss Ralston is in there and, doubtless owing to the vigour of the storm and the thickness of the door, has not even heard your arrival or, if she has, is not aware of who it may be.'

The Earl nodded and went to rap sharply on the door. 'Charlotte,' he called. 'It is I, Julien. Please open the door.' Response came there none and a particularly vivid flash of lightning brought a slight smile to his lips. 'I could wager on it,' he said to Bellingham, 'she is huddled under the covers, for she has an abhorrence of thunderstorms.'

He was about to abandon his efforts and return to the fire when the key grated in the lock and the door was opened a few cautious inches to reveal a wan and wild-eyed Charlotte. Her expression when she saw him was one of such utter relief that he almost laughed, but when she flung the door wide and caught at his hand to draw him in, his amusement faded.

'Julien, Julien, I am so frightened!' she gasped.

'Yes, Charby, I know, it is an odious thunderstorm, but you cannot blame Sir Francis for that!'

'Maybe not!' she retorted, with a glare at her discomfited escort. 'But – Julien, please come in. I must talk to you.' The Earl looked eloquently at Bellingham, who shrugged in apparent resignation, and turned away. No sooner was the Earl inside the room than she shut the door firmly behind him and burst forth.

'Julien, I don't care what tale he pitches you, this was no accident! Look about you, is this the dwelling of a groom and his wife? And the dinner set out there,' she indicated a table by the fireplace. 'When I saw that being prepared, I knew we had been expected.'

It was certainly a set-out that gave no indication of two unexpected travellers having to take their pot-luck. There was a casserole of game, chicken, tongue and ham, an apple-pie and a tansy pudding, while a bowl of mulligatawny soup kept hot in front of the fire, along with a couple of bottles of burgundy. The table appointments were of crystal and silver and the whole room, while not large, gave an impression of extreme luxury. The wide bed had a white fur coverlet thrown over it, two deeply cushioned armed chairs were on either side of the fire, and two smaller chairs set to the table. Another door, leading to a small closet, stood open, revealing a washing stand with ewer and basin of fine porcelain – remarkably like Sèvres to the Earl's expert eye. The floor was covered with several thick rugs and the curtains at the two small windows were of heavy damask. No, the Earl had to admit, not precisely the style of room one might expect in a dwelling of this sort, but there was no object in alarming Charlotte further by adding his doubts to hers.

'Now, tell me what happened,' he said in his most calming manner, leading her over to the fire.

'Well,' she began, endeavouring to emulate his self-possession, though at every rumble of thunder a fresh shudder shook her slight frame. 'At first everything was just as it should be. We viewed the physic gardens while the groom rode on here to visit his wife. Then we had a nuncheon and Sir Francis said we would go across the Common to join the Brighton Road. The sky was becoming overcast and he assured me that if it came on to rain, that was the best place to be, for he had no doubt we could hire a covered carriage at one of the posting inns.' Julien nodded. So far he could not fault Bellingham's reasoning and was inclined to allow him the benefit of any doubt that might exist as to his motives. 'Then we got here just as it started to rain heavily so, of course, I was willing to stay for a time until the weather should clear. I did not trouble my head overmuch at first. We played backgammon and spillikins and all manner of foolish games and Sir Francis can be most entertaining when he puts his mind to it. Then it became dark and the rain never ceased so he said that he and Harper would have to return to Mitcham and find some sort of covered vehicle to get Mrs Harper and I back to the inn. Harper went out to put the horses to and returned to say the animals must have been terrified by the high wind and noise of the rain, for it appeared they had thrashed about in the stable and cracked the pole of the phaeton. There was no using it and anyone who wished to go to Mitcham would have to ride there.' She paused for breath and gave a long sobbing sigh. The storm had moved away but could still be heard growling in the distance. A log fell from the fire and Julien kicked it back before its glowing sparks could scatter over the rugs.

'And then?' he prompted gently.

'Then Mrs Harper suggested that she prepare us a meal and, perhaps, by the time we had eaten it, the weather would have taken up. I did not know what to say for it appeared that Sir Francis was willing to do all in his power to invest my situation with as much propriety as possible. We had been sitting by the fire outside in these armed chairs,' she indicated the two by the fire, 'and I had not seen this room until Mrs Harper asked me if I would care to retire and – and put my appearance to rights. Then I observed the table set as you see it and Sir Francis put his head round the door and said, "Oh, this is famous! What do you say we eat in here, Miss Ralston?" And he bade Harper bring in the chairs and Mrs Harper set out the food. I remarked that she seemed very well-provisioned and she said, with a knowing sort of smile, that she never knew when Sir Francis might not descend upon her, and somehow then, I began to get a little alarmed and to wonder if this was not – well, I do not know what you would call it, Julien!'

'Bellingham's little love-nest!' he supplied for her. 'Which could account for the fact that you were not shown this room at first. He possibly thought to get you away before ever you saw it. So then you locked the door?'

'Yes, and that put him quite out of countenance, but I said he must go back to Mitcham and take Harper with him, and then the storm came on and I was terrified, and I knew mama and – and everyone would be distraught!'

'Sssh!' He put a comforting arm around her but he was scarcely listening to what she was saying for the oddity of the situation was becoming more and more apparent. Bellingham, he could swear, was no ravisher and was, beyond question, sufficiently the gentleman to know that when he got a lady of his own social standing into such an impasse, however inadvertently, he must offer her the protection of his name. The Earl cleared his throat. 'Charlotte, was there an understanding between you and Bellingham?'

'Understanding?' she almost snapped. 'Of course there was not! Nor had I led him to believe that he might deal with me in this fashion!'

'Then,' said the Earl unwisely, 'I am forced to the conclusion that he is innocent of any ill intention towards you.'

'Oh, are you?' she retorted, her quick temper flaring. 'And I suppose all this,' with a wave of her hand to embrace the room and laden supper table, 'is kept ready nightly on the chance that Sir Francis might call?'

'Well, perhaps not nightly,' admitted the Earl, who thought he saw Bellingham's predicament, but how was he to explain to Charlotte that this would be the last place Sir Francis would wish to bring her if, indeed, it was designed for his more amorous adventures? 'He might have had the intention of returning here later this evening.'

'To meet his local light-of-love, I suppose!' She was not being so nice about expressing the possibilities. 'And why, if he was so innocent, did he make no effort to seek assistance before now?'

'That I do not understand,' admitted the Earl. 'I should have thought he could have sent his groom back to Mitcham before dark. Let us go and ask him, shall we?'

But when they went into the outer room, Sir Francis was not to be found, nor were Mrs Harper or her husband. The kitchen bore evidence of a hasty departure while the only other room in the cottage was devoid of furniture and quite empty.

'This is the outside of enough!' Charlotte burst out. 'Can they have taken advantage of the lull in the storm to set out? But why Mrs Harper, too?'

'And how, if the pole of the phaeton is cracked?' Julien snatched up his driving coat which had been set to dry in front of the fire and, dragging it on, plunged out into the streaming darkness. He was back in a few minutes. 'Both cabriolet and phaeton are gone – all the horses, too!' he gasped, shutting the door with real effort against the furious wind. 'Nothing for it but to walk to Mitcham for assistance.'

'*Now* will you believe what I have been trying to tell you?' she raged at him. 'I dare swear there was nothing ever wrong with that phaeton!' At that moment the thunderstorm elected to return in force, and a flash of lightning accompanied by an almost instantaneous clap of thunder, literally threw her into the Earl's arms. 'Julien, you cannot leave me alone! And you cannot walk to Mitcham in this weather, it is all of three miles, and – Julien! You are soaked to the skin, all down your front!' The next moment he was being pushed into the bedroom and forcibly divested of his dripping coat. 'Now your boots – how do you imagine you could walk in Hessians like wet flannel? I will put these in front of the fire outside while you take off the rest. There's a towel to rub yourself dry and take a blanket off the bed to wrap round you.'

'I am not going to drape my wet small clothes around your bedroom fire!' he protested.

'It is your bedroom fire, too!' she pointed out and left him to digest that fact while he stripped off his damp garments.

'You may come in now, ma'am!' he called presently.

'Julien, you have still got your shirt on!' The Earl, swathed from the waist down in a blanket, protested that his shirt was mostly dry. 'No, it is not, take it off at once!' Reluctantly, he did as he was bid. 'This drenching after all you have suffered could prove *fatal*! Come, sit in this chair and drink a glass of wine.' She gathered up the rest of his clothes and carried them to the fire in the outer room. 'There!' she said, coming back and closing the door, 'when that fire dies down I will bring them in here, for there is not enough wood to keep both fires going so we must save it for this one. Meantime, I am quite ravenous. Can you carve this chicken or shall I?'

'I will do it,' said the Earl and sneezed violently.

'Julien! You are not going to get one of your dreadful head-colds?'

'If that is all I get having pursued you over half the county in a gale, then I must consider myself very fortunate!'

'I cannot think why you did, you know,' she said, pouring herself out a glass of wine.

'You cannot think why – ' Julien, knife and fork suspended in mid-air, was so stunned by this blatant ingratitude, that words quite failed him.

'Yes, well – don't stop, please, Julien. I am so very hungry. But I was able to lock myself in here and the groom and his wife were here as well – of course, you could not have known that, could you? I allow it was not at all the thing, but if you consider our present situation, well, it is much worse, isn't it? Not only are we quite alone but you are certainly going to have to sleep in this room with me because there is no alternative, and I will not have your early demise set at my door on the score of prudishness. In any case,' she added, 'wh-who is going to believe us if we said we did not?'

'Did not what?' Julien was attacking the chicken with a ferocity quite unsuited to the task.

'S-stay together to keep warm,' she ended rather lamely.

'I take it, then,' said the Earl, as if the matter was one of supreme indifference to him, 'that, as on a previous occasion, you would prefer to accept an offer from another gentleman rather than from me.' She looked bewildered.

'Wh-who is talking of accepting offers?'

'I am!' he rapped back. 'You do not imagine we can spend the night here without your becoming my wife? As you so truly remarked, who is going to believe us if we said we did not?'

'No one, I daresay,' she agreed. 'B-but, Julien, there is Braybridge!'

'What has Braybridge got to say to anything? 'Fore God, if he hasn't got the wit to guard over his lady then he don't deserve to keep her!'

'But I cannot – Julien, you do not perfectly understand – '

'Charlotte,' said the Earl patiently, as if addressing a slightly backward child, 'what *you* do not perfectly understand is that Bellingham will have spread the story all over town before tomorrow. No doubt he is incensed with both of us for having doubted his good intentions and will think it a ripe jest to turn the tables on us.' He placed a plate of chicken and ham in front of her. 'Is that to your liking, ma'am?'

'Yes, thank you,' she said, but made no attempt to eat the food, just sat staring in front of her so that Julien was put in mind of what her mother had said about Charlotte being entrapped in a nightmare. If so, she was not alone, for a more nightmarish situation than the present could hardly be imagined.

'Charby,' he said gently, 'it won't do at all to starve yourself, you know.' At that, the tears spilled down her cheeks.

'Julien, I must marry Braybridge. I have no other choice.' This declaration so disconcerted the Earl that his attention strayed from his carving. 'Oh, you have cut your finger!'

He, sucking his skinned knuckle, eyed her almost malevolently. 'What do you mean that you must marry him? Have you – has he – Charlotte, what *do* you mean?' He half-rose as if to shake the truth out of her, but the imminent descent of his protective blanket required him to clutch at it with both hands and resume his seat in somewhat undignified haste.

She, grasping at any straw rather than be forced to tell him the truth, sobbed out: 'Yes, yes, indeed, that's it! He – he has c-compromised me quite dreadfully!'

'You never were a good bouncer,' said her childhood friend with distressing lack of sentiment. 'Come now, I want the truth, so don't try to gammon me with some unlikely tale of seduction!'

'I cannot tell you the truth, Julien. P-please take my word for it that I m-must m-marry Braybridge.'

'Has it occurred to you,' said the Earl, applying himself to his meal in what she considered to be the most cold-blooded manner, 'that he may be unwilling to accept you for his wife after to-night?'

'Oh, if only that might be so!' she breathed.

'So,' said the Earl, setting down his knife and fork. 'You have no desire to marry Braybridge but conceive it to be your duty to do so. I cannot believe that your mother should be in such desperate straits.'

'My m-mother?' she gasped.

'That was the reason you gave me once before for embarking on this – unsuitable engagement,' he reminded her.

'There is another reason,' said Charlotte in a very small voice. 'My lord claims to be – to have – to entertain a partiality for me. He is – he is set upon marrying me.'

'I see,' nodded the Earl. 'Then he is going to be out of all reason angry with me. Where Bellingham is concerned in this business, guilt can only be presumed, whereas I am trapped *in flagrante delicto*!'

'Trapped!' she echoed wildly. 'Can that be possible? Bellingham is his friend, and he would be sure that mama would send you in search of me!' She rose to her feet, her food still untouched. 'Braybridge hates you, Julien – oh, you have my word on that! I am afraid, so very afraid of him.' If the Earl thought that an odd expression of opinion for a lady about to engage in matrimony with the gentleman concerned, he said nothing of what was in his mind, but waited patiently for further revelations, watching Charlotte as she paced about in extreme agitation. 'I have no right to burden you with my troubles,' she went on in a low hurried voice, 'you have Anthea to consider and if any harm came to you on account of my affairs – Julien, are you quite astray in your head? How can you possibly propose marriage to me, no matter how provoking the circumstances?'

'Because Anthea and I are no longer engaged.'

For a fleeting moment the joy she felt at this announcement dispelled every anxious thought from her mind, but he was pouring another glass of wine and being very careful not to look at her. 'You have my s-sympathies,' she got out at last.

'Thank you.' The silence in the room was broken only by the hissing of the raindrops down the chimney on to the burning logs. Then Charlotte resumed her seat and they ate their meal without speaking, she because she longed to tell him of her anxieties but feared the outcome of such a revelation, he because of the difficulties of the situation in which they found themselves. Though any reasonable man would accept that it had all come about through no fault of his, yet he was very ready to believe that Braybridge might not prove reasonable. Charlotte, for her part, was thinking hard. If Julien was free of Anthea then would it not be wise to tell him the truth since he was, in any event, quite irretrievably implicated in the whole melancholy business? Here her thoughts suffered a check.

'Julien,' she said nervously, 'will Braybridge call you out, do you suppose?'

'I must confess that I think it very likely,' he admitted.

'Then I am assured you have the right to know of my difficulty. It has not to do with my mother, but my father.'

'Sir Greville?' The Earl looked his astonishment.

'Yes, my lord knows of something to his discredit and holds over me the threat of making it public should I refuse to marry him.'

'The devil he does! And you mother, does she know of this? But, of course, she cannot, else she – '

'And she must not know!' Charlotte interrupted him. 'It would quite overset her.'

The Earl tapped his fingers impatiently on the table. 'Your father's fondness for gaming was no secret,' he said. 'So what is this crime of which Braybridge holds him guilty?' She saw then there was nothing for it but to tell him the whole. The Earl heard her out in silence. 'This puts a very different complexion upon the matter,' he confessed. 'But you, you foolish child, can you suppose for one moment that your mother would permit you to make such a sacrifice? When all is said, you are alive and your father is not.'

'B-but, Julien, dear mama would suffer such anguish!'

'I doubt that,' he assured her. 'The whole affair sounds to have been an unhappy accident. If your father believed the pistol not to have been loaded – who was the other gentleman concerned?'

She shook her head. 'I cannot say. Braybridge was careful not to give me his name.'

'Then this we must discover for, as it rests, we have only his lordship's word for it.' He paused, considering. 'The affair must have taken place soon after I left for the Peninsula for I cannot recollect hearing anything of it, though I remember young Cotterell, a puppy as flash as he was foolish.' He stretched out a hand across the table to her and, after a little hesitation, she put hers shyly into it. 'Have no fear, Charby. We'll come at the truth if you will but trust me.'

'I have ever trusted you, Julien!' she cried, but hung her head in confusion at his wry smile.

'Have you, Charby, have you?' he asked, and sneezed again.

'Oh, Julien, you *have* taken a cold – but, of course, the very thing, hyssop! I purchased some at Mitcham to-day and it is a noted remedy for coughs and chills. I'll boil it in some of the broth from the chicken!' Grateful to have something practical on which to exercise her mind, she sped out of the room and returned clutching a pan and looking rather scared. 'I think I saw a rat out there! When you set out for Mitcham in the morning I am coming with you. I'll not stay here alone!'

'How far do you imagine you would go in that footgear?' He directed a scornful glance at her dainty yellow kid boots, just showing below the trimming of her robe of worked jaconet muslin. Over this she wore her usual neat spencer, also in yellow, while her French bonnet and elegant blue velvet pelisse lay on the bed. 'It must be agreed that neither of us is suitably attired for tramping three miles of muddy track, unless – that farm the ostler spoke of! It cannot be as far as Mitcham, and surely they would have a horse I could hire.'

'You are not to think of going out to-night, you would never find it in the dark.' As if to support her argument, a loud rumble of thunder sounded overhead.

'I shall go at first light,' he promised her. 'In the meantime, I shall sleep here in this chair.'

'And be so stiff and chilled in the morning that you will be quite incapable of going anywhere? Julien, be sensible! What difference can a distance of six feet make to anything? You can sleep, wrapped in blankets, under the fur cover on one side of the bed, while I am between the sheets on the other. There are an amount of pillows in the cupboard here which I will place down the middle of the bed to serve as a – as a palisade between us.'

The Earl eyed the big comfortable bed with some longing. He was excessively weary and feeling far from amorous, being mainly concerned with conserving his strength for what promised to be a trying day on the morrow. In any case, as there was no possibility of investing the situation with any degree of propriety, he might as well avail himself of what comfort there was for, if he should be stricken by a chill or other crippling ailment, Charlotte would be quite unable to fetch assistance, and an already difficult problem would be rendered almost insoluble.

He allowed her to hustle him into bed and was persuaded to drink of the chicken broth infused with hyssop which she had prepared. After that she bustled about, making up the fire, bringing his clothes in from the outer room to dry, clearing away the food and generally so busying herself he was brought to realize that, in spite of her brave talk and barricade of pillows, she was very nervous of getting into bed. The only solution was for him to appear to have fallen asleep and, shutting his eyes, he breathed slowly and deeply until rewarded by the knowledge that she was standing beside him. Timidly, her hand touched his still damp hair but, rigidly controlling his emotions, he lay unmoving until, satisfied that he slept, she went round to the other side of the bed, slipped off her spencer and robe, and slid carefully between the sheets.

CHAPTER FOURTEEN

THE rigours of the day took their toll and Charlotte, at least, enjoyed an excellent repose. Once only during the night when the lightning, fiendishly resolved to wreak its worst upon them, struck and felled a tree near to the cottage, did she wake and stretch a trembling hand over the pillows to have it taken at once in Julien's strong clasp.

'Don't be frightened, Charby. That will be the end of it, I swear.' And, mercifully, it was.

When she awoke in the morning there was a fringe of light showing below the curtains and the terrors of the previous evening seemed but an evil dream. There was no movement from Julien so, gently detaching her hand from his, she got out of bed to dress herself quickly and silently. Then she cautiously drew a curtain to look out upon a wet and steaming world with a pallid sun endeavouring to break through the mists. Putting the bellows to the still glowing ashes in the fireplace, she presently had a good blaze going and set about making tea.

'You are mighty busy about your affairs, madam housewife!' He was awake and watching her with sleepy amusement.

'Good-morrow to you, my lord!' said she, dropping him a mock curtsy. 'How do you feel in health?'

'Tolerably well, I thank you,' he said with small regard for the truth, for his eyes burned and his head felt as if bursting. 'Is it still raining?'

'No, but everything is in a quagmire. I am sure I do not know how we shall go on. And your clothes are in a sad state – indeed your driving coat is fit only to be thrown away. I doubt the hood of your cabriolet afforded you much protection.'

'Well, I was driving into a gale for most of the way,' he protested mildly. 'One would need a suit of armour to withstand that style of thing.'

'Julien, I think we should eat and get away as soon as is possible. I will go to the kitchen while you dress. I do trust your – your inexpressibles are quite dry, but double kerseymere does retain the damp so.'

'I only hope they have not shrunk,' said the Earl, 'else walking is going to be even more uncomfortable than I had deemed possible!'

Happily, no such catastrophe had occurred and when the Earl emerged a little later he was, though rather flushed, looking much his normal self. Charlotte set him to slicing ham and he was in the midst of this task when a noise from outside made them both raise their heads and listen intently. It came again, the unmistakable sound of a horse blowing through its nostrils and the faint clink of a bridle and bit.

With a warning glance at Charlotte, the Earl strode to the door and flung it open. Upon the threshold, his riding-whip tapping ominously against his boot, stood Lord Braybridge.

Charlotte it was who first recovered her composure. 'Please to enter, my lord,' said she with commendable coolness. 'We were about to partake of breakfast. Do you care to join us?'

The Earl stepped back to allow Braybridge to come in and she was put in mind of nothing so much as a pair of hounds, circling stiff-legged round each other. Then Braybridge turned to survey her with a studied insolence that brought the blood to her cheeks.

'I must congratulate you, ma'am,' he said. 'To be in such command of yourself after so unnerving an experience is, I am persuaded, a rare accomplishment.'

'If you mean the thunderstorm,' said she, all innocence, 'I must confess that, had not my lord of Clandon been here to bear me company, I was like to have been scared half out of my wits.'

'Indeed!' he snapped, walking to the open bedroom door and looking in upon the still unmade and rumpled bed. The barricade of pillows brought a quizzical frown to his face, but the meaning in his voice was unmistakable as he turned to her again. 'And right well he bore you company, I see!'

'And right speedily you found your way here, my lord!' she retorted, seeing Julien's fists clench by his side. 'Did Sir Francis ride all the way to Meudon Hall last night to acquaint you with our unhappy predicament?'

He bowed ironically to her. 'What joy to have a wife with such quick understanding!'

'A wife?' she echoed wonderingly. 'Hardly that now, my lord, for surely I have fallen too low in your esteem.'

He almost smiled. 'It won't do, my dear Charlotte,' he said, jerking his head towards the bedroom. 'Those pillows tell their own story! I could almost pity you, Clandon, for having to pay for something never attained!' He ran a scornful eye down Julien's tense figure. 'Or perhaps that wretched animal from which you so gallantly rescued my wife-to-be did its work better than I knew? If so, no *blame* can attach to you – say pity, rather – ' He got no further for Julien's left fist shot out, dealing him so shrewd a facer that my lord took some time to pick himself up from the floor. He stood for a moment, fingering his jaw tenderly. 'For that, Clandon, if for naught else, I must demand immediate satisfaction.'

'I am very willing to oblige you, my lord.' Julien was endeavouring to keep a tight hold on himself, but Braybridge's gibes and Charlotte's wan face combined with the threatened onset of a streaming head cold to make reasoned thinking a shade difficult.

'As neither of us, I am assured, would wish the lady's name to be bandied about, I suggest we dispense with the formality of seconds and settle this matter now.'

'You take a high hand, Braybridge, but one thing has escaped your notice. I have not come provided with a weapon.'

'Nor have I my duelling pistols,' admitted the Viscount in a pleasantly candid manner. 'But, no doubt, Bellingham will have something to our liking.' He strolled over to a wall-cupboard and took out two delicately balanced swords. 'Do these meet with your approval?'

Julien weighed one in his hand. 'I cannot recall that I have ever given Sir Francis cause to be my enemy,' he commented lightly, 'and can only suppose that you have uncovered some indiscretion that renders it impossible for him to withstand your commands. That is a favourite ploy of yours, is it not?'

Braybridge's eyes narrowed. 'So there have been confidences in the night?' he murmured.

'Nor am I as easily gulled as a frightened girl!'

'All the more reason to silence you, then!' The menace behind the words was implicit and Charlotte stifled a horrified gasp. 'But, I am given to understand, you have been indulging in fencing practice so, doubtless, you will be in prime fettle!'

This last remark made the Earl even more keenly aware of the tightness of the net drawn around him. With pistols he had a good chance of success; with swords his nimbleness of foot would come into question and his left foot was far from strong. But none of this showed in his face as he stripped off his coat and handed it to Charlotte, smiling down into her wide anxious eyes.

'Do you stay here and don't be distressing yourself,' he said easily. 'This will not take long.'

'I pray you may be found to be right,' she whispered. 'Take care, Julien.'

He pressed her hand lightly and walked out to where Braybridge awaited him. His heart sank as he saw the sodden treacherous ground on which they must engage. To suggest that the duel be conducted within the confines of the cottage was impossible because of lack of sword room, so he would have to make the best of things and hope for a fortunate thrust before his foot wearied of the sport. This, as became plain from the outset, the Viscount had no intention of allowing to happen. He was a competent swordsman, one with whom Julien would have relished a bout with the foils in other circumstances, and he was at pains to adopt a defensive attitude and leave it to the Earl to force the pace which, as Julien well understood, he must do, else they would be at the business for longer than he could sustain.

The Earl fought with smooth dexterity, but every attack was checked by Braybridge's close guard and, before long he knew his breath to be coming faster than he could like. It was plain from the exultant gleam in his adversary's eye that he had based his hopes on that very circumstance. Julien, despite his outward calm, was deeply anxious for, if he should be overborne, what was to become of Charlotte?

As if in answer to his unspoken thought, a chaise came bowling up the muddy track and turned in smartly at the gate. Before the groom had time to let down the steps, the door burst open and out sprang Bellingham. The Earl, who was facing the gate, had full cognizance of this unexpected development, and Braybridge, quick to turn his momentary inattention to advantage, moved in to attack. Julien, in parrying the thrust, was forced back upon his left foot which, slipping on the wet grass, twisted and gave way, throwing him to the ground. As he fell, he heard a shot ring out and Sir Francis shouting: 'Put up your sword, Braybridge, or by God, the next one'll have your name on it!'

'What the devil are you about, Bellingham?'

The Earl hardly heard Braybridge's furious protest for his attention was directed to the chaise from which, to his utter astonishment, he perceived Lady Ralston being handed out by an elderly, portly gentleman, at sight of whom Braybridge muttered a muffled curse and flung his sword to the ground.

'My dear Sir Francis,' Lady Ralston was saying, 'you did warn us that it was only a cottage but not that it was situate in the midst of a swamp! Good-morning, gentlemen. Charlotte, my love, those yellow boots! It is a great deal too bad of you to wear them in such adverse conditions!'

'I – I have nothing else to w-wear, mama!' stammered Charlotte, darting a look of helpless entreaty towards the Earl who, with Bellingham's aid, had struggled to his feet.

'To be sure you have not,' agreed her mother comfortably. 'The next time you have the intention of spending a night from home do not fail to instruct one of the maids to put up some things in a valise for you.'

'Yes, mama,' said her dutiful daughter. 'W-would you care for some tea?'

'A capital notion,' nodded her ladyship. 'Julien – oh, dear boy, you are covered in mud! – may I beg your arm over this last stretch? And, indeed, my manners are deserting me! You are not acquainted with Lord Wigton, I believe.'

Julien found himself bowing to the portly gentleman and escorting Lady Ralston into the cottage while, at the same time, being acutely aware of Bellingham holding a pistol levelled at Braybridge. The Viscount appeared disinclined to enter the cottage, but a sharp prod from the pistol barrel induced him to change his mind and, with the air of one accepting the inevitable, he went in, followed closely by Sir Francis.

'Th-there is only one room to sit in and it is not very tidy, mama,' explained Charlotte nervously.

Lady Ralston walked into the bedroom, taking in at one glance the table laid for breakfast, the kettle boiling away on the small fire, and the bed with all its attendant implications, then she nodded as if satisfied.

'This will do very well. Do you make the tea, my dear.' With a few quick twitches she straightened the fur coverlet and sat on the end of the bed. 'Lord Wigton, please be seated, and you other gentlemen as you can. Now, where shall we start?'

'With me, I fancy,' said Bellingham.

'Yes, but do put that weapon away, if you please, Sir Francis. I cannot suppose it to be at all necessary.'

'Yes, ma'am,' said Bellingham politely but laid the pistol on the table, close to his hand, while Braybridge sat stiffly upright, arms folded, with an expression of icy disdain on his face. Charlotte's courage failed her as she thought of how he must relish what was to come, for it was not to be supposed that his lordship, if thwarted in his purpose, would be so obliging as to keep silent. Sir Francis cleared his throat and looked apologetically at the Earl. 'You have my word for it, Clandon,' he said, 'that had I the least notion of what was Braybridge's intent, no persuasion of his would have induced me to lend him my support. He informed me he had a mind to teach you a lesson for what he was pleased to term "over-familiarity" with Miss Ralston – though, for the life of me, I could not conceive how throwing you together in this cottage was going to advance his cause for, having no knowledge of your injury, I judged you to be at least his equal in whatever weapon he chose.' He hesitated. 'There was another reason, too, why I had no wish to disoblige him.'

The Earl raised an enquiring eyebrow. 'The usual one?' Bellingham laughed shortly.

'Yes, I am deep in the suds and most of it owed to him. He offered to tear up my vowels if I would help further his plans by keeping Miss Ralston here until you arrived and then making off with the carriages. Thereafter I was to join him at the Greyhound at Streatham – the tale of going to Meudon Hall was but a trick to have you think him out of the way – and later we were to return here, I to remain out of sight while he conducted his business with you. But the storm upset his plans and he was content to wait until morning, knowing full well that it would not be possible for you to summon assistance. I asked him what he would be at, to leave his lady in such straits. He then informed me plainly that he had the intent to kill you and take Miss Ralston to London, where his chaplain would marry them under special licence.'

'But why a special licence?' asked Charlotte, perplexed. 'We were to have been married within a se'ennight.'

'There is some quirk of the law, so I understand,' explained Bellingham, 'that does not allow of a wife testifying against her husband.'

'And what, may I ask, was to be done with my cadaver?' enquired the Earl.

'Oh, as to that, I did not enquire, but when I protested at being drawn in so deep he said he would be well content if I would but hold my tongue. Well, that did not precisely commend itself to me, but I had little choice in the matter and every confidence that you, Clandon, could handle him, though it was past my understanding that he should permit you both – ' His eyes strayed to the bed and the barricade of pillows. 'Well, perhaps he was right, after all!' he allowed, with an awed glance at the Earl's rigid countenance.

'W-what happened then?' asked Charlotte hastily.

'I set out for London, resolving to put as much space between me and the cottage as possible. I was half-way there before it occurred to me how neatly I had been tricked. This cottage is my property, there would be nothing to show for Braybridge's presence here, while the landlord and ostler at the White Hart could bear witness to last night's happenings.'

'And you would have been in a devilish awkward fix if my lifeless form had been discovered here,' agreed the Earl.

Bellingham grinned disarmingly. 'I'll own freely that it was in the hope of saving my own skin rather than consideration for you that sent me to Clandon House!' he admitted. 'For who was to say that I had not returned here at first light to confront you? I had some vague notion of warning your staff that you were in danger and of establishing my presence there while you were still breathing! At the door, I met Lord Wigton about to take his leave of Lady Ralston.'

'Thank you, Sir Francis,' said her ladyship, sipping her tea appreciatively. 'Shall I continue from there? Lord Wigton is an old friend of your father's, Charlotte, and I paid him the courtesy of sending him a card for Penelope's wedding but he wrote me that he lived very retired nowadays on account of his health, and seldom set foot in London. I replied to his letter the other day, expressing my sympathy and promising that if ever I was in the vicinity of Basingstoke, where he lives, I would give myself the pleasure of calling upon him. I further mentioned that this might be sooner than otherwise could be expected since my eldest daughter was about to marry Lord Braybridge, and with all three girls disposed of, time could well hang heavy on my hands. Conceive of my astonishment when I returned to Clandon House last night to discover Lord Wigton awaiting me.'

Lord Wigton coughed portentously and spoke for the first

time in a slow ponderous voice that gave the impression of creaking from lack of use.

'Braybridge,' said he weightily, 'allow me to tell you that you are a contemptible fellow.'

The Viscount smiled thinly. 'Your age and state of health give you leave to use such expressions, my lord, not I!'

Wigton ignored him and turned to Charlotte. 'Tell me, my dear, did he bring any pressures to bear upon you so that you felt obliged to marry him?'

Charlotte hesitated and looked at Julien, who nodded reassuringly. 'Yes,' she allowed. 'He – he told me a tale of my father having – having – '

'Shot someone?' Her mother might have been passing the time of day, so collected was she. 'My poor child! Your father told me of it the day after it happened. Indeed, he was so distraught that he could not well have concealed it, but he never told me the names of the other gentlemen concerned. He protested that it was all due to their efforts that the affair had been brushed over, and he would be forever in their debt.'

'A very proper sentiment,' drawled Braybridge. 'Or have you cause to complain, Wigton?'

'I have had cause to think, my lord, in the succeeding years but, as poor Greville died soon after the event, I could not be assured that to air my suspicions could be of any benefit to his family. When I heard that you were to wed his daughter the matter took on a very different complexion, and my talk with Lady Ralston convinced me that you were using your knowledge to further your own ends.'

'Allow me to remind you, Wigton, that whatever you say can only be conjecture.'

'I'll take you up on that, my lord. It was fact and not conjecture that those pistols were unloaded when Greville brought them into your house. It was also fact that you loaded one, intending to try it out or so you declared, but then your other guests arrived and it was set aside.'

'I have no wish to throw a rub in the way of your brilliant

reasoning, but what has any of this to say to anything?' Braybridge still maintained his air of scornful indifference, but his eyes were watchful. 'Ralston shot the boy and, by so doing, saved himself an amount of money.'

'He saved you a great deal more!' countered Lord Wigton. 'It was you who owed the greatest amount to Cotterell – oh, I know what you would say!' He held up a hand as Braybridge attempted to speak. 'That we were over eager to fall in with your suggestion of making it appear that the gun went off while Cotterell was examining it. As I saw it there was no other course to follow. We knew it was no intended thing, but how to prove it? What should you have done, I wonder, if Greville had not snatched up that pistol?'

'Such surmise is singularly profitless!' Braybridge rose and smiled faintly upon the company. 'Your servant, Lady Ralston, Charlotte, gentlemen. You have put your case and there the matter stands. Good-day to you.'

He was about to leave them when Charlotte stepped forward. 'A moment, my lord. I have something for you, and this time I will not have it back!'

'Who knows?' he said, accepting the diamond from her with a show of graceful resignation. 'Maybe I will yet find a lady of a mind to wear it.'

'May Heaven help her if he does!' said Charlotte devoutly as the door closed behind him. 'Oh, mama, dearest mama, are you not utterly cast down by all this misadventure?'

'It is the greatest mortification to me,' said Lady Ralston sadly, 'that all my daughters appear to regard me as being quite hen-witted! If anyone should lay claim to that distinction, it must be you, Charlotte! Could you not have confided in me before sacrificing your future on such an altar?'

Before Charlotte could think of a suitable response Julien, who had found the room apt to recede and advance upon him in the most tiresome manner imaginable, swayed and caught at the back of a chair to steady himself.

' 'Pon my word, Clandon, you are looking in devilish queer

stirrups!' exclaimed Bellingham.

'He is hurt and I daresay he has taken a chill,' declared Charlotte. 'Julien, please sit down – Sir Francis, the brandy!'

'My boot!' gasped the Earl, all colour drained from his countenance. 'If you could – get it off!'

Bellingham's well-intentioned efforts caused the Earl to hold on to Miss Ralston with greater fervour than might have been thought proper but she, concerned only for his pain, continued to ply him with brandy and soothing words until his foot was laid bare.

Lady Ralston shook her head over it. 'I fear it is back to Dr Bolton, Julien,' she prophesied. 'And oh, dear boy, you are so hot, so feverish!'

'Mama, he is not going to be ill again?' cried Charlotte.

'He *is* ill again!' said her mother firmly. 'See to it that Lord Wigton and Sir Francis have something to eat while I contrive a compress for this foot.'

'Do not be putting yourself out, Aunt Emmelina,' begged the Earl. 'It is nothing that a few days' rest cannot cure.'

'I'll not allow it to be so,' she said. 'If not taken proper care of this foot could be a drag to you for all your life.'

'Be kind enough to explain to me, Clandon, why you give her ladyship the title of "aunt",' said Wigton in his pontifical way. 'I had thought to know most of the Ralston family connections and can recall none that links them with the Revels.'

It was as well that Lady Ralston took it upon herself to explain this odd circumstance, for Julien's attention was directed upon Charlotte who was attempting to slice more ham and making such a mull of the business that Sir Francis was obliged to render her assistance by closing his hands over hers in order to guide them more surely. Charlotte, it must be allowed, was blushing and protesting but hardly to a degree, the Earl considered, as might be said to discourage such attentions, and the flush on his cheek could not, in Lady Ralston's opinion, be put down altogether to his mounting fever.

CHAPTER FIFTEEN

HAPPILY, Lady Ralston's worst fears proved to be illfounded; nonetheless, it was more than a week before the Earl left his bed and then to the disapproval of Dr Bolton who insisted that he resumed the use of his stick. Throughout this trying time Lady Ralston had proved herself to be a very Cerberus, forbidding all visitors and permitting only Chivers to wait upon his master. The Earl found this constraint most irksome, and the knowledge that Charlotte was out each day, driving or riding with Sir Francis, caused him to suffer an excessive irritation of the nerves.

'Oh, as to that,' Lady Ralston was swift to assure him, 'I must own myself grateful for his attentions. Braybridge may be outfaced but he is not a man easily to be deflected from his purpose and he still carries a special licence in his pocket. What if he should bear her off by force?'

The Earl did not think it to be likely and said so. 'He knows I would shoot him down if he attempted any such thing.'

'You are in no case to shoot anyone,' she objected. 'Besides, why should you be called upon for ever to act as Charlotte's champion?'

'Perhaps she would prefer Bellingham to perform that service for her?' The Earl was still smarting a little from the recollection of that morning at the cottage when, he felt, he had not shown to the best advantage. 'It would appear she has not informed you, but I offered Charlotte marriage that night we were together.'

'Very gentlemanlike of you, Julien, to be sure, but there is not the least need for you to be putting yourself out in such a way. We few who know the circumstances could not hold you to blame. I can assure you Charlotte does not.'

'I am obliged to you but I would be glad of a chance to speak to her, if she could bring herself to visit me.'

'She has called each day to enquire for you,' Lady Ralston informed him. 'It is I who forbade her to see you lest – well, I felt any agitation might excite your fever. But I have no doubt she will call again to-day,' she added kindly, 'and now there is no reason why you should not have your little talk.'

He looked at her in quick suspicion but her attention appeared to be wholly taken up with her embroidery, and when she spoke again it was to discuss the recently opened Dulwich College Art Gallery which she had visited the previous day in the company of Melissa, Philip and Mr Edmond Vereker.

'I did not know the old gentleman was in town. Dangling after you, is he, Aunt Emmelina?'

To his amusement, she blushed and bridled. 'That is no way to be speaking of Mr Vereker, Julien!' she reproved him. 'No, nor of me either!'

When Charlotte called that afternoon she was accompanied by all three Verekers and in the general confusion of greeting and expressing delight at finding the Earl out of his bed, Lady Ralston found an opportunity to draw her eldest daughter aside and address a few words of advice to her.

'Do not, I beg of you, be teasing him, Charlotte. He is in no state for it.'

'But, mama, I am persuaded he is only offering for me out of a sense of duty. He – he has never truly forgiven me for my lack of faith in him.'

'I cannot altogether blame him for that!' said her mother tartly. 'So you can well be grateful for any circumstance that makes you his wife!'

The asperity of Lady Ralston's tone did nothing to steady Charlotte's ravaged nerves and when, the elder Mr Vereker's curiosity being gratified by a tour of the house which necessitated several persons attending upon him so that no detail should be overlooked, she found herself alone with the Earl, her first impulse was to formulate some excuse to join them.

'Don't run away, Charlotte. If you would be so kind as to allow me a few moments of your time, there is something I would say to you.' So remote and formal was his manner that she could find no words to answer him but waited, with downbent head, for him to continue. 'It may have escaped your memory, ma'am, that a week since I made you an offer of marriage and wish to assure you that my sentiments have not undergone a change. May I be informed of your – ' he stumbled slightly, 'if you are disposed to grant me a favourable reply?'

'My lord,' she said tremulously, 'am I to assume that this is to be a "marriage of convenience" as heretofore?'

'Say rather a marriage of necessity,' he corrected her.

'But it isn't necessary, truly it isn't! I know we were alone together and it was n-not at all p-proper, but I have known you all my life – '

'What has that to say to anything? I am not yet quite senile, whatever you may imagine!' His irate tone betrayed the depth of his feelings on that subject. 'If you do not think marriage necessary to preserve your good name, I consider such an outcome imperative for the preservation of mine!'

Dear God, she thought, would he but hold out his hand and smile at her in his old friendly way, then she would know herself to be forgiven! But Julien, as nervous as a lad with his first love where she was concerned, dared make no such gesture.

'I allow there may be a little awkwardness in your having been so recently attached to Braybridge,' he went on, 'and, in any case, you will not be pleased to have your bridegroom hobbling down the aisle at your side.' The question in his voice put her in mind of what she ought to be saying.

'I – I am profoundly grateful to you for your obliging offer, my lord,' she faltered, 'and will do all in my power to make you a conformable wife.'

'You have made me a very happy man, Charlotte,' he said and, in an effort to conceal his emotion, limped over to the window to be rewarded by the sight of Sir Francis, dressed in the first stare of elegance, alighting from his phaeton. 'I perceive Bellingham is about to descend upon us,' he remarked. 'Shall he be the first to learn of our good news?'

Lady Ralston, when approached upon the matter, gave it as her opinion that nothing could be done for the moment other than make Charlotte's severance from Braybridge generally known. 'I have in mind to take her on a visit to her cousins at Sarum for at least a month. When we return I am hopeful that all speculation will have subsided and the announcement of your engagement may be released soon after.' She advanced her argument in so reasonable a manner that Julien was forced to acknowledge the good sense of it. 'When had you thought of getting married?'

The Earl, who had planned to fill Chalice with his friends at Christmas, put it to her that the last day of the year would be a suitable time to celebrate their wedding. Their guests would still be with them and would not have to make a special journey in the depth of winter, and as Chalice would be en fête in any case for the ushering in of 1815, he was in high hopes that the occasion would pass off as a tolerably gay one. Lady Ralston, well-pleased at the turn things had taken, expressed herself as being in full agreement with this notion.

'No need, then, to publish your intent until December,' she declared, 'just so as your guests may be forewarned.'

And with that Julien, who would have been happy to publish his intent then and there, had to be content.

* * *

The Christmas visitors began to arrive on the twenty-first of December, the first of them being Colonel and Lady FitzJames and their children, accompanied by Lord Wychfield.

'It is a fine thing Christmas Day being a Sunday,' declared the Colonel. 'It saves one church going!'

'I may say,' said his lady, adjuring her offspring to go quietly upstairs with their nurse, 'that you will probably regret the descent of this horde upon you, but I could not desert them at Christmas, not even for you, Julien.'

'It will be good for Chalice to have young things about it again,' said the Earl.

'They will be warming it up for its future occupants, eh, Sultan?' the Colonel quizzed him.

The Earl was saved the necessity of replying to this by the arrival of the Duchess's great coach, escorted by Robert and Penelope's chaise and, soon after them, Lord and Lady Oakley, with Miss Branscombe.

The time passed easily enough for the weather was excellent for shooting and riding and, since every household of any standing in the district was determined to offer hospitality to the Earl and his guests, there was hardly an evening to be spent quietly at Chalice.

Christmas Day was a memorable occasion with a gargantuan feast provided both for tenantry and guests. There were Norfolk turkeys, saddles of mutton, haunches of venison, barons of beef, chickens, ducks, geese, hams from Westphalia, truffles from France, caviare from Russia, and even Dee salmon which had been kept in the Earl's ice-house since the summer. In addition to all this were the pastrycook's confections, the apple-pies, the pâtés, the sugared sweetmeats and an infinite variety of cheeses all washed down with champagne, burgundy, hock and every wine for every taste down to the local home-brewed ale.

Thereafter the days to New Year's Eve merged into such a whirl of festivity that Charlotte could hardly believe it when she found herself being dressed for her wedding by Melissa and Penelope, aided by her mother's maid and Mrs Tremlett's niece, who was to be her own maid. Her sisters saw to it that this was a light-hearted ceremony, but Penelope was at pains to warn Charlotte that, after the New Year had been rung in, she and Julien must disappear and go upstairs and lock themselves in their rooms.

'The gentlemen have the notion of perpetrating some jest upon you, of what sort I cannot tell, but it would be best, I think, if you could elude them.'

'Doubtless it would amuse them to revive the old fashion of

tucking you both up in bed together!' remarked Melissa scornfully.

'Oh, no!' Charlotte looked her horror. 'I – we – I – it would be most distasteful to us both.'

'Then you must go when everyone is wishing everyone else a prosperous New Year. I will warn Julien also. Now, let me look at you. Dearest sister, you look so lovely, I can hardly believe it is you!'

This somewhat backhanded compliment from Penelope sent them into whoops of laughter, and when Lady Ralston looked in a moment later it was to find the bride mopping her eyes and declaring she could not go weeping to the altar.

The sight of the fairy figure in white gauze embroidered with tiny pearls, over white satin, with a white bonnet similarly embroidered and lined with blue silk, coming towards him on her Uncle Warner's arm, brought a lump into Julien's throat as he stood waiting, with Ned beside him, in his chapel at Chalice, to take Charlotte for his wife. The guests at Chalice and Heatherstone Hall filled the building, while outside, in the waning December light, was crowded every tenant and employee of the Earl's that could stand on his or her feet.

All too soon, it seemed to Charlotte, the vows were made, his ring was on her finger, the ceremony was over and she was his Countess. Then they had to run the gauntlet of the waiting crowd, the laughter, the congratulations, the embraces and the tears. Even Robert's grandmama, the Duchess, had a suspicion of moisture in her fierce eye as she wished them well, while Lady Ralston, her dearest wish fulfilled, was crying unashamedly on Melissa's shoulder.

After came the reception, when their healths had to be drunk by all, so many persons had to be spoken to and thanked for their bride-gifts and good wishes, and here Charlotte was grateful for her knowledge of Chalice and its people, for she was rarely at a loss for a name or a word and Julien was beside her to prompt and encourage when needed. He, saving only his dark blue coat, was dressed in white, and appeared so heart-rendingly handsome that she scarce dared look at him. She could not know what beauty happiness had conferred upon her, and old Mr Vereker expressed the opinion of all when he said:

'A perfect matched pair. They'll run well in harness together.'

At last they got away to change their dress for dinner. Charlotte slipped gratefully into a gown of sheer dark green silk over an amethyst satin underskirt. She hesitated long over what jewellery she should wear for nothing seemed quite to match the graceful elegance of the simple dress. Then, hearing the Earl's voice at the door of her room, she gasped:

'Oh, dear! He has come to take me down to dinner and I cannot decide!'

'What cannot you decide, my lady?' The caress in his voice quite overset her, though she reminded herself that, of course, he had to appear loverlike on his wedding-day.

'My lord, this gown – I fear I will have to wear another or else preside over your table quite unadorned in a manner unbecoming to your Countess.'

'My lady,' he said, his own good taste appreciating the exquisite simplicity of her appearance. 'What adornment can be necessary when all is utter perfection?'

She blushed at the graceful compliment. 'You are too obliging, my lord, but my first appearance at your table,' she shook her head, 'I would like it to be just as it should be.'

'Then, if it please you, be seated at your mirror and let us see what we may contrive.'

'Oh Julien!' she gasped as he laid an open jewel-case on her dressing-table and took from it a slender collar of amethysts and bracelets of the same sort. 'They are perfect! But how did you know the colour?'

'I asked your mother what you would be wearing,' he said simply. 'Now, my lady, does that please you?'

Only the smiling presence of her maid prevented her from throwing her arms around his neck and telling him how much it pleased her, but she managed to express her gratitude entirely to his satisfaction, and they went down to join their guests in perfect harmony with each other. At least, thought Julien, as he watched her take her rightful place at the head of his table, I can give her every material pleasure, and all the worldly consequence she could desire, perhaps that will compensate for what is missing. And he wondered, as he had so often done before, just what was missing, and if his wife loved another man since she could not love him.

Charlotte scarce tasted any of the delicious food set in front of her at dinner, but no one could have faulted her on the score of looking after her guests. She was animated and gay and, every so often, she glanced down the length of the table to meet Julien's encouraging smile. Then he had to lead her out to start the dancing and, in no time at all, it was the end of the year. Bells were ringing, people shouting, every possible pot and pan was being clanged outside, so the musicians gave up their efforts to make themselves heard and joined in the general mêlée. Then the Earl's hand closed on hers and she was drawn out of the great hall, down a little-used passage where Sefton stood guard with a candle at the foot of a staircase she could not remember ever having noticed before.

The old butler beamed upon her. 'This way, my lady. It will take you to your rooms in safety. I fear, my lady, that your maid has not been apprised of this circumstance, lest she should drop a word in the wrong ear.'

'I promise you,' said the Earl, taking the candle from him, 'that I am very skilled at dealing with hooks and buttons. Come, we must make haste before the pack comes slavering at our heels!'

Once safely in their rooms, Julien had no sooner made sure that all the outer doors were locked than there arose a loud outcry from below which heralded the arrival of a large, vociferous party on the landing. To their entreaties and thumps upon the doors, the Earl and his Countess vouchsafed no reply, just stood listening and laughing silently, his arm about her shoulders. At last, when their tormentors had tired of the game and gone away, he released her.

'Are you – can you manage?'

'Of course,' she said quickly. 'You must know I am not at all used to having someone to wait upon me.'

There came a scratch upon the door and Chivers' voice saying: 'It is I, my lord, can you admit me?'

'Provided you are alone!' retorted the Earl. 'Go to the door of my room. You had best watch and listen,' he added to Charlotte, 'for if this is a trap to get me to open up, then you must lock the door between our rooms.'

'And leave you to their mercy?'

'Better than having us both at their mercy!' said he with so meaningful a glance that it brought the colour to her cheeks. But a moment later she heard his and Chivers' voices conversing amicably together and quietly closed the door.

She undressed and quickly got into her night attire, but it seemed an interminable time before she heard a light knock on the connecting door and his voice asking if he might come in.

'Is everything to your liking, my lady? I trust you are not too fatigued after such a day.'

Resplendent in a magnificent blue and gold dressing-gown over a blue nightrobe, he came to take her hand and smile reassuringly at her where she sat, bolt upright in the vast bed, her bedgown of palest cream silk with deep flounces of lace around the wide neckline showing off her delicate colouring to perfection. Julien thought her the most exquisite and desirable creature he had ever laid eyes upon, but no hint of such improper feelings showed in his demeanour as he sat on the side of the bed and talked to her of the events of the day.

'And you were quite right, you know, the Duchess and Mr Vereker dealt together famously. What a compliment to us – to you, rather – that she made the journey at such an inclement time of year.' Charlotte was bravely playing her part in this curiously detached wedding-night scene. 'Penny and Robert will not be best pleased if she decides to winter with them at Wimbledon.'

'Oh, she has every intention of going to London to stay with Ainsford – her son, you know.' The clock might have been moved back eight years, Charlotte reflected, when Julien always came to bid good-night and gossip with his young friends if taking wine or a meal with Lady Ralston, the only difference being that now they were at Chalice and she was his wife.

'Julien, have you taken to wearing bedgowns? I thought you always hated them so.'

'Chivers was of the opinion that it would be – well, it would not be quite the thing if I did not wear one to-night.'

'Oh!' Charlotte found herself with nothing to say.

'Sleep well, my Countess,' he said, kissing her quickly on the forehead. 'Our guests will be leaving us to-morrow and we will have more time to ourselves.'

As he was leaving her now she realized, in horrified disbelief. He was half-way to the door when the sound of a stifled scb arrested him. Then the sight of his little love, sitting there deserted, with the tears spilling over on to her cheeks, was too much for his resolution. He took her close in his arms, her head nestled on his shoulder.

'What is it, Charby? Tell me, darling.'

'W-whatever will people think if you do not stay with me to-night? And no use saying they won't know because the servants will talk!'

'No doubt I can find some pillows to lay down the middle of the bed!' The laugh in his voice drew an answering gurgle from her.

'But, Julien, we are married now!' His arms tightened around her.

'And I hope will be for many years. So there is all the time in the world for you to adapt yourself to the circumstances. I would not do anything that you do not wish for, my dear.' Another sob greeted this noble declaration. 'Charby, are you terribly unhappy?' It was difficult to assess whether the shake of the copper curls was intended as a yea or a nay, so closely pressed were they under Julien's chin. He took a deep breath. 'Are you – do you love some gentleman?'

There was a brief silence and then a very smothered 'Yes!' came from the region of his chest.

'Then why could you not marry him?' The Earl realized that his worst fears had been well-founded, and his heart, which had been beating outrageously at the joy of holding her in his arms, now felt like lead. 'Is he perhaps already wed?'

Charlotte raised her head. 'He is now,' she said.

'A necessary marriage? He was obliged to marry for money rather than wed you whom he loves?' He was doing all in his power to ease her confession but she would have none of it.

'Oh, no, he never even thought of me in that way,' she explained.

'Who is this fellow,' demanded her lawful wedded spouse wrathfully, 'that he should cause you pain from sheer heedlessness – blindness more like, that he could not perceive what a jewel was his for the taking?'

That such sentiments were considerably beyond the line of what might be expected in a gentleman making a marriage of convenience did not occur to the Earl, but his lady did not fail to observe his indignation and took courage.

'Julien,' she whispered, 'have you ever been in love?'

'What? Yes, yes, I have.'

'Are you in love now?' she asked, greatly daring.

He held her to him again so that she should not see his face when he replied: 'Yes, I am.'

'Oh, Julien dear, could you not have married her?'

'I did,' he said simply. 'To-day.'

For a time she lay supine in his embrace, hardly daring to breathe, so precious was the moment. Then, wriggling out of his arms, she faced him.

'Do you know what you have just said?'

'Yes, I do beg your pardon.' He brushed a hand across his forehead as if confused. 'I had no intention that you should be troubled by my feelings. I do assure you that it is nothing for you to distress yourself for, my emotions will ever be subject to your wishes.'

This dignified speech had a startling effect upon his Countess. The tears began to fall again and, leaning forward, she threw her arms about his neck, crying out, 'Oh, Julien, you dear goose!'

'Don't cry, Charby,' he implored her. 'I never intended that you should know, but now that you do, pray pay no heed and we shall go on together famously.'

She ignored his protestations. 'Now that you have confessed to me, would you not wish to know the name of the being I adore and have adored for all my life?'

'Only if you wish to tell me – you've adored him all your life? Then this is no recent attachment? Who is this fellow? Should I not know him?'

'You should, but I am beginning to doubt that you do!' she teased him.

'His name?' he flashed at her, suddenly tried beyond bearing.

'Julien Robert Valentine Revel, ninth Earl of Clandon.'

He went deathly pale and when he spoke it was scarce above a whisper.

'But, sweetheart, you mistake, this cannot be. I hope you have always had a fondness for me but love, the kind of love that exists between a man and a woman – '

'Can spring quite naturally from a childish adoration as I discovered when you came home from the Peninsula.'

'I cannot believe it!' He was still refusing to accept the happiness that was being offered to him so unreservedly.

'When did you first love me?' she asked, gently leading him on.

'When I saw you engaged to Braybridge – no, long before that, I think, but it did not come to me until you were promised to another.'

'Ah!' she murmured against his cheek. 'I hoped it might make you jealous!'

'Well, it did!' he retorted. 'As jealous as you were over Sally! What a fool I was not to have guessed then!'

'Yes, you were, darling – Julien.' A little later, when he had left off kissing her and she could draw breath, she said shyly: 'If you are not going back to your own room would you not be more comfortable in bed?'

And Sultan, that accomplished lover of women, astonished himself by saying meekly: 'If you will allow me, my love.'

'Allow you?' snorted his exasperated Countess. 'If you do not I think I will fall into a frenzy!'

As, of course, nothing of so distressing a nature could be permitted to befall his lady, the Earl took every possible precaution to ensure she maintained a sane and reasonable outlook upon life to their mutual content.

ANNOUNCING
Masquerade
MAY TITLES